DON'T SAY HER NAME

A C.T. FERGUSON CRIME NOVEL

THE C.T. FERGUSON MYSTERIES
BOOK 12

TOM FOWLER

WIDENINGGYREMEDIA

Paperback ISBN: 978-1-953603-47-0

Editing by Chase Nottingham
Cover design by 100Covers
Published by Widening Gyre Media

CHAPTER 1

ONE OF THE perks of having a secretary is delegating tasks I don't like.

It's a pretty long list. I've never been fond of a lot of the minutiae involved with running a business. For the last few months, I've been able to offload these items to T.J., who has always accepted them while maintaining a veneer of happiness. Appearances matter.

"It's a good thing you paid for that accounting class," she said as she looked over a few sheets of paper. The idea of reviewing actual printed documents made me feel much older than my almost thirty-two years. I don't know where T.J.—recently twenty—picked up the habit, but I would need to ask her about it sometime. The large monitor connected to the laptop on her desk would have been perfectly good.

"Sure," I agreed. I took a couple financial classes in college . . . for all the good they did me today. I ranked them somewhere between algebra and trigonometry in the *Things People Promised Would be Useful but Are Totally Not* category.

"We're profitable." She pointed to the bottom of a column. The agency was indeed in the black. I offered an impressive nod. When I started working as a PI, I didn't charge my clients. My parents' foundation paid me instead. In the months since the arrangement ended, I'd managed to carve out a decent paying clientele.

And I did it all without investigating a single cheating spouse.

T.J. tapped her pencil on another column. "Charging businesses more helped."

"It was a good idea," I said. "Just like the previous seventy-nine times I told you."

"I'm going for an even hundred." T.J. offered a smile full of teeth and mock sincerity. "Probably get there in another month."

"How's your filing coming along?"

She rolled her eyes. "I still wonder what year it is when we have to use paper."

"They're backups," I said, declining to point out the irony of what we currently reviewed. "I never used to care much about stuff like this. Getting audited by the state would suck, but knowing where all our data is will help if it ever happens."

"You were just waiting to have someone to delegate it to," T.J. said.

"And here you are."

"It's fine." She pointed to a tall black file cabinet whose number of paint chips and scratches far exceeded its drawers. I bought it for twenty dollars when Manny got rid of it. He owned the car repair shop below us, and my business occupied the second floor of the attached office. The price did not include him or his crew helping me move it up the stairs. I would've paid triple for the assistance. "I've finished all our recent cases. Still going over some of your old ones. You might have tried writing down some notes."

DON'T SAY HER NAME   3

"I take the Paperwork Reduction Act very seriously," I said.

T.J. crossed her arms. "That's a federal thing. I remember reading about it." She tried to glare at me but didn't quite get there. The right corner of her mouth betrayed her. Despite the unseasonal warmth in the fall air, T.J. wore a light sweater over her jeans. Her blonde hair was pulled back into a ponytail which reached her shoulder blades. She was pretty but not so much my male clients would stop at her desk to gaze upon my secretary.

"Maryland might adopt it. I like to be prepared."

"Uh-huh," she said with a healthy amount of skepticism. "Anyway, if you want to talk numbers again, we're doing well. A little better each month, in fact."

"Good." T.J. had worked for me almost five months now. After the 180-day mark, I'd need to start paying her full salary. Until then, my friend Melinda's Nightlight Foundation paid half. I might even be able to give her a raise or a bonus. She'd certainly earned it. My smartwatch vibrated on my wrist, and I glanced at its screen. *Jewelry appointment,* it reminded me. "I'm going to head out early today."

"Can I go, too?" T.J. asked.

"No," I said. "I'm delegating staying late to you."

She narrowed her eyes. "It's not like you to leave early. Where are you going?"

"An appointment."

"Hmm." She checked her screen. "Nothing on our shared calendar. Your watch buzzed, so it's something you don't want me to see."

"I'm seeing a doctor," I said. "I have this five-foot-nine blonde growth which annoys me every afternoon."

T.J. grinned. "Fine. Have your secrets. You know you'll tell me eventually."

I walked to the door. "Eventually. Maybe. Remember, you're staying until closing time."

"Yeah, yeah," she said. "Get out of here."

I got out of there.

———

I stopped my Audi S4 in the parking lot. Rich's blue Camaro sat a couple spots to my left. Of course, he was already here. My cousin and I were opposites in many ways. He could always be counted on to arrive early, whereas I would walk in the door and make everyone check their watches. Good thing there would be plenty inside. Most of the shops in the northeast Baltimore strip mall were unremarkable, but my eyes fell on the one I came for: Small's Jewelers.

Over the years, I'd met Stuart Small a few times. He and my parents were acquaintances but not friends. When I made the appointment, I verified he wouldn't run and tell them I'd stopped in. I got out of my car and walked in. A friendly chime chirped when I crossed the threshold. True to form, Rich glanced at his watch when he saw me. My cousin wore a nice navy blue suit befitting a police lieutenant. He bought off-the-rack, but I'd be happy to wear his dress clothes if they fit me. Alas, he stood a little shorter and thicker than me. "You're almost on time," he said.

"My secretary had a lot of questions."

"Maybe you've trained her a little too well."

In reality, I hadn't trained her much at all. T.J.'s natural curiosity drove her to go the extra mile, and I think she wanted to succeed for Melinda's foundation. Instead of explaining all this to Rich, I simply said, "Yeah, I guess so."

"I've been here a few minutes." He spread his hand around the store. Display cases lined both long side walls of the small shop. Another few were arranged in a U shape near the center, where the proprietor stood near an old-fashioned cash register. I considered anything other than an iPad or similar tablet to be archaic, but Stuart's machine dated back at least two decades. The overhead lighting sparkled off the many gems around the store. "Haven't seen anything with more than a five-figure price tag. Gloria might be disappointed."

"Early in our relationship, maybe. She's changed. Grown up some."

"Yeah." Rich nodded. "You both have." He was almost seven years my senior, and I'd earned plenty of barbs over time for being immature. It meant a lot for Rich to acknowledge the strides I'd made in the last four years. "I'm still not sure why I'm here today. Do you really care about my opinion on jewelry?"

"I figure you know about as much as I do," I said. "I can't bring my mother. My father's as clueless as we are. Joey, too. Melinda probably knows a few things, but it would be weird to shop with her." I shrugged. "Guess you win by default."

"Lucky me."

"Besides, we might be doing a role-reversed version of this in a few months."

Rich snorted. "Don't put it on your calendar. I'm not sure Jeanne and I are there yet."

"You know, if you need some advice from a man who's more experienced with this sort of thing . . . "

"Piss off," Rich said with a grin. "Let's look at rings. I want to watch your eyes water when you see some of these price tags."

We approached a case full of diamond rings. The prices written on tiny tags started in the mid-four figures and escalated sharply from there. After a circuit of the interior, I had a few options in mind. They lined up with the ones I liked on the store's website. For whatever it was worth, Rich approved of my choices. Stuart approached us. I was about to talk to him when my phone vibrated in my pocket. T.J. called. I ignored it. The owner and I exchanged pleasantries, and he retrieved the rings I wanted to see. Stuart looked to be about sixty, making him an age peer of my parents. What remained of his black hair was half gray. He was a short and slender guy who always wore a smile. Then again, happiness came easy when everything you sold cost thousands of dollars.

"I like these," he said, and I wondered how many times a man in his profession upbraided customers for their selections. I would take the under on once *per annum*. He picked up a ring with a slender gold band and three diamonds. "This one is probably my favorite. I don't know your girlfriend, but I can't imagine she wouldn't love it, too. You can tell her the stones represent your pasts, present, and the future you'll build together." To his credit, Stuart didn't comment on the most expensive of my choices.

My buzzing phone interrupted us again. I excused myself and walked to the far corner of the shop to answer it. "I left early for a reason," I said to T.J.

"I know, but there's a potential client here."

"I don't remember seeing anything on the calendar."

"She didn't make an appointment," my secretary said. "Couldn't convince her they were necessary in an empty office."

"I'm a little tied up right now. Can she come back in the morning?"

"She says her dad's missing."

"How long?" I asked.

"Hang on." Muffled voices came through the connection. A few seconds later, T.J. said, "Twelve years."

"Does she expect me to find him tonight?"

"I doubt it."

"Then, ask her to come back in the morning. It's been over four thousand days. One more won't make a difference."

"Did you need to know anything about the ring?" Stuart asked. I turned around to find him standing a couple feet away.

"What? Where are you?" T.J. demanded. I could picture her frowning and leaning forward in her chair.

"I'll see you in the morning," I said and broke the connection.

"I don't mean to be pushy," Stuart said, "but I have someone else coming in a few minutes."

"I presume resizing is easy if we need it?"

"And free."

"For the price, it'd better be." He plastered a generic smile on his face. The three-stone model had been one of my favorites from my online browsing. I'd been careful to do it when Gloria and T.J.—the nosiest women in my life—weren't around. "Sure. I'll take it."

"I'll get everything together for you," he said and walked away.

Rich took his place a moment later. "Wow. You actually bought a ring. I'm impressed. I'd never pegged you for the marrying type."

"Until recently, I don't think I was," I said.

"Now, you just need the perfect moment," Rich said. "Can't seem too contrived. Maybe a place you've been before. She can't be expecting it, and Gloria's smart. She needs to think it's a possibility without figuring it'll happen."

"You're trying to put pressure on me." My cousin grinned in response. "I can't *wait* until our roles are reversed."

"Who says I'd bring you with me?"

"There's no reason to be rude," I said. "Who do you know more fashionable than me? I'm your best bet." I walked to the register, blanched at the total, and put it on a credit card I'd be paying off for the next several years. Much of the money I'd put away over the last several months went into relocating my office and getting it ready for prime time. At least Gloria would be happy. Rich was right, though. I needed to find the perfect moment, and doing so involved putting one over on my very smart girlfriend.

Maybe I should have gone back to work.

———

I went home from the jeweler, much poorer on the credit report but wealthier in spirit. Parking has always been dicey in the Federal Hill area of Baltimore. Luckily, my end rowhouse featured a concrete pad in the back. Gloria's car was already there. Her Mercedes coupe looked, sounded, and drove like a rocket, and anyone who missed these attributes could get clued in from its bright red color. I pulled in beside her and walked in via the rear door.

Gloria was on the couch working on her laptop. She smiled and stood, and we kissed a few times. "You're home early."

"Light afternoon. One of the perks of being the boss is getting to leave when you want."

"And your bookbag is still on your back."

Considering its unusually valuable contents, I wanted to keep it on. Gloria wasn't the type to go rooting through my stuff, but I didn't want her to find it in case she needed a pen and chose my bag to look for one. I slung it off my shoulders and set it at its usual spot near the coat rack. "Better now?"

"You're a creature of habit." She grinned. "Most men are. I guess I notice when something is different."

I sat on the couch, and Gloria plopped down beside me. "How's your arm?"

"Itchy." She frowned as I handed her the laptop. Gloria

slipped and fell on a wet tennis court ten days ago and frac-tured her left wrist. She sported a cast from her hand to her elbow. "I'm not sure I'll make it three more weeks."

"You'll manage," I said. "It'll be time to get back on the court before you know it."

"You're just happy you'll have a chance to beat me for a change," Gloria said with a smile.

"Don't think I won't hit everything to your backhand side. I'll take a win however I can get one."

She closed her computer. "Let's go out to dinner tonight."

"All right."

"We should go upstairs first, though." My girlfriend's hazel eyes sparkled. "You're rarely home so early."

"Might as well work up an appetite," I said. As we raced upstairs, I wondered when I would find the right moment to give Gloria the ring which remained in my living room.

CHAPTER 2

THE NEXT MORNING, I arrived at the office before T.J. It didn't happen often. She showed up on time reliably, and I gravitated toward the opposite end of the spectrum. Today, I managed to be a little early. I set a pot of coffee to brew. Clangs, whirrs, and other sounds came from downstairs. Manny and his crew started work before either T.J. or I did, and the products of their labor were much louder. Thank goodness for decent insulation and a thick floor.

T.J. rolled up before the coffee finished. She'd replaced her old, battered Civic for a newer Mustang about a month ago. It suited her better even if it lacked both the V8 and a manual transmission. Unfortunately, it was painted yellow, and T.J. did not seem to care for me referring to her car as a banana on wheels. It wouldn't make me stop, of course. I'm a man of principle, and cars resembling tropical fruits needed to be called out.

Her footsteps rang on the metal stairs, and T.J. walked through the door a moment later. She shot me a quizzical look right away. "You left early yesterday, and now you're here before me today." T.J. dropped her bag beside her desk and sat in a leather chair which was a smaller version of mine. "This is unusual."

"When you're the boss, you don't need a set schedule."

"Mm-hmm. Where'd you go yesterday? You definitely went somewhere else when you left."

"By definition," I pointed out, "any place I went would be somewhere else."

"Semantics just mean you're losing the argument," she said with an artificially sweet smile. When I didn't say anything, she added, "I heard someone else's voice."

"I appreciate your dedication to the science of detection, but I'm not going to tell you everything I do. Just like I don't expect you to tell me everything you do."

"Something happening to you affects me, too. What if you're dying?"

I scoffed. "I'm not dying."

"You sure?"

"When you've had a lung lobe and your spleen removed after getting shot," I said, "you make pretty frequent trips to the GP. I'm fine."

T.J. looked at me through narrowed eyes. I returned the favor. "I'm skeptical," she said. "Something's up with you."

"A man needs a little mystery."

She checked her monitor. "The potential client I mentioned last night is coming soon, by the way." T.J. smirked. "Her dad is probably still missing. I don't think anyone found him last night while you were off doing whatever."

"After all this time, he's statistically unlikely to be alive."

"I think she knows."

"Good," I said. "This should be quick."

A few minutes later, a weeping potential client and sympathetic secretary ensured our conversation would not, in fact, be quick.

It started out like a normal visit. The woman knocked on the door at the appointed time. T.J. let her in. I'd been expecting someone older, probably around my age. The potential client looked to be fresh out of college. She had dark brown hair with blonde highlights near the ends . . . like she'd colored it months ago and let it grow out ever since. When she shrugged out of her light jacket, her clothes covered a body which would have made her popular in college. A pretty face went with it, though circles under her eyes made her look tired.

Our guest sat in one of the chairs in front of my desk. T.J. asked if anyone wanted coffee, received two affirmative replies, and prepared two cups. She sat next to the potential client. "I'm Tara," the woman said. "Tara Street. Thanks for meeting me this morning." She added a snarky emphasis to the last two words. If Tara expected me to apologize for not coming back in yesterday, she'd be waiting a very long time. In the best interests of everyone, she moved on quickly. "You probably heard my father is missing."

I nodded. "For quite some time."

"Yes. Twelve years last week." She sniffed. "I was eleven when he left."

"I have to point out . . . after such a long time, the odds are very small he's still alive."

"I know." A tear slid down her cheek. T.J. grabbed the tissues before I could, and Tara plucked one from the box. "The police never found a body, so it took a while to make his death official. Years, in fact." She shook her head. "I never bought it. I knew he was alive somewhere. We just . . . weren't enough for him." The water works started in full at this point, and we all sat quietly while Tara cried and eventually composed herself.

"Did anything happen that might've caused him to leave?" T.J. asked. Her tone was gentle, and Tara offered a small smile.

"He and my mom used to fight sometimes. No worse than any other couple now that I look back on it. At the time . . . as a kid . . . it seemed awful."

"And he just disappeared?" I said.

"More or less," Tara said. "He left for a night or two here and there. Usually after some bad fight." This sounded worse than the typical squabbles of a couple, but I kept my opinion on Tara's parents' marriage to myself. I hadn't even popped the question yet. Who was I to offer insights even if they were very likely to be correct? "He tucked me in one night. Normal stuff. The next morning, he was gone."

"Did your mother tell you he died?"

"Not the first morning." Tara dabbed at her moist eyes with a new tissue. "I think she was in shock, too. By the time I got home from school, though, she broke the 'news.'" Tara added air quotes to the final word. "I don't know . . . I just never bought it. My father was healthy. Didn't hang out with the wrong people. We lived in a nice neighborhood, and he didn't have a dangerous job. I've always been good at math. The odds of him dying all of a sudden seemed really long."

"They probably were."

"I talked to his family," Tara said. "My mom didn't know about it. My uncles told me about their ancestors, especially the men. No one died young going back a few generations."

"You were pretty smart for eleven," I said.

"An affinity for numbers and years of watching *E.R.*," she said with a grin. "I saw a lot of family histories."

"All right, let's presume he's still alive. Do you have any idea where he might go?"

"None." Tara's head wagged, and her two-toned hair wiggled around her face. She brushed a stray lock behind her ear. "I thought a lot about it . . . asked his relatives, whatever friends I could find. Even if people entertained the idea he was still out there somewhere, no one knows where he might've gone."

"Sounds like he didn't tell anyone he planned to leave," I said.

"Not that I could find." Tara paused. "I know you're going to tell me this makes it more likely he's dead. I understand the percentages. Are you good at math, C.T.?"

"I have a master's in computer science."

"Excellent." She smiled. "You're not the first private investigator I've talked to. The others were at least nice enough to decline taking any money for telling me my father was probably dead. They wouldn't even entertain the idea."

"What's his name?" T.J. asked.

"Kevin Patrick O'Kelly," Tara said. "About as Irish as you can get. I took my mother's last name when I turned eighteen. Even if my father wasn't dead, he abandoned us. I wasn't carrying his name around with me."

T.J. jotted a note. It always amused me how easily she embraced technology for most of what she did, but she used an old-school spiral steno book during client meetings. "Is your mother still alive?"

"Yes." Tara's voice cracked, and she waited a few seconds before talking again. "She's washed her hands of all this. We don't discuss my father anymore . . . haven't for years, really. She'd probably be horrified if she knew I was here talking to you about him."

"How old would he be?" I said.

"He'd recently turned forty when he left. It's another reason I think he's still alive. He hit a milestone, realized he wasn't where he wanted to be, and blew his life up."

"Early fifties today, then. By actuarial tables, odds are good he's still out there. What did he do for a living?"

"He was a civil engineer," Tara said. "I think that's where I got my math aptitude. My father was always good with it, too." She snorted. "Mom used to tell him he could've been a bookie if he had any interest in sports. I don't think he could spare any time for it. I remember my father working a lot."

"Working a lot can kill," I said. "It's why I try to maintain a light load. At my current pace, I might end up being immortal."

Tara smiled at my crack. She took a white envelope from her purse. "I was told I should give you this if our chat went well."

I recognized the logo for my parents' foundation from across the desk. At least they hadn't insisted I work with Tara. I took the envelope and opened it. My father wrote a short note encouraging me to take Tara's case because she was awash in student loan debt, coming off a very bad relationship, and needed the chance for some stability in her life. I didn't know how a man who didn't want to be in his daughter's life a dozen years ago could improve it today. "My parents sent you."

"Yeah," she said. "Something about a new arrangement they'd made with you. Whatever. They're good people. Said I didn't need to pay you."

"Nope," I confirmed. "They'll take care of it." My folks and I set up this arrangement when I began working as a PI. After my shooting, our relationship developed a pretty thick layer of ice, and I struck out on my own. In the months since, we tried a semi-revival of the original system. Tara would be the first client they'd referred to me. "I'll be sure and rack up a lot of expenses just for them. Premium fuel all the way."

Her eyes brightened, and she leaned forward in the guest chair. "You'll help me, then?"

"We're at your service," I said. Tara extended her hand, and I shook it. "Leave your information with T.J., along with anything relevant you can think of involving your father." The two adjourned to the smaller desk where my secretary took notes. A few minutes later, they exchanged a quick hug, and Tara left.

"I almost wish she'd led off with your parents referring her," T.J. said.

"I'm glad she didn't. Might have biased me against her."

"I thought you were getting along with the folks?"

I shrugged. "A fair bit of the ice has thawed. I just don't want them interfering."

"How are you going to find Tara's dad?"

"Her father," I said. "People's word choices mean things. She never called him her dad. I imagine she can't."

"Fine," T.J. said. "How are we going to find the missing man?"

"I don't know," I said. "Let's have more coffee so I can think about it."

————

"So how do we find this guy?" T.J. leaned in toward my desk to see what I was doing. At the moment, finishing a cup of coffee and reading email comprised the whole of my activities.

"We start by not presuming we will," I said. "If he's alive, he's gone to great pains to stay hidden. I think it's likely I can find him because I'm smart and resourceful." T.J. rolled her eyes, but I continued despite her injection of negativity. "If he didn't want to leave a trail, he could've gone off the grid. Not many people can really live an unplugged life, but if he's one of them, it's a big wrench in the works."

T.J.'s knee bobbed. If we were at a poker table, I'd call it a tell. "Why don't we assume we can find him, then?"

"Why are you so desperate to?"

"Who says I am?" she asked.

"You're practically leaning into my face, and your leg is bouncing like you're a kid waiting to get a shot at the doctor's office."

My secretary composed herself, straightening up more and keeping her limbs still. "How many girls like me you know who came from good homes?"

"You're not Tara," I said. "There might be a few similarities in your stories, but you're different people. No one is only the sum of their experiences." T.J. pursed her lips. "Besides, I don't know anyone quite like you. You're unique." I paused. "Thank goodness."

She smiled and gave me a light punch in the shoulder. It hurt more than normal because I got a vaccine a few days ago. The perils of not having a spleen. "Where do we start?"

"The usual place. Google." I entered Kevin Patrick O'Kelly and got several results. With about ten percent of the US being of Irish descent, a set of three common names produced a fair bit of hits. I narrowed by location. Now, we saw a manageable number to sift through. Finding the right person didn't take long. Tara looked like her dad, and T.J. pointed to his picture around the same time I noticed the resemblance to our latest client.

This Kevin Patrick O'Kelly entered the world in New York City fifty-two years ago, settled in Maryland as a teenager, and married the former Katherine Street when he was twenty-four and she twenty-three. Five years later, they welcomed their only child Tara. Short of his civil engineering job at Grayson Environmental, there wasn't much else to see. O'Kelly's file stopped accumulating when he hit forty, and several sites mentioned a disappearance concluding with his declared death.

One of our results was an obituary in the *Baltimore Sun*, but I ignored it for now. They never contained useful information unless you wanted to send flowers or attend a viewing. Apart from the death notice, I found nothing else which confirmed O'Kelly's status as a member of the choir invisible. No police blotter indicated a violent demise. Not a single article or blog mentioned his loss, not even the company where he was employed for years.

"You still think it's likely he's dead?" T.J. wanted to know.

"There's a chance," I said. "Based on what we see here, though, I think it's more likely he's still alive." She grinned. "This is very preliminary, though. We'll need to look deeper."

"We're going to find him."

I appreciated T.J.'s confidence, but I wasn't ready to proclaim any guarantees to our client yet.

CHAPTER 3

WE DIDN'T FIND a lot of actionable facts the rest of the day. T.J. and I called it a night around the usual time with no suspicions raised. I drove home, arrived to find Gloria receiving a dinner delivery, and settled in to a quiet evening. Sitting together on my couch didn't seem the right time to get the ring and pop the question. It needed a better setting and something more memorable than chilling after take-out. For her part, Gloria seemed not to notice my brief internal conflict. I wondered anew if she even expected me to propose, wanted to get married, and all. We were happy the way things were. Why change?

I couldn't come up with better reasons than complacency and inertia. They're often fine, but they didn't do enough here. I would need to keep looking for the right place and time. After a few hours of TV, we headed upstairs and went to bed. As usual, I woke up before Gloria the next morning. I changed into my running attire and hit the mean streets of Federal Hill for my morning constitutional.

Before I got shot, I could do about four miles in thirty-five minutes without much trouble. Running seemed impossible for a while post-surgery, but I'd gotten most of my stamina back. I doubted I would ever be one hundred percent again, but maintaining the mid-nineties when you're already at a high baseline works out well. Now, I'd built up to about three and a half miles in those same thirty-five minutes. I finished my final lap, paused for a few deep breaths, and walked toward my house.

An engine roared from my left. A car sped the wrong way up Hamburg and nearly ran me over before continuing along Riverside Avenue.

I stopped and tried to read the vehicle's license plate, but it moved way too quickly. All I could tell was it was a green sports car. Probably a Mustang. Considering my neighborhood would be ill-suited as a speedway, I had a hard time believing this near miss to be accidental. Who would want to run me down, though? I'd only recently started a new case, and the odds of Tara's dad still being alive, knowing I looked into him, and ordering me squashed flat were astronomical.

Once my pulse returned to normal post-workout levels, I walked the remaining block to my house. I didn't see the Mustang again.

Once within the friendly confines of my house, I went upstairs and got in the shower. As the hot water ran over me, I thought about the Mustang incident of a few minutes before. Could someone I put away months or even years ago be gunning for me now? I couldn't dismiss the possibility. Most of the criminals I tangled with ended up in jail for a long time or—occasionally—dead. I couldn't think of anyone who had the reach to order vehicular homicide from a jail cell.

The longer I stayed in the steam, one name popped to mind: Gabriella Rizzo.

It struck me as unlikely. Despite the bad blood which simmered after her father's death, the queen of Baltimore organized crime and I had reached a truce. We would basically leave each other alone. While I wouldn't put it past Gabriella to lie, we'd known each other a very long time. I doubted she would send someone to turn me into handsome roadkill near my house without a good reason, and I hadn't provided her any.

I emerged from the shower a hundred percent cleaner but no less confused. Downstairs, I turned the coffee pot on and started breakfast. The caffeine and egg aromas made their way upstairs, and Gloria's feet hit the floor a moment later. I flipped the omelet, and Gloria joined me in the kitchen. She gave me a minty kiss good morning before pouring herself a mug of coffee. I prepared my own and carried it to my small kitchen table while the toast browned. We soon enjoyed half an omelet and two slices of whole wheat toast each.

"You're diving into the new client today?" Gloria asked after she'd taken a few mouse-sized bites.

I nodded. "T.J.'s all gung-ho to help her. I think she sees herself in Tara in some way."

"I'm doing some location scouting." Gloria grinned. "We have a few standby places, and I love them, but this city is full of cool old buildings. A bunch of them can hold at least fifty people."

"You sound like a movie producer," I said. "Make sure you wear sunglasses to keep up your mystique."

She sipped her coffee and chuckled. "I will."

I watched as Gloria cut her omelet into small pieces. Her left hand couldn't do much of the work, and the cast ruined the visual, but I imagined how the engagement ring would look on her finger. A mundane breakfast chat wasn't the time to find out. "What?" she said. "You're staring at my hand."

"Sorry," I said. "I . . . was wondering if I should've cut the omelet for you before I brought it. Your bites are the same size mine were when I was eight, so I think I could do it."

Gloria smiled. "I'm managing but thanks." I stole a few more glances at her ring finger while we ate. I now worked a new case, and Gloria had her own fledgling business to run. We'd settled into a quasi-domestic life together. I knew I wanted to marry her, and I presumed she felt the same, but I couldn't broach the subject without unleashing the world's biggest spoiler alert. I would just need to wait for the right moment.

And hope I recognized it when it came.

———

When I arrived at the office, T.J. was already there. She'd completed her most important job of the day—making a fresh pot of coffee. After I'd enjoyed about half my cup, she rolled her chair to my desk. "Any epiphanies come to you last night?"

"Who am I?" I said. "Doctor House?" She gave me a puzzled look. "*House, M.D.* It's streaming. Watch the show."

"Professional development?"

"Of a sort."

I'd ignored the obituary yesterday. Might as well read it today especially in the absence of epiphanies. Even if Kevin Patrick O'Kelly were still out there somewhere, his Maryland trail went cold a long time ago. Getting on the scent again would take some work, and nothing else jumped out at me as a starting point. I found the death notice again quickly enough. T.J. leaned in a little, and we both read it.

Kevin Patrick O'Kelly, a civil engineer in Baltimore, has been missing for five years and is now presumed dead.

He was born forty-five years ago in New York City, the son of John Patrick and Sheila O'Kelly (nee Murphy).

The family moved to Maryland when Kevin was fourteen, and he was a proud graduate of the A Course at the Baltimore Polytechnic Institute. Four years later, he earned a B.S. In Engineering from Johns Hopkins University.

He was employed at Grayson Environmental for eleven years prior to his disappearance. His family searched for him to no avail. Police have uncovered no leads though they never treated his disappearance as suspicious.

He is survived by his wife Katherine (nee Street) and daughter Tara. No information is available on a viewing at this time, though the family does plan to hold a funeral.

"Doesn't say much." T.J. frowned. "I was hoping we'd learn a few things."

"I think we did," I said. "He was missing for five years before the family officially presumed him dead." The state typically wanted a seven-year gap. Maybe the family convinced them to make the proclamation early. "We didn't know how much time had passed before." I pointed at the screen. "Also, the police never considered his disappearance suspicious."

"Don't you generally assume they screw things up?"

I grinned. "A little uncharitable, even for me. I think it's worth taking a second look at their work in most cases, yes. An investigation has a lot of moving parts, as my cousin likes to say, and a bunch of people will have their hands in it. So there are quite a few chances to introduce an error."

"Fine." T.J. waved a hand. "Maybe someone introduced an error here."

"It's possible." I shrugged. "We can't do much but look at a report after all this time has passed. Even if they missed something obvious, it's been years. Trails are cold. Evidence is long gone. My point, though, was the cops didn't think foul play was involved."

"They think he simply left on his own," she said.

"Basically. Seems to be Tara's impression of events, too. She was young, and it was a dozen years ago, but even if she's remembering something wrong, the police back up what she told us."

"You read a lot of obituaries?"

"No," I said. "My grandparents used to, though. I'd hear them talking about it with some of their gossipy old friends. Every now and then, I'd read some to see what all the fuss was about."

"And?"

"And whoever writes them adds as much detail as they can. Even after the fact . . . it's easy to update the notices online." I pointed to the top of the page. "This one didn't get anything added. I wouldn't say it's lacking for details, but it's missing some things other obits include."

"What's it all mean?" T.J. asked.

"Don't quote me on this, but I'm more convinced Tara's father is still alive."

"Too late." She scribbled something on her notepad. "I've already got you on the record."

"You're fired," I said.

CHAPTER 4

THE POLICE DIDN'T FIND Kevin O'Kelly's disappearance suspicious. I told T.J. we might want to check their work, so I tasked her with contacting hospitals. The law required doctors to report gunshot wounds to the police, and any assault usually resulted in the cops coming. If O'Kelly ended up on the wrong end of a violent crime, hospitals would have the records, though they'd go back quite a few years. Maybe even before the era of digitizing documents as my secretary pointed out in a huff.

I didn't expect her to have much luck, but it was a low-risk, high-reward play. In the meantime, I searched funeral home records for viewings. Despite the obit not mentioning one, it could have happened. The impression I got from Tara was her mother was fed up with the whole mess by the time they declared her father dead. If she put anything together, it would've been small. I wondered how many places which could have held such a gathering closed since it happened. None of the data I could find indicated a viewing ever took place, and every director I talked to on the phone gave me a negative response.

A dead man can have a funeral—being deceased was kind

of a requirement, in fact. O'Kelly seemed about as Irish as a man could be, and most Irish people of his generation who settled in Maryland were Catholic. I checked churches next and stifled a laugh as T.J. grew exasperated with someone in a hospital records division. I couldn't blame her. I'd probably need to go a few verbal rounds with a priest before long, and given the choice, the worker bee in the hospital basement sounded preferable.

A few minutes later, I uncovered a funeral notice. Kevin O'Kelly was laid to rest at Oak Gardens in Baltimore County. No family members were buried there. The priest who presided over the service had since changed parishes a couple times, but Reverend Anthony Mannion was easy enough to track down. One of my early cases involved a priest with the wrong kind of history, so I checked out Mannion and found him to be on the side of the angels.

T.J. hung up a few minutes later. "Nothing." She shook her head, and her blonde ponytail wagged behind her neck. "Some hospitals didn't even have digital records back then. It's like the stone age only stopped a few years ago." She paused to blow out a breath, but her tirade would not be stopped. "A few people were helpful. Most gave me the impression I wasted their time. Maybe I did. Nothing on this guy going to any hospital in the area before he disappeared."

"Maybe the police got it right," I said.

"Yeah. It's also possible he went to someplace like an urgent care facility. There wouldn't have been as many of them back then, but I think it would be hard to get a good list of the ones that were."

"And there's no chance you'd talk to someone who worked there a dozen years ago. Never mind the issue of print versus digital files."

"You gave me a shit task on purpose, didn't you?" T.J. said.

"It was a worthwhile avenue to pursue." I shrugged. "Not every lead turns into something."

"What about you?"

"Couldn't find any viewings," I said. "Seems like the obit had it right. I did track down a funeral notice. The priest is still around, too. I guess I need to pay him a visit."

"Catholic?"

"Yep."

T.J. grinned. "You going to confession while you're there?"

"You really want me to be gone the whole day?" I said. Her expression didn't change.

———

The Reverend Mannion's most recent post was Saint Michael's Catholic Church in Silver Spring. I figured the drive would take close to an hour, and it did. Silver Spring was a smaller city than Baltimore. This meant its traffic problem—not counting the constant one provided by the Capital Beltway—operated at a smaller scale but was still an issue. I passed a few restaurants, a Baptist church, and a Whole Foods before finding the parking lot. I left my car in an empty spot and walked around to the front of the building.

Like many similar structures, most of the exterior was brick, and a tall steeple extended well above street level. I passed a Nativity scene made from statues on my right. You don't need to put out the Christmas decorations if you display them all year. Tall columns framed three sets of doors with the center pair sized for giants and young giraffes. In the interest of making the most dramatic entrance possible, I chose the middle set.

Inside, St. Michael's went with white and dark brown as the color scheme. The pews looked new or recently refurbished, and their color matched both the top of the lectern and the wood of the crucifix hanging behind the altar. A door on either side led to different parts of the church—I presumed one connected to the rectory. It was late enough on a weekday for morning services to be over. No one else was here. I sat in a pew and took it all in. While I've never considered myself religious, the architecture and quiet of a church made for a serene setting.

A few minutes later, a priest emerged from the door on the left side of the altar. As he drew closer, I pegged him at about six-two, making him as tall as me. He was a little heavier and probably twenty years older. Most of his curly black hair had turned silver. The reverend was white with a ruddy complexion. His face matched the photo I found for Anthony Mannion. He stopped at the pew before mine and offered me a collegial smile. "Here to talk to God?"

"Actually, I'd rather talk to you." I took out my badge and ID. "Better chance of a timely answer."

"Did something happen to one of our parishioners?" Father Mannion possessed the kind of voice which could put people at ease. I imagined his sermons were popular with the congregation.

"It's . . . from something a long time ago. We can talk here if you want, but it might be easier in your office."

"I've been there most of the morning," he said. "I think I'd rather do it here." He gestured to the pew, and I scooted down to allow Father Mannion room to sit. "Can you tell me why you're here, Mister . . . Ferguson, was it?"

"It was and still is," I said. "Call me C.T. About twelve years ago, when you were still in the Baltimore archdiocese, you presided over a funeral for Kevin Patrick O'Kelly."

It took a few seconds and a deep furrowing of his brows, but the reverend nodded. "I remember. It was a cool, misty morning. Not very well-attended."

"Did you know the deceased?"

"He'd been a parishioner for a while. Hadn't seen him in a few years. His wife told me he'd been missing, and she had him declared dead. I have to say it was my first time doing a funeral where I didn't know if I was actually interring a dead person."

"Did you normally check the coffin to be sure?" I said.

Father Mannion grinned. "The families frowned on it, so I stopped." At least he had a sense of humor. "Like you mentioned, it's been years. Why bring it up after all this time?"

"It seems Kevin's daughter thinks he's still alive somewhere."

"Children have difficulty accepting their parents' early deaths," the priest said.

"She would have been eleven," I said. "Still young but old enough to understand what was going on."

"I have no reason to think they declared him dead in error."

"I figured you wouldn't. It's going to be hard to establish anything after all this time."

"Good luck, Mister Ferguson," Father Mannion said. "I wish I could help, but I'm just a simple priest trying to save souls. I'm not Father Brown."

I smiled. "Where's Chesterton when we need him?" This visit turned into a predictable dead-end. The priest showed up for a funeral and performed the service as requested. He didn't know anything else about Kevin O'Kelly's disappearance and proclaimed death. I wondered if he could tell me anything which might have led the man to vanish. "Did you know Kevin well?"

"I guess." Father Mannion shrugged. "He and Tara came to church a lot. I worked with the youth group at the time, and they were both active in it. He and a few other parents used to chaperone most of the outings we took the kids on."

I wondered what boring and sanitized destination would be right for a church youth group but thought better of asking. "Did it surprise you when he simply stopped showing up?"

"Of course," the reverend said. "Hard not to suspect the worst. Even a dozen years ago, you had to figure someone missing for more than a couple days either wants to stay gone or met an unfortunate end."

"Maybe you have more of Father Brown in you than you realize," I said. "Do you remember anything being suspicious or unusual before he disappeared?"

"No. In fact, we'd just done a youth mass the week before." The priest paused for a deep breath and frowned again. "I don't remember anything unusual. Kevin was always a little intense. He had a demanding job plus his family. I'm not sure he had an 'off' switch."

"What about his wife?"

"Didn't see her much." Father Mannion spread his hands. "Not everyone wants to get involved in church functions . . . or even come to mass." He focused his brown eyes on me. "You seem comfortable in church, C.T. Are you Catholic?"

"I was raised Lutheran," I said.

"Pretty close."

"The Vatican's official position on heretics must have evolved. Better hope your bishop doesn't have the hymnals bugged."

He chuckled. "I wish I could help. There's really nothing I can think of, though. After all this time, I have to wonder if I've forgotten some detail."

I slipped a business card out of my wallet and handed it to Father Mannion. "If you think of anything, call me."

"I will," he said. We shook hands, and I walked out of the church. Other than Kevin O'Kelly's piety, I didn't learn anything in my time here. If Tara's father were still out there somewhere, it would take more than talking with people who knew him a dozen years ago to find him.

CHAPTER 5

I DROVE BACK to Baltimore in much lighter traffic. Talking to the priest hadn't been the bad experience I expected. As a bonus, my hair didn't catch fire as I entered the church. Maybe this would be a good day, and I would solve the case quickly. T.J. texted and asked how things went. I told her I'd already made it to Columbia on my way back. She asked me to pick up lunch somewhere. My enthusiasm for the rest of the day waned as I sat in a drive-through line.

At the office, I heated our food in the microwave before we ate. A few minutes after we finished, the door opened, and Tara walked in. T.J. smiled and greeted her while I turned away to roll my eyes in private. Client updates were the worst part of my job, and delivering them in person only compounded the misery—as did providing them so soon in the process. When I spun back around in my chair, I wore the most sincere smile I could under the circumstances.

So much for the good day I'd looked forward to not even an hour prior.

Tara and my secretary chatted, and T.J. painted an optimistic picture. Great. The two women looked happy as they sat on the other side of my desk. "I was just telling Tara about the investigation," T.J. said.

"How is it going?" the client wanted to know.

"How do you think it's going?" I said. They both frowned. I would soon be the villain in the rose-tinted play they co-authored behind my back. "It's been one day."

"Yeah." Tara nodded, and T.J. joined her. "Have you found anything?"

"If your father is still alive—"

"He is."

"*If* he is, he's gone to great lengths to stay hidden for twelve years. I think I'm the smartest person in the room wherever I am, but uncovering all this in twenty-four hours is asking a lot. It's a ton of inertia to overcome."

"Has anything led you to think he's dead?" Tara asked.

"No," I said, "and by the same token, nothing I've seen has convinced me he's alive. If he is, the cold trail is a feature, not a bug." Confusion clouded her features. "It's by design. Anyone who reinvents themselves and stays hidden wants to make it difficult for people to find them."

Tara lapsed into silence, so T.J. picked up the slack. "We've talked to a lot of people. Checked hospitals in case the police overlooked anything, funeral homes . . . C.T. even found the priest who performed the funeral."

"Oh, Father Tony." Tara smiled. "How is he?"

"Fine. He's in Silver Spring now. We had a nice chat. It's the longest I spent in church since the last funeral I attended. He knew of no reason to think your father's body wasn't in the casket when they lowered it into the ground. He also didn't have anything useful to tell me about the time before your father disappeared."

"So it was a bust."

"More or less," I said. "He seems like a sincere guy, and

his church can always use more of those. I'm going to need to broaden my search. I need to talk to your mother."

"No." Tara shook her head. "I want to keep her out of it."

I rubbed my forehead. This impromptu meeting served as the most recent example of why client updates were the worst. "Track with me here. She was married to your father."

"Yes."

"Happily, as far as you know. Apart from a few arguments."

"Yes," Tara said.

"You maintain your father disappeared rather than died." She bobbed her head. "In what universe is talking to the man's wife not a good idea?"

"I'm not sure she's up for it."

"Do you want to find your father?" I said.

"Yes," Tara said again.

"Then, she's going to need to be."

Silence filled the room. I could almost feel T.J.'s disapproval. She still saw something of herself in Tara and wouldn't be pleased I didn't trip over myself to be polite and helpful. "Fine," our client said after a moment. "I'm not going to help you find her, though. You want to talk to her, you put in the work. You're the detective."

Tara left, and T.J. glared at me as the door slammed shut. "Did you have to be rude to her?"

"She's being unreasonable."

"She wanted to know what was going on."

"She also could have hired someone any time in the past dozen years."

"They declined to take her case. She told you." T.J. crossed her arms. "What's our next move?"

"The only one which makes sense," I said. "Find the mom."

———

I wanted to conduct a little more research into Tara's father, so I put T.J. on the task of finding her mother. Living off the grid posed challenges for most people. The smallest thing could serve to trip you up and get you back on the radar. If Kevin O'Kelly meant to stay hidden, he did a damned good job of it. I couldn't find anything in his name since his disappearance. Even if he remained alive and fled Maryland, he did so without alerting any local, state, or federal entity to his movements. Even his Social Security number stayed dark for a dozen years.

While I pondered whether Tara's father relocated with a new identity, T.J. rolled her chair next to mine. "I think I found her." We wheeled over to her desk, and she pointed to her screen. "I looked under Katherine O'Kelly first. She used the name even after he left. Once she had Kevin declared dead, though, Katherine went back to her maiden name." T.J. frowned. "I'm pretty sure I've located her."

"I'm guessing it's not in a good place," I said.

"No." She clicked a link, and the website for the Saint Dymphna Psychiatric Recovery Center opened. "She's apparently the patron saint of mental illness."

"I appreciate you anticipating my questions." T.J. smiled. "Kind of an unfortunate thing to be associated with, though. I'd rather be the patron saint of sunrises or puppies."

"I don't think there's a lot of choice involved," T.J. said.

"True. I'm pretty sure you can't become a saint until you've died, usually in some horrific fashion. Limits the odds of an objection."

"Anyway." She scrolled down the page. The facility sat nestled in the woods of northern Baltimore County. It wouldn't be a bad drive from Gloria's house. Photos of the grounds, common areas, and residential rooms filled the page. Next came part of the prayer to the eponymous holy woman. *Saint Dymphna, martyr of purity, patroness of those who suffer with nervous and mental afflictions, beloved child of Jesus and Mary, pray to Them for me and obtain my request.* Finally, headshots and bios of the doctors completed the main page. "I don't know how long she's been there, but their posts discuss the excellence of their long-term care."

"Tara definitely didn't want us talking to her mother," I said.

"Which is why you're gonna do it."

"It's part of the reason, sure. I also hope she might be able to tell me something."

"Should I get you on the guest list?" my secretary asked.

"Please. Feel free to tell them my parents' foundation will make a donation if it helps."

"Will they?"

"Seems right up their alley," I said. "Besides, what kind of son would I be if I didn't spend their money?"

T.J. shook her head and picked up the phone. She got transferred a couple times, and an edge crept into her voice after the third. I appreciated her professionalism in normal circumstances but also how she lost her cool dealing with other people's bullshit. Another moment and a fourth reroute of her call led to T.J. delivering the world's most sarcastic thank you and breaking the connection. "It seems they have some strict visitation policies." She set her phone down and blew out a deep breath. "They're not willing to amend them for private detectives or missing persons investigations."

"Let me try someone." I found the number for Saint Michael's Catholic Church and dialed it. A pleasant-sounding woman answered. I asked to be connected to Father Mannion and told her who I was. She wished me a blessed day as she passed me along. Once I'd reintroduced myself to the reverend, I got down to business. "Kevin O'Kelly's former wife is in a psychiatric hospital."

"I'm sorry to hear it," he said.

"We might be in luck. They're Catholic. Saint Dymphna's."

"I know the place. Used to visit there occasionally when I worked closer to the area."

"Great," I said. "I'd like to talk to her. If Kevin really is out there, she might know something. I won't badger her. Can you call and ask them? My secretary tried and failed. A priest might have better luck."

"I'll certainly give it a shot. Is this the best number to reach you?" I told him it was, and we said our goodbyes.

"Calling a priest?" T.J. said with a grin. "Next thing you know, you'll be at a Sunday mass."

"Unlikely," I said. "There's no need to test the church's lightning rods."

A few minutes later, Father Mannion called back. He told me the staff didn't like the idea, but he'd put in a good word for me, and they relented. I thanked him and hung up. "Looks like I'm a go. They're expecting me in about an hour."

"And the good father might be expecting you this weekend," T.J. said.

"If he is, he's going to be disappointed."

"All this time talking to a holy man must be rubbing off on you."

"The next time you sneeze," I said, "my blessing will be ten percent more sincere."

It took about thirty-five minutes—most of them spent on I-83 North—to get to Parkton, a pretty remote area of Baltimore County. The Saint Dymphna Psychiatric Recovery Center was about five minutes from Our Lady of Grace Church, tucked away on a side street several blocks off York Road. It didn't look like the gray, ominous institutions popularized in movies and TV. If anything, I guessed the building had once served as a school—probably a middle school judging by the size of the grounds. Windows broke up the brick facade at regular intervals. One end of a jogging track peeked out from the far side. A fence which would not have existed in the facility's previous life encircled everything.

I turned the car off and stared at the structure. A chill crawled down my back. Almost thirteen years ago, my older sister died, and I dealt with it quite poorly at first. My parents —trying to be helpful and proactive—took me to see a shrink named Janishefski. He practiced his vocation in a building similar to this, but I remembered it being bleaker and gloomier. The sun never shone when I went to see him. After a couple months, I realized he was useless and stopped going.

Scenes from Arizona played in my mind as I climbed out of the S4. After I got shot, my parents moved me to a rehab facility in Phoenix. There, I basically learned how to walk again, and a psychiatrist named Parrish oversaw my mental recovery. We shared a love of classic science fiction novels and an intolerance for bullshit. It meant she didn't put up with mine, which turned out to be what I needed. I'd even leaned on her a couple times remotely since leaving the center.

I hoped Katherine Street got to see doctors more like Parrish than Janishefski. Still leaning against the car, I took a deep breath. I didn't expect to deal with these memories when I set off for Saint Dymphna's. There was probably no shortage of shrinks inside who would love to get me on a couch to talk about it. "I won't cheat on you, Doctor Parrish," I said to no one as I pushed off the Audi and headed toward the front doors. I fought another shudder as I approached.

CHAPTER 6

ONCE INSIDE, I spoke to the receptionist. She was the kind of severe-looking woman who would have made an excellent middle school secretary. After scrutinizing my PI and driver's licenses, she directed me to have a seat nearby. It felt a bit like waiting for the principal. I almost asked her if I should call my parents, but I doubted she would accept the question in good humor. The large reception area also held two small offices—exactly the kind a pair of school administrators would occupy.

I recalled a few times I'd been sent to take the long walk down the hallway when a short man in a white lab coat came through the open door. "Mister Ferguson?"

I stood. "In the flesh."

"I'll take you to see Miss Street now." The badge hanging from his lanyard identified him as Doctor Blair. He probably would have made an excellent physical science teacher. He certainly looked strong enough to hoist a few large rocks from the earth and display them on his desk. "She's been here for a while now and made great strides. I'll be nearby, but I won't be sitting with you while you talk. Katherine has earned a little privacy."

"I never thought of it as something we need to earn," I said as we turned down a corridor. Painted doors lined each side, and it was easy to tell they'd been classrooms at some point in the past.

He half-turned and showed a gentle smile. "In here, things can be different. Katherine dealt with a lot after her husband left. She held it all in for years. Since she's been with us, we've helped her come to terms with a lot of it." I didn't think any of this pointed to a reason someone needed to earn privacy, but debating the psychiatrist didn't seem like a good play.

We walked another thirty feet or so before stopping at another former classroom. This one featured two large round tables set near the front and back walls. A pair of small desks sat near the windows. A woman who looked more than old enough to be Tara's mother sat in a chair at one of the tables. Her face was thin, and her stringy hair hung in a mess around her head. I wondered exactly how great her strides had been as Doctor Blair extended a hand toward the slouching Katherine Street. "I'll be at the desk," he whispered before heading toward the farther one.

I pulled out the chair next to Katherine and sat. She eyed me up without speaking. "Miss Street," I said after a moment. "Thanks for meeting me today." I showed her my PI license, which she looked at wordlessly for a few seconds. "Your daughter came to see me a couple days ago."

She nodded. "I know. She told me she was going to do this." Katherine frowned at me, and a small smile played on her pale lips. "You're handsome."

"Thanks. My girlfriend thinks so, too." Her expression soured a bit. "I doubt Tara hired me for my looks."

"That girl is determined to find her father. Says she needs closure, needs to understand what happened." She snorted. "I told her it don't matter. If he's dead, he's dead. If he's alive, he walked out on his family. What the hell's the point of tracking him down now?"

People liked to know where they came from, but I didn't raise this point with Katherine. If she grew agitated, Doctor Blair would whisk her away to a medically-induced tranquility, and I'd never sniff these hallways again. "I grew up with both my parents," I said. "If I didn't—especially if one of them left all of a sudden—I'd probably want to know what happened."

"I guess," she mumbled.

"I know some of this might be unpleasant, but I want to help your daughter. Anything you can tell me will be useful."

"Tara's always been smart." Her face brightened. "Once they started giving out awards in school . . . second grade, I guess . . . she won a bunch. Could have gotten a free ride to a good private high school, but she wanted to stay with her friends. Were you in the National Honor Society, Mister Ferguson?"

"Yes."

"What the hell are you doing working as a detective, then?"

I shrugged. "High school recognition doesn't guarantee good life choices later."

Katherine cocked her head and stared at me. "You got in trouble with the law?"

"We're not here to talk about me," I said.

"Oh, but I want to." She sat up straighter and rubbed her hands together. "You want something from me. Tell me something about you."

I didn't care for the *quid pro quo* arrangement, but I doubted I could talk her out of it. Calling Doctor Blair wouldn't help, either. "After college, I did some traveling. Eventually, I made it to Hong Kong. I ended up working with a group of hackers against the Chinese government. It took them a while, but they found us and threw me in jail."

"You made it back in one piece, though."

"Yes. Thankfully, a family friend knew someone in the state department. Without a connection, I might still be behind bars. I spent nineteen days in prison over there, and it's not an experience I'd care to repeat."

She bobbed her head. "I'm sure."

"There's my story of lawlessness and rebellion," I said. "Your turn."

Katherine didn't say anything for a moment. Her posture relaxed, and she ended up slouching again. "You want to talk about Kevin," she said in a voice which had lost much of its happiness in the span of twenty seconds. "Everybody here wants me to talk about Kevin."

"We can go at your pace."

She sat in silence for at least a minute. Her pace looked like it was going to be glacial, and while taking a lot of time for an uncertain return chafed at me, I didn't let it show. "How'd you find me?" Katherine said. "I don't think Tara would've told you. She's not proud I'm here."

"She didn't tell us," I said. "My secretary found you. I talked to a priest about visiting . . . Father Mannion."

A small smile crossed her features. "Father Tony was always nice to me." She resumed her silence for a few seconds before continuing. "I don't like talking about Kevin, you know. My life kind of went off the rails when that asshole left. I never thought I'd be in a place like this."

"I'm sorry to bring it up. Take your time."

Doctor Blair watched us but didn't intervene. After another short delay, Katherine said, "I was always skeptical about him being dead. Always. Maybe Tara picked it up from me. At first, I told her that her dad went away on a business trip. She bought it for a while, but a lie like that only works for so long." Katherine paused, and I remained silent while she collected herself. "I didn't hear from him after he split. Not a word. His phone stopped working the next day. I gave up trying to reach him after a while."

"You think he's still alive?" I asked.

"Still?" She shrugged. "No idea. I'm pretty sure he wasn't dead when we buried him, though."

Having been declared dead before, I understood—and I knew how challenging it could be to reverse. "Any idea where he might've gone?"

"No. I tried everyone he knew. Family. Friends. Guys from college he hadn't talked to in years who showed up on his Facebook page. I think he had some help. I don't want to say he faked his own death because he basically just disappeared. Everything we did after was for legal reasons. Anyway, yeah, I reached out to people in a lot of different places. Nobody had seen him."

Or no one would admit to it, at least. Still, the result was the same. "Did he ever mention wanting to travel to a particular city or destination?"

"He loved LA," Katherine said. "Disneyland, Hollywood . . . all of it. I tried everyone I knew in California. Even hired a private eye out there. That was a couple grand I'll never see again." She frowned anew at me. "How much are you charging my daughter for this ghost hunt?"

"My rates are being covered by a charitable foundation. She found me through them."

"Good." She jabbed a bony finger at me. "I don't like it when people rip my daughter off."

Doctor Blair cleared his throat, and Katherine relaxed. I didn't think I'd learn anything else from her, and continuing the conversation might be harmful for her mental health. "I think I have what I need." I stood from the uncomfortable chair. "Thanks for your time, Katherine. Good luck in your recovery."

"Mm."

Doctor Blair offered me a nod but didn't get up. I could take the hint. I showed myself out.

———

I drove away from Saint Dymphna's glad to put it in my rearview. It seemed like a decent enough place, and Doctor Blair gave the impression he was a competent practitioner who cared about Katherine Street. Still, I preferred to visit these kinds of facilities on my terms—which were as infrequently as possible and only when necessary.

A few minutes into my drive toward the city, my father called. "I just gave Tara a status report earlier," I said. "Don't tell me you want one, too."

"No. Son, someone slashed all our tires."

"What? Where are you?"

"The foundation," he said. "Your mother's here with me."

"Hello, Coningsby," she said, though her voice sounded like it came from the bottom of a well. I wondered if I should send Lassie after her.

"We were going to pick up lunch for the staff," my dad continued. "All the tires are cut."

"Have you called anyone else yet?"

"No."

"All right," I said. "When we hang up, call the police. They'll take a report. If you parked where you normally do, the cameras might've picked up something."

"I'll also need to get the car towed," he said.

"Do you need me to come get you?"

"We'll be all right. You said you took Tara's case?"

"I did. Look, Dad, I don't want to keep you. You're going

to need to make some more calls. Let me know if you need a lift or anything."

"We will. Thanks, son." He broke the connection.

I dialed Tara, and she answered right away. "C.T., do you have any news?"

"A question, actually. Did you tell anyone you'd hired me to look into your father?"

"What? No." She paused. "Why? What happened?"

"My parents had all their tires slashed," I said. "I'm used to people coming after me and trying to discourage me from solving a case. Going after my folks would be new, but you're connected to me through them."

"I hope they're all right," she said, "but I didn't tell anyone. Doesn't seem like anybody else's business."

"I agree. Thanks. I'll fill you in more later." I pressed the red phone button on my steering wheel. My parents were philanthropists who worked with a variety of charities and causes. They shouldn't have any enemies. The cynic in me wondered if the Mustang which nearly ran me over tied into this most recent incident. No one knew I worked this case, however. T.J. and I wouldn't tell anyone, Tara hadn't, and my parents never said anything in the past until I'd wrapped up my work.

It looked a lot like someone came after them and me. Probably the same someone. But who?

CHAPTER 7

WHEN I WALKED BACK into my office, T.J. polished off a slice of pizza. "Box is on top of the microwave," she said after chewing a bit. "I got hungry."

"I'm glad you ordered something."

"I used the business credit card."

I opened the white box, snagged two pieces of pepperoni, and set them on a paper plate. "I guess we'd better make this a working lunch." I glanced around the area. "Don't you always get a salad, too?"

"I ate it," T.J. said.

"The whole thing?"

"It wasn't very big."

I set my lunch on my desk and checked the nearby trash can. A large plastic container with bits of lettuce and shredded carrot took up most of the space. I pulled it out. "Not very big?"

T.J. tried to give me a sweet smile, but I wasn't falling for it. "I told you I got hungry. Didn't know when you were coming back."

I dropped it back into the can. "At least you saved me some pizza."

"What'd you learn from the mom?" T.J. wheeled her chair to my desk. She frequently did this even though our stations were only a few feet apart. After the past five months, I chalked it up as part of her charm.

I answered her after eating a large bite. "She never thought he was dead. Just figured he disappeared. I got the impression she didn't care why."

"The answer's kind of implied." T.J. shrugged. "His wife and kid weren't enough for him, so he split. Happens every day across the country."

"I'm not sure it's so simple."

"It usually is."

I didn't know a lot about T.J.'s background. When I first met her a couple years ago, she worked as a prostitute. Melinda—who left the same kind of life behind—started a foundation to help girls get off the streets and make their way in the world. T.J. had been her first job placement. I'd gotten the impression a few times her childhood was unpleasant. In reality, well-adjusted girls from good homes rarely turned into hookers. Still, I wondered if she would tell me more at some point. I wasn't going to press her on it. "She looked for him. Talked to his friends, people he knew. Said he loved LA, so she checked with everyone she knew out there and even hired a PI."

"I hope he's alive, and we find him," T.J. said. "He can write his ex-wife and daughter a couple of nice checks."

"One thing at a time," I said. "Katherine told me he basically just disappeared. Never came home. He didn't do anything elaborate like fake his own death."

My secretary cocked her head at me. "What about your friend Joey? Doesn't he help people get away and start over?"

"Sure, but twelve years ago, we were both in college."

"You're old," T.J. said.

"And you're a pig when it comes to salad."

She shrugged but eventually bobbed her head. "Maybe you should talk to Joey."

"Great," I said. "I get to pay for two lunches in one day."

"He's probably eaten already."

"It's never stopped him before. When it does, I'll get worried." I ate some more pizza—which had now assumed room temperature—and texted Joey. I got a reply quickly.

"What'd he say?" T.J. wanted to know.

"He'd love to talk with me," I said. "And—of course—he's hungry."

———

Conveniently, Joey wanted to meet at Brick Oven Pizza. It was a short walk from the office. I wasn't keen on the menu choice after eating lunch a few minutes ago, but I'd survive. I walked in to find Joey seated against the wall. Like many establishments in Baltimore, Brick Oven Pizza occupied what was once a rowhouse. The windows and portable AC units—not in use this time of year—served as a dead giveaway. The walls contained interesting art and maps of the city which carried over onto the tabletops.

Joey Trovato was a black Sicilian of good humor and better appetite. We'd been friends for ages, and in the time I knew him, I never saw anyone eat more. Despite his ability to put away food, Joey wasn't obese, and some honest athleticism hid under the layers of carbs and grease. "Good to see you," he said as I pulled out a chair and sat. A half-empty plate of jalapeño poppers sat on the table, and a waitress dropped off an order of pizza-looking potato skins. Steam wafted off them, and they smelled good. "I got a large pie coming, too, if you want some."

"I'm paying for it all, I presume." Joey confirmed this with a nod as he crammed most of a potato skin into his mouth. The temperature of food rarely deterred him from devouring it. "Might as well have a slice or two."

I let Joey eat for a couple minutes—it seemed rude to interrupt a master at work—before we got down to the reason for my visit. "It's always cool to have lunch with you," he said, "but I know you asked me here for my professional opinion."

"Yes." I acted as if I held a clipboard. "How would you describe the clogging in your arteries after the appetizer round?"

"Two percent more than before." A crumb fell from Joey's mouth as he talked around his food. And he wondered why I didn't eat with him more often.

"I'm trying to find a man who's been missing for a while," I said. The same cute blonde waitress dropped off Joey's pizza. She smiled at me before walking away. The pie would make a vegetarian weep. Pepperoni, sausage, ground beef, bacon, and ham dotted the surface of the golden-brown cheese. "Did they not have venison, too?"

"Maybe it's not deer season," Joey said. He used the triangular spatula to put a slice on his plate. In a rare moment of restraint, he let it cool while I talked.

"Anyway, the guy's daughter thinks he might still be alive. Ex-wife does, too. They declared him dead, but there was never a body or even a real investigation."

"When did it happen?"

"Twelve years ago."

Joey chomped his slice before answering. "He didn't come to see me, then. Twelve years ago, I was in college with you."

"Early start on your chosen profession?" I asked.

"No."

"Any idea who might have helped this guy disappear, then?"

"No." He shook his head. "I didn't exactly do an apprenticeship before I started." Like me, Joey helped people when life dealt them a bad hand. He created convincing new identities and assisted his clients in fleeing whatever they needed to get away from.

"You had to learn a few things from someone," I said.

"Sure," Joey said. "He was old-school, though. The shit he did wouldn't work in the modern world." He shrugged. "Besides, Old Mike is dead. Even if he worked with your guy, we couldn't exactly ask him about it."

A dead end. I consoled myself with a slice of pizza. It weighed about five pounds from all the meat on it. Lifting it to my mouth a few times would count as my bicep curls for the day. I took a bite and had to admit I liked it. It made me feel like a barbarian to eat it. Still, the crust came out crisp and just strong enough to hold the herd of deceased animals lying atop it, the sauce had a zing to it, and the cheese—what little of it I could see past the toppings—was exactly the right color. Another work of art from the brick oven.

"The ex-wife said he loved Los Angeles," I said, trying to salvage a nugget of information from this lunch. "She called everyone she knew out there . . . even hired a private eye. No dice."

"I guess he didn't go to LA, then," Joey said.

"I'm so glad I'm footing the bill. Your piercing insights are a bargain at twice the price."

He grinned. "I wish I could tell you more. If this guy is still alive, and if whoever helped him was smart, he wouldn't go anywhere he had family or friends. No place on his bucket list. Those are the basics."

"He was a civil engineer," I said. "We should presume he's smart."

"Lot of places he could be, I'm sure. Look, I can see you want to find this guy. If I can help once you know a little more, gimme a call."

"You just like me for the free lunches."

"They help," Joey said.

———

I didn't know much about Oak Gardens as a cemetery, but they put time and effort into their website. T.J. and I checked it out after I walked back to the office. She entered Kevin O'Kelly's name, and we saw a picture of his headstone along with a map indicating where a visitor would find his alleged final resting place. "Nice of them to draw a map," she said.

"We're running out of options. If this guy is alive, he could be just about anywhere."

"Have we eliminated all the places he might have family or friends?"

"No," I said, "but it's not reliable. We'd be going off what Katherine and Tara tell us, and maybe doing a little cross-checking and verifying of our own. There's no way we'd get a complete or accurate list. No matter how much work we did on it. Not after a dozen years."

My secretary pursed her lips. "Are you going to the cemetery?" I nodded. "Why?"

"We're operating off the presumption he's alive. Might as well see if the casket has anything inside it besides dirt and stale air."

"You think they're just going to let you dig up a grave?"

I snorted. "I don't plan on doing any digging. I'm sure they have a guy with a backhoe."

"Still," T.J. said, "you can't simply roll in and ask to open a casket."

"I'll use my charm and good looks." She rolled her eyes. "They have a long track record of success."

T.J. smiled and leaned back in her chair. "I wish you luck, then. I get the feeling you'll need it."

"I guess we'll see." I left the office, got in my car, and drove to Oak Gardens. It was in Essex, so I took Eastern Avenue most of the way. Driving through Greektown made me hungry even though I'd just eaten twice. The cemetery itself looked small but typical. A black five-foot chain-link fence surrounded the grounds. A narrow paved road snaked through the plots. Near the entrance, a small building and parking lot marked the office. I left my car in one of many empty spots, walked inside, and found no one at the desk.

The office looked even tinier than mine. There would only be room for one person unless two were fans of really cramped quarters. The waiting area such as it was consisted of two basic plastic chairs whose picture could have accompanied *uncomfortable* in the dictionary. I left the petite building and walked down the road. It didn't take long to find the caretaker. He was a tall man in dingy overalls which probably hadn't been clean since his first hour on the job. A backhoe was parked nearby, but this burly fellow looked like he could dig a bunch of graves by hand equally fast. "Help you?" he said when I approached.

I showed him my badge and license. "I'm looking for Kevin O'Kelly."

He jerked his thumb to the right. "About two hundred yards over there."

"His daughter hired me," I said. "She and his ex-wife think he disappeared and want me to find him. I'm inclined to believe them."

"Why?"

"There's not much evidence he's dead."

"You mean besides the grave and headstone," he deadpanned.

"Anyone can bury an empty casket. I'd like to take a look at it."

He chuckled and crossed his meaty arms. "Let me get this straight. You drove down here to ask me to dig up a grave so you can see if there's really a body in the box."

"Sounds about right," I said. "When can we start?"

"Soon as you come back with a court order."

"I couldn't get one. It's still early in the investigation."

The caretaker shrugged. "Can't help you, then."

"There has to be another way." I gestured around the open grounds. "You don't exactly seem overwhelmed here. My guess is whoever runs this place gives you a pretty long leash."

"So?"

"So maybe we don't need a court order this time."

"You're a PI?" he said.

"I am," I confirmed.

"Fine. Maybe you can help me. You do something for me, and I'll unearth Kevin O'Kelly for you."

I groaned. "I thought side quests were only for video games."

"Not sure what a side quest is," he said. "You want me to put my neck on the line, I need something from you. Pretty simple."

I thought about giving him the company line about not investigating cheating spouses but thought better of it. The caretaker didn't wear a ring, and I felt confident he could snap most philanderers over his knee if he caught any. "Fine. What is it?"

"My daughter. She got knocked up by some college asshole. Rich kid. He said he'd pay for everything, but he hasn't yet. He owes her three grand for her doctor visits so far. You collect the money from him, I'll dig up a grave for you."

"You can't find the guy yourself?"

"Probably," he said. "I'd be inclined to strangle him, though, and I can't go to jail. My daughter needs me and my insurance." He scoffed. "For all the good it does us. Her bills are after whatever they pay . . . which ain't enough."

I rubbed the bridge of my nose. This would take a little time. Considering how long Tara's father had been gone, it was a plentiful resource. I didn't want to get bogged down in some family squabble, though the idea of giving some stuck-up prick a bloody nose held a fair amount of appeal. Did I need to see an empty casket? We'd been operating off the presumption Kevin O'Kelly was alive. Katherine would have known if a body got lowered into the earth years ago. Still, confirmation would be nice. She wasn't the most reliable of people, and she probably kept her daughter in the dark.

"Fine," I said again and added a sigh. "Give me the name."

CHAPTER 8

"YOU AGREED TO *WHAT?*" T.J. shrieked as I drove back. Thank goodness for Bluetooth. I might have gone deaf if I held the phone to my ear. As it stood, I'd need to trust Bang & Olufsen's quality control process for speakers.

"I'm thinking of it as a side quest," I said.

"You're not the hero of a video game."

"A lot of video game heroes have detractors."

She sighed. "It's probably for the best. We've been assuming this guy is alive. Some jerk of a boss told me I should challenge my assumptions."

"He sounds very smart," I said. "Handsome, too, no doubt."

"He's a little full of himself," T.J. said.

"I'm on my way back, but I want you to start looking into this guy. His name is Trevor Duckworth the Fifth."

"The Fifth? Should be easy enough. How far away are you?"

"Ten minutes."

"All right. I'll have something ready."

I thanked her and broke the connection. As the son of wealthy parents, I grew up knowing a few people with fancy names. My rule: if a number followed someone's name, he was likely to be an asshole, and the probability increased in direct proportion to the cardinality of the number. I placed the odds of Trevor Duckworth V being a jackass at over ninety percent even before I knew his status as a deadbeat dad.

When I walked into the office a short while later, T.J. tapped away on her keyboard. "I found some info on this guy." She stared at her screen. "Good family and all. Most people probably wouldn't believe he got some girl pregnant and ghosted her."

I stood behind her and leaned down to see her screen. "Lacrosse player for Hopkins. Another strike against him."

"It's a fine school," she said. "Good program, too."

"When you win a national title with Loyola, you don't bother with JHU."

I couldn't see her face, but I knew T.J. rolled her eyes. "He's a sophomore. Not a starter." She scrolled down. "Look at this. 'Campus police searched his room after getting reports of Duckworth selling drugs. They found nothing.' Interesting, right?"

"Very." If it were true, it meant Trevor would have cash. Collecting the money he owed Lacey Green and her father Vernon would be easier. While at a stoplight on the way back, I learned Lacey attended Essex Community College. Her Instagram showed her continuing pregnancy. She never came out and said how far along she was, but I guessed five months. "You can't be a dummy and go to Hopkins." T.J. glanced askance at me. "What? You're right. It's a good school. Our boy Trevor must keep be careful with his stash."

I walked to my own desk and sat. Weed, powder, and pills were easy to get on most campuses in America. Students knew where to go. They couldn't talk about it openly, of course. Many of them would use messaging apps, and the smart ones would make sure their communications were encrypted. Others—including a dealer trying to drum up business—might make coded posts online. I searched a few likely places.

T.J. wheeled over to my desk. "Where are you looking?" "The random corners of the Internet," I said. "No one is stupid enough to come out and say you should buy your oxy in room three-ten or whatever. If you look, though, you can figure out what they're saying. I'll look on the dark web if I need to, but for now, I'm focusing on Reddit, campus Facebook groups . . . things like those. They're useful to have in your toolkit."

"I'll remember them," T.J. said, and I knew she would. While I took programming classes and even earned a master's in computer science, a lot of my hacking knowledge was either self-taught or extrapolated from something legitimate. I would read or see something and try it. Mistakes served as good teachers, and I certainly made my share as I refined my craft. Since she began working for me, T.J. showed an interest in learning a lot of the things I do, and she certainly had the smarts to pick it up. She'd already been to classes for accounting, plus whatever training she got from Melinda's foundation before she started. In a year or less, she could be dangerous.

"Here." I pointed to the screen. A thread on a Hopkins campus life subreddit would never serve as a smoking gun in court, but it worked for our purposes. *TD can get you the best acne medicine*, it proclaimed. Several replies asked where to obtain this remedy.

"I don't get it," T.J. said.

"Let's step outside the world of pills for a moment. Oxy is a brand name. Several companies have used it for years. The one we care about makes pimple and acne treatments."

She nodded. "Clever."

"Easy to say you just wanted to get rid of a few zits if someone takes note of it," I said. I searched for more similar posts. Several popped up. Whoever made them did so every couple days. The town crier used the handle BigBarker. A quick Google search told me this was Brian Barker, who was indeed big. If he didn't play offensive or defensive line for the Hopkins football team, he could have.

"You think he's the muscle?" T.J. asked.

"Makes sense. He might even do more of the actual selling, and I'm sure he's a rather imposing figure when money is due. Trevor doesn't put himself at risk as much if he has a fall guy."

"Looks like you're going to need to visit Hopkins."

"It's no Loyola," I said.

———

I waited a while to drive to Hopkins. Trevor and Brian would be more likely to work in the evening and at night. It suited me. If I were going to tangle with one or both of them, I preferred to attract as little attention as possible. Before I left, T.J. and I gained access to the campus housing registry. They'd failed to apply a web server update, and something so seemingly minor often turned out to be enough.

JHU sat nestled between the Charles Village and Hampden neighborhoods of Baltimore. This meant a lot of cool eateries and cultural attractions surrounded the campus. The superior Loyola University was about a mile north. From what I gathered, Trevor and his muscle plied most of their trade in two residence halls just off Charles Street. Both lived on the other side of campus. This meant they kept their product where they worked. Carrying it across the grounds introduced all sorts of risks. These were college kids, so maybe they didn't think things through. Still, I figured I would give them credit for being smart.

Even if they didn't go to Loyola.

I'd switched to my Caprice Classic, a late-'eighties sedan which would look more at home in a college environment than an Audi S4. It blended in well with most of the other vehicles in the lot, though none were its exact mishmash shades of blue. My vantage point allowed me to see students come and go from both buildings. If I needed to, I could check the online haunts T.J. and I found on my phone to see if our two targets were already inside.

I learned early how waiting was an essential part of the job. Things rarely happened on the schedule I wanted. It took over an hour, but a late-model BMW 7 Series sedan with tinted windows rolled into the lot. My estimation of the dealers' intelligence dropped. Sure enough, two white guys who looked like they made their second home at the country club got out. Each wore a polo shirt and khakis. Trevor, the smaller of the two, still wore his sunglasses even though their usefulness expired about an hour ago.

As they neared the Caprice, I got out and put myself in their path. Both stopped and tried to glare at me. It didn't work. "Trevor Duckworth."

"The Fifth," he added as if it made the situation better.

"You owe Lacey Green five thousand dollars."

He scoffed. "I don't know who she is."

"Her father works in a cemetery. You might want to be more careful who you knock up. I don't think he'd give a second thought to throwing you in a grave."

This made Trevor fall silent. His compatriot picked up the slack. "Hey, yo, Trev. Want me to deal with our friend?"

"Yeah." Trevor walked around me and headed toward the nearest residence hall at a fast walk.

"Get back in your shitty car," Brian Barker said.

"Give me five grand, and I'll leave."

He raised his fists. I did the same. A bout with flinching following my shooting led me to adjust my fighting strategy. I either needed to go all offense right away or settle into a particular type of defense. I glanced around. No one milled about. Still, I couldn't let this go on too long. Trevor could use the time to hoof it out of the building. Brian wound up for a big punch. I rocked back on my heel and leaned away from it. His face twisted in surprise. When you're used to ending a fight with a single blow, your arsenal is limited.

Before he could launch another attack, I kicked him in the front leg. It wasn't a debilitating blow, but it made him drop his hands. My next kick took him squarely in the face. To his credit, he staggered backward but didn't fall. I clocked him in the side of the head with an elbow, which did the trick. He'd gone down between a couple SUVs which would help shield us from prying eyes. Brian rolled to his side. I kicked him in the ribs. When he grunted and tried to cover up, I grabbed his arm and twisted. "What the hell, man?" he said through gritted teeth.

"Where did Trevor go?"

"Piss off."

I gave it a little more torque and got a string of curses in response. "I don't care about your drug business," I said. "Your friend needs to pay his debt, and I'm going to collect. How useful you remain to 'Trev' in the next two months is up to you. My guess is he won't employ you as his muscle if your arm is in a cast."

"Piss off," he said again.

"I went to Loyola, but I have to admit Hopkins has some good science programs." Another bit of pressure caused him to groan anew. Brian reached for me with his other hand, but I'd been careful to stand out of range. "Should we test my hypothesis? Another twist should snap at least one bone."

"All right, all right." His breath came in gulps. "Trev knows the RA in there. We use an empty dorm room on the bottom floor towards the far end. One-sixty-six."

"Thanks," I said. "I'll take the key now."

"What?"

"You can either hand it to me yourself, or I can fish it out of your pocket after I break your arm."

"Fine, fine. Fuck you, man." He rummaged in his pants pocket and produced a single key—on a ring advertising an area Mercedes dealer, of course. Gotta stay on brand.

"Toss it toward me." He did. "Have a nice nap, Brian." He frowned before I punted him in the head, and his lights went out. I picked up the key and walked into the residence hall. Just like he told me, room 166 lay near the back side of the building. A student left via the door as I approached. I tried the knob. Locked. The key got me inside quickly. "Hey, yo, Trev," I said with as much seriousness as I could muster.

Trevor turned and regarded me with wide eyes. I kicked the door shut behind me with my heel. "Get out of here," he said, but his voice lacked any conviction.

"Sure. Pay me the five grand, and I'm gone."

"You think I carry so much cash?" We stood in a mostly empty dorm room. Instead of two beds and a bunch of cheap furniture, the space held a large desk and a few storage cabinets. Several bottles of pills lay on the desktop. I imagined a lot more inventory hid in drawers.

"You have a lot of stock here," I said, "and I'm pretty sure you're not taking Venmo for someone's Vicodin fix. Brian's taking a nice nap in the parking lot. You can either give me the money, or I'll find it once you're unconscious. If I do, though, I might just clean you out. Call it a risk of doing business."

He stared at me. I doubted anyone had confronted Trevor Duckworth the Fifth with such an undesirable choice before. His biggest disappointment in life might have been the time the resort ran out of jumbo shrimp and only offered him the same regular ones the normal people ate. "Fine." Trevor unlocked a drawer, pulled out a massive stack of cash, and counted out five thousand dollars. He slapped it down onto the desk and didn't lift his hand when I moved to collect it. "Tell that bitch I'm not paying for anything else."

Trevor let go of the money when I clocked him in his smug face. He stumbled and fell. "Her name is Lacey, you asshole. And you'll pay as much as she needs you to because you're going to be responsible for once in your life. Daddy's fancy lawyer can't make this one go away." I stuffed the bills in my pocket. "If I hear you've been delinquent again, I'll have to come back. Do you want me to come back, Trevor?"

"No," he said in a small voice as he wiped blood from his nose.

"Good. Then try not being such a prick for a change." I walked out of the dorm and back toward my car. Brian Barker got up and left in the meantime. I climbed into the Caprice and drove away from Hopkins.

———

Leaving Hopkins, I went back to Oak Gardens. Only one car sat in the lot as I pulled in. I counted out a thousand dollars and left the bills in the glove compartment. It would make a nice bonus for T.J. As before, Vernon Green was nowhere to be found inside the office. I located him out on the grounds, shovel in hand and a day's worth of dirt on his clothes. "You're back early," he said despite the late hour.

"I work quickly." I held up a bunch of cash.

"Three thousand?"

"Four," I said. "Trevor Duckworth the Fifth was happy to kick in an extra grand for your troubles."

"You hit him?" Vernon's hands gripped the shovel tighter, and the wooden handle groaned in protest.

"Just once. He tried getting entitled and defiant. He has another guy working with him . . . the muscle. He caught the worst of it. Neither of them will be a customer of yours anytime soon."

"Pity," the caretaker said. "I want to finish replanting one thing, and then I'll get the heavy equipment and dig up your guy like we agreed."

"Sure. I'll wait in the office." I walked back into the small building and plopped down in one of the uncomfortable chairs. Owing to a lack of exhumation experience, I had no idea how long this would take. It couldn't be quick. I slipped my phone out of the pocket and texted T.J. *At the cemetery. Waiting for the magic to happen. I'll have something to give you in the morning, btw.*

She responded quickly. I wondered what hours she kept. Regardless when something went down, T.J. always seemed ready to jump in. She deserved a bigger bonus than I'd be giving her. *I hope it's not a souvenir from the graveyard.*

I grinned. *Now, I need to find something else. Caretaker is going to dig up the grave in a minute. I'll let you know tomorrow what he finds.*

Again, her reply came without delay. *Bullshit. Tell me tonight.*

I told her I would. While I waited, I checked both personal and work emails but didn't find anything urgent. About a half-hour later, a horn sounded from somewhere outside. We were close enough to the road for it to be a car driving by. A few seconds later, it blared again, this time three beats in succession. I walked toward Kevin O'Kelly's plot. Dirt and Maryland clay covered the backhoe's large shovel. Its lights shone on the tombstone and excavated grave.

Vernon hopped down from the cabin. "It'll be faster if I just climb in there, pop the lid, and check."

"Whatever works best for you," I said. "You're the one doing me a favor."

He smirked. "We helped each other."

I handed him a business card, which he accepted and slid into a grimy pocket on his overalls. "In case you need anyone to go and collect from Trevor again."

The caretaker nodded and then lowered himself into the six-foot hole. He flicked on a handheld flashlight to provide extra illumination. Opening the coffin was easier than I expected.

It was empty.

CHAPTER 9

THE CONFIRMAIIUN of Kevin O'Kelly not being buried at Oak Gardens didn't give me an epiphany. I expected it. Even T.J., who had jumped at every chance to do anything with this case, didn't get excited. If anything, she was concerned with breaking the news to Tara. I didn't think we'd be telling her something she didn't know or strongly suspect, but we resolved to do it the next day. As much as I disliked client updates, they sometimes needed to happen.

I went home, washed lingering graveyard dirt off of me in the shower, and climbed into bed beside a sleeping Gloria. She didn't even stir when I crawled under the sheet. In the morning, she padded downstairs as I made coffee and breakfast. We didn't get a lot of time to chat—I needed to drive to the office, and she had a fundraising venue to check out. I imagined the process of exploring wedding venues with her. It would probably consume my evenings and weekends for months. We might get married before I turned forty.

After a few goodbye kisses, I headed to work where T.J. already waited. She'd given up on telling me I was late when I arrived after she did, but she still shot me a frosty look when it happened. Which was most mornings. As I made my way to the coffee machine, she asked, "Didn't you say you had something to give me?"

I poured myself a mug. T.J. repeated her question. I held up a finger, took a sip, and let the hot liquid work its caffeinated magic. A few seconds later, I said, "I don't want to answer questions before coffee."

"You had some at home," she pointed out.

"Not enough. Never enough." My secretary crossed her arms. "I was hoping to build some suspense first."

"You should've gotten here before me, then."

"Long night," I said. I took the wad of money from my pocket, kept it hidden from a curious T.J, and crammed the bills into a small envelope. I sealed it shut and tossed it to her. She caught it like a wide receiver hauling in a pass.

The envelope ripped open, and her eyes went wide. "What the hell?"

"It's a bonus. You've probably deserved one for a while. Trevor Duckworth the Fifth agreed and was nice enough to provide the funds for this one."

"I've never received a bonus before." T.J.'s eyes glistened in the overhead lights. "I'm not sure anyone really appreciated what I did . . . back then."

"Don't get soft on me now," I said. "We're still working a case."

She nodded and composed herself. "When do you want to talk to Tara?"

"When we have something to tell her."

"You don't think she wants to know her father isn't buried in his grave?"

"I think she hired us because she strongly suspects he's alive. It was nice to get the confirmation, but we've been working off the same presumption. I don't think giving her information she's already expecting is very helpful."

"Fine." T.J. crossed her arms—a pose I saw at least once a

day and deserved even more often. "What's the next move, then?"

"We need to go harder after the dad," I said. "We know he's not buried in the county. We can also presume he's not around here somewhere."

"California?" she said.

"Maybe. Just because someone likes visiting a place doesn't mean he'd want to live there. I love Hawaii, for instance, but I'm happy to go there as a tourist." I sat at my desk, and T.J. wheeled her chair close. I was happy to teach her things because of her genuine interest in wanting to learn and also because it allowed me to delegate more if I needed to in a pinch. "All right." I unlocked my computer. "We'll focus on areas away from Maryland. What else should we do?"

She pursed her lips. "Check civil engineering firms?"

"Is he likely to do the same job?" I said.

"It's what he knows."

"He's also smart enough to consider people could find him. I think he pulled a career change."

"Into what?" T.J. said.

"Don't know. Guess again." She stared at the screen. After a few seconds, I provided a hint. "When did he disappear?"

"About twelve years ago."

"So . . ."

It took a few more seconds, but she made the connection. "We should look for men whose history started around that time."

"Good," I said, and T.J. smiled at the praise. "Sometimes, people will build a couple years of bogus transactions into a new identity. They don't stand up to much scrutiny, but they're enough to throw off initial searches like ours. I'm going to look back fifteen years." A moment later, I'd setup all my search parameters at a major online data warehouse.

It took a few seconds, but the results came. And kept coming. Pages of them. Hundreds. "Lot to sift through," T.J. said when the count finally stopped increasing.

"You take last names starting with A through Y. I'll tackle Z."

"Nice of you to do one-twenty-sixth of the work."

"I couldn't leave you with all of it," I said. "It'd be unfair."

"How are we really going to go after this?" she said.

I stared at the screen. By the time the counter stopped rolling, we'd racked up well over a thousand hits. With a staff of two working on things, Kevin O'Kelly could die of old age before we found him. "We need some more expertise," I said.

———

The exterior door opened a few hours later. "I know you're on your own now," Joey said, "but I didn't expect I'd need to provide the expertise *and* the lunch." He kicked the door shut with his heel and carried an overstuffed bag to T.J.'s desk. "Good to see you again." She smiled, stood, and they did the European air-kissing thing.

"For Christ's sake," I said, "you two aren't in Victorian England."

"She's prettier than you," Joey said, and T.J. blushed.

"She's just better when it comes to batting her eyelashes at strange men." Both grinned, and T.J. stuck her tongue out at me. "What'd you bring?"

"Strombolis."

"We just had pizza."

"This is folded pizza," Joey pointed out. "Totally different." He unpacked three white cardboard boxes from the bag. Grease made parts of each translucent. Despite my objections to such a similar meal, I enjoyed the aromas in the air.

"Is there a vegetable in there anywhere?" I said.

Joey shrugged. "I think they put some green peppers in your stromboli. I figured you'd be a wimp and want the one with the veggies."

"Not all of us have 'heart attack by forty' among our goals."

Once everyone received the right meal—the slightly healthier version for me, a meat lover's for Joey, and plain cheese for T.J.—we tried to cut into the crust with the dreadful plastic forks and knives the restaurant provided. T.J. retrieved some stronger single-use cutlery from our snack area, which made the process much easier. "What do you have so far?" Joey said around a mouthful of his lunch.

"A lot of noise and not much signal," I said after chewing and swallowing. Someone needed to be civilized. Joey walked behind me, and I showed him the results on my screen.

"You're not kidding."

"How do we narrow all this down?"

"Can I see your search criteria?" I showed him, and he looked at the results again. "Not bad. The issue is a lot of these are going to be people who established a credit history in your timeframe simply due to age. Like someone who got their first MasterCard and car loan after college."

I chided myself for not considering this. It was a simple enough oversight, and it took an expert pointing it out for me to see it. "I guess I need to be more exact."

Joey nodded after another massive bite. "The narrower your search, the better your results." He smiled. "Didn't you ever take a database class?"

"Yeah, yeah." I made some adjustments in my parameters. This time, I added an age limitation, looking for men over thirty-five whose credit history came out of the blue. Combined with the three-year cushion, this should give me more meaningful information. I set the new query to run, and we reviewed the results. There were more than I expected, but it was still a manageable number. I wondered how many of the names on my screen came to see people like Joey—or got new lives from the government in witness protection. I would destroy this data after we found what we needed.

"Surprised you got so many hits," Joey said as he scrutinized my screen. "You might be able to filter some out, but this is a lot better than before. Just goes to show you there'll always be a market for what I do."

"What's our next step?" T.J. asked.

"Find the best candidates," I said. "We can go by age, location, current job . . . should get us a smaller pool. From there, we'll dive deeper."

"You probably don't need me for the second part," Joey said. "I'll send you a bill for my wisdom."

"How could any man put a price on such a treasure?"

My longtime friend chuckled. "Oh, I'll figure something out."

———

My secretary and I finished our lunches—she put about a third of hers into the fridge—and got to work on our results. I'd been hoping to see a handful of hits, and while we had quite a few more to sift through, it would be faster and easier than the first round. After applying a more precise age filter, I emailed T.J. the results and suggested we each explore half with her starting from the bottom.

We were a few minutes into our investigations when my cell phone vibrated on my desk. Joey. I wondered what he wanted so soon after driving away. "If you're trolling for leftovers, you'll need to talk to T.J."

"I almost got T-boned at an intersection," he said.

"Wow." T.J. frowned and looked over at my exclamation. "Where were you?"

"Driving down Eastern Avenue. The light went green as I came up, intersection looked clear, and so I went. Damn near got hit from my right."

"What happened?"

"I zigged . . . the other guy zagged," Joey said. "Good thing."

"I'm glad you're all right," I said.

"Me, too." He paused and sighed. "The whole thing was weird, though. I guess he might've completely whiffed on the light changing, but it had been a few seconds. I don't know. From what I could tell, the guy didn't seem surprised he nearly plowed into me."

"Sounds like you think he might've been gunning for you."

"Ridiculous, I know . . . but the thought crossed my mind."

"What kind of car was it?"

"A green Mustang," he said.

I almost dropped my phone. The memory of a green Mustang nearly running me over a couple days ago played again in my mind. I'd never been a big believer in coincidences, and my job disabused me of the last notions I might have clung to. I didn't want Joey to freak out, so I didn't say anything. He did, though, when I'd been silent for several seconds. "Hey! You still there?"

"Yeah," I said. "Sorry. Glad everything turned out. You get the plate?"

"I wish," Joey said. "It all happened so fast. By the time I processed what went down, the car was too far away." He let go a deep breath. It sounded a little shaky. "I know it sounds kinda crazy, but I wondered if it was really an accident, you know?"

"I hear you." We hung up, and I set my mobile down on the desk.

"Everything all right?" T.J. wanted to know.

"Yeah." I nodded and hoped it looked convincing. If a green Mustang nearly mangled me, the odds of a different car of identical make and model nearly barreling into Joey were astronomical. The first incident happened before I even started working our current case.

Who harbored a vendetta against me? And why did it extend to Joey?

CHAPTER 10

I FELT DISTRACTED as I looked over our list of names. Maybe Joey had been in an honest near-accident. It would have happened quickly. He didn't get a plate. How could he know the other driver didn't look surprised? Every time I tried to rationalize it away, I kept coming back to the green Mustang. It was a long-running popular model. Green would be an uncommon color choice, however. T.J. plugged away on the list. I could spend a little time on something else.

My parents' foundation was in a building on Calvert Street. I'd helped them set up their computer systems before I started working as a PI, and I maintained them while I toiled away as a contract employee. They added security cameras about a year in, and I integrated those into everything. I opened a remote connection to their network and tried the credentials I used before our professional relationship dissolved.

They still worked.

I checked my phone for when my father called me and searched for events earlier in the day. Sure enough, two men walked into the frame just after ten o'clock. The building offered a shared parking lot for its tenants, and my parents enjoyed a designated space. The pair lingered in the area, careful to keep their backs to the building at all times. A few late arrivals trickled in. Once no more cars arrived, the two pulled masks over their faces.

It happened quickly. One man went to each side of the car. The camera's resolution didn't provide a great picture. It looked like the two punched the tires. They must have carried short blades. The whole operation only took a few seconds. They kept their masks on as they walked out of frame. Damn. I'd been hoping to catch a look at one of them or their car.

Maybe the city's traffic cameras could help.

I'd accessed them several months ago. A competent IT shop would have disabled credentials or forced some change to keep me out. Of course, I got in right away. The user interface proved much clunkier than the one my parents' setup used, but I got it sorted out. Calvert Street ran one way northbound, and the intersection immediately after the entrance to the foundation had a camera. I backtracked to the day in question, set the time for a few minutes after, and let the footage play.

With rush hour over, keeping track of the cars was manageable. A few minutes later, I saw it. A car pulled out of the entrance next to my parents' location and sped up Calvert Street. It was a green Mustang. I paused the playback as it came into the intersection. The windows were dark enough to make any kind of facial identification impossible. I could make out two occupants, and they filled out the seats pretty well, but I couldn't discern anything else. The Mustang lacked a front license plate—Maryland law required them fore and aft. As far as I could tell, it was the same vehicle which nearly ran me down a few mornings ago. I took a screen capture to share with Joey.

"What are you looking at?" T.J. asked from over my

shoulder, and I almost jumped out my chair. "Is this related to the list I'm apparently working on by myself?"

"No," I admitted once I felt sure my heart wouldn't burst from my chest.

She leaned a little closer. "Two guys in a Mustang. So what?"

"A car which looks a lot like this one almost plowed me down on a run a few mornings ago. This footage comes a few minutes after all four of my parents' tires were slashed while they were at the office. And today, shortly after he left here, an identical car almost T-boned Joey farther along Eastern Avenue." TJ frowned. "Mustangs are popular. You have one. Green has to be a rare color, though. This is the same car . . . probably the same asshole behind the wheel every time, too."

"You think it's related to Tara's case?" she said.

"No. We hadn't even met with her when I almost got squashed flat." Tara did tie everything together, though. My parents referred her to me—the first time the foundation worked with me since our split. Joey helped both today and yesterday. Before I met with her, she stopped in to the office while I was out ring shopping with Rich.

"But I did," T.J. pointed out. "Maybe someone doesn't want us working for Tara."

"Maybe." It seemed a little flimsy, but I couldn't deny the possibility. "If so, you might be on this bastard's radar, too. Keep an eye out for green Mustangs."

T.J. nodded. "This kind of thing happen a lot?"

"No. Normally a couple goons show up and try to discourage me from nosing around. Using a car is a new tactic."

"Lucky us."

"Yeah," I said. "Lucky us."

———

After a fruitless afternoon, T.J. and I both left for the day. I arrived home to find Gloria on the sofa working on her laptop again. "You can use the office, you know," I said as I walked into the living room. "There's an actual desk in there."

"I know." A devilish smile played on Gloria's lips. "I'm . . . intimately familiar with your desk. And your chair."

"Yes." I cleared my throat. "I suppose you are."

She set her computer aside, stood, and kissed me. "The sofa's fine. I'm not toiling away here. I'd rather stretch out a little and be comfortable."

"I do have a pretty good couch," I agreed. Gloria went back to her laptop. Before I could make it to the kitchen, she summoned me back.

"Can you look at something?"

"Is this what the kids are calling it these days?"

Color came to her cheeks, and she fought a grin. "I made a video about the organization and the kinds of events we want to do, charities we plan to support, all that. Want to see it?"

"Sure," I said as I plopped down beside her.

"All right." A Media Player screen opened. Gloria sat behind a desk, her right hand atop it and her left below it. "We wanted to hide my cast," she told me. "The director felt it was important not to shoot me just from the neck up. It looks more professional this way."

"I could do your next video."

"Really?"

"Sure. We'll need a lot of time on the casting couch first, of course."

The grin came through this time despite Gloria's efforts. "Of course. Can we watch this now?"

"Sure." She started playback. In the short movie, Gloria wore a dark blue dress with gold stripes. I'd rarely seen it outside of her closet. She discussed why she got into fundraising, what she hoped to do, and the kinds of people she wanted her events to help. The lighting and audio were both good, and Gloria looked beautiful and sounded like she really knew her stuff. "Really good," I said when it ended after about ninety seconds.

"You think so?"

I nodded. "I'd work on a thirty-second version for social media. Pare it down to the very basics."

"The director's already on it."

"Good. You hungry?"

"Definitely," she said.

I got up and poked around in the kitchen to see what I might make for dinner. If I cooked a good meal and timed everything right, I might even get to propose to Gloria. She wouldn't care if I got on bended knee in the middle of some fancy restaurant. Rich was right—Gloria and I had both grown up in the last few years. In the fridge, I found fresh linguine I didn't remember buying. Gloria probably got it delivered at some point. A new package of ground beef stared at me, as well.

Within a few minutes, I'd made a dozen meatballs and put them in a skillet to start cooking. "Smells good," my girlfriend called from the other room. Once the meatballs had browned all around, I set them to bake for a few minutes while I added a jar of marinara, some Italian seasoning, and a small can of tomato paste to a pot. Soon, the sauce bubbled while my water boiled for the pasta. I whipped up a quick salad in the moments of downtime.

When Gloria walked upstairs to put her laptop away, I scampered to the office, grabbed the engagement ring box from a locked drawer, and stuffed it into my pocket. My shirt covered it enough to avoid suspicion. After tossing the salad, I put the linguine into boiling water and tended to the sauce. Gloria came back downstairs, walked into the kitchen, and sucked in a huge breath. "Mmm. The aroma's better than carry-out," she said with a grin. "Maybe you should cook more often."

"Maybe I should." I frowned as she turned to sit at the table. She'd stolen my planned opener. I wanted to mention how much I liked cooking for her, hoped she'd say she'd gotten used to it, and then capitalize on the good sentiments by popping the question. I'd find another opening. Talking to people—especially girls in my single days—always came easily to me. I set the salad bowl in the center of my small table and then returned with two plates of linguine and meatballs.

Gloria breathed in the aromas again before she cut everything into small bites. It took a little extra work thanks to the cast on her left hand, but she'd gotten good at it. As before, she caught me looking at her. "I'm fine," she said. "You keep staring at my hand . . ." Her voice trailed off as if she expected me to follow up with something.

Just imagining how it would look with a ring on it, I replied in my head. Instead, I said, "Every time I think I should cut something for you, you surprise me." I paused and took a bite. "You've been surprising me for a few years now, you know."

She grinned. "I'd like to think we've made each other better."

"We have. It's one of the great things about our relationship. And it's why . . ." I didn't finish when her phone vibrated on the table.

She frowned and silenced it. "It's why what?"

"It's why I wanted . . ." The mobile cut me off again.

Gloria rolled her eyes and looked at the screen. "Hell," she muttered. "We just picked the venue, and now there's some issue with it." She looked at me and then at her steaming plate. "I'll try to be quick. Sorry. This has to get resolved ASAP."

"I understand," I said. And I did—the demands of my job pulled me away from meals sometimes. The timing of this intrusion couldn't have been worse, though. I'd fallen into a rhythm in the conversation, and I got the feeling Gloria expected it to go a certain way. Proposing was a moment I wanted both of us to remember, and the fundraiser challenge ruined it. I would need to find another.

———

After my engagement overture plans met a grisly demise, I didn't sleep well. I dreamt Gloria found the ring, scoffed at it, and stormed out. This made me wake up before my alarm went off. Gloria snoozed beside me, her face absent any evidence of scoffing, snickering, or similar behavior. I carried the ring downstairs with me, locked it in my desk drawer again, and got on with my morning.

Coffee came first. I didn't feel like making breakfast, so I skipped it. Gloria woke up as I dressed upstairs. "You look tired," she said in a voice carrying the alluring husk of sleep.

"Didn't sleep well." I yawned to emphasize the point. We chatted a bit, I told her caffeine waited in the kitchen, and we shared a few goodbye kisses. I drove a little out of the way to pick up some Royal Farms breakfast sandwiches. The smell of them on the passenger's seat tempted me, but I left the bag shut. I made it to my office to find T.J.'s car already in the lot. This meant more java would await me upstairs. Maybe it wouldn't be such a bad day, after all. I walked in to find my secretary sipping from a mug at her desk. I set my backpack and the bag of food down, prepared my own coffee, and sank into my chair.

"Rough night?" T.J. asked.

"I'll survive."

"Good. You can't die so soon after giving me a bonus. People might get suspicious." She stood and pointed at the bag.

"Help yourself," I said.

"You're giving me first choice?"

"Consider it your second bonus."

"I think I'd rather have another thousand dollars."

"How can anyone put a price on freedom of choice?" I said. She snagged a sandwich out of the bag. Three remained, along with an equal number of hash browns. I picked a bacon, egg, and cheese flatbread. "Have you looked over the names and profiles on the list?"

T.J. nodded. "Even called one." I paused in mid-bite. "Don't worry. He's in England. It's later there."

"I know how time zones work," I said. "I'm just not sure there's a lot of value in reaching out to the people on our list directly."

She frowned. "Why?"

"Think about it. If someone cold-called you and asked if you'd been secretly living under another identity for twelve years, what would you say?"

"No . . . obviously." T.J. sighed. "I guess I didn't think it through."

"It's not a bad question to pose in person," I said. "You can at least gauge someone's reaction when you can see them. Over the phone, though, lying is really easy."

"Spoken like a liar." I raised my mug in salute. "What's the play, then?"

This time, I took and finished a bite of my sandwich. "Information gathering. We've compiled names and data. Now, it's time to look deeper. Hopefully, one of them is Kevin O'Kelly. If so, it means all the rest aren't. There should be signs somewhere."

"Can't you just invite Joey over again?" T.J. said. "He seemed to speed us up last time."

I shrugged. "I guess we could. My parents are footing the bill, so we have the lunch budget."

She jabbed her finger toward the grease-marred paper bag on my desk. "There's still food in there."

"It's early for Joey. He needs his beauty sleep more than most."

"Fine." T.J. picked up her phone. "I'll call him, then."

"Why do you have his number?" I said.

"In case something happens to you. I want to be prepared." She dialed my friend. It took her a couple minutes of persuasion, but he eventually agreed to head our way soon. I wondered how many other phone numbers T.J. kept in case of emergency. It was another example of her sound thinking. If this kept up, I'd need to give her an additional bonus soon. Preferably while Melinda's foundation still paid half her salary.

"I even got him to accept two breakfast sandwiches and two hash browns as food payment," she said.

"Well done."

"That means the other hash brown is mine. A reward for a job well done."

"You're fired," I said.

———

Joey arrived at ten-fifteen. It was about two hours earlier than I'd seen him vertical in a while. He yawned as he walked in and made a beeline for the coffee pot. I bid him good morning and got a grunt in response. Joey grabbed the paper bag from my desk, peeked inside, and put it in the microwave. A minute later, he enjoyed his first breakfast sandwich. "I'll be ready to work soon."

"We'll wait," I said. "I know it takes a little while for the grease to lubricate all the parts."

Joey grinned around a mouthful of food. He put two flatbreads and a pair of hash browns away in record time. After polishing off his mug of caffeine, he made of show of cracking his knuckles. "All right. Let's go."

I brought up the results from yesterday as everyone crowded around my desk. Even after narrowing down the first search, we still had a bit over a hundred possibilities. "I think we'll need to eliminate these logically," I said.

"Like how?" Joey wanted to know.

"This guy was smart. He had a good job and worked enough overtime to save some money but not enough to coast for a dozen years. He'd need a job or a business."

"Can we remove anyone who's not currently employed?" T.J. said. I did so with two mouse clicks. Now, we stared at seventy-seven names. "Not bad."

"For my next trick," I said, "I'd like to make even more disappear. The impression I got from Tara is her dad knew he was smart. He was an engineer. He's not going to own a little bistro or be a fourth-grade music teacher. Whatever he's doing, it's going to be a job where people can see his big brain at work."

Joey made a point of looking at everything in the room except me. "Wow. It must suck to know such a person. I can't imagine."

"Me, either," T.J. added, staring at the ceiling.

"Have I told you both how much I dislike you?" I said.

"Sure," Joey said, "but I'll never get tired of hearing it." He and T.J. shared a nice chuckle. I grinned and shook my head.

"How do we account for this?" my secretary asked. "I doubt *smug* is a searchable field."

"It's not. We need to go through the reported jobs one at a time."

Joey offered a single nod. "All right. Let's go."

We eliminated a few candidates right away. It would take an hour to go through all the names at this rate. "I found a couple I like," I said, bypassing several entries to highlight Donald West. Joey and T.J. scanned his information. He was fifty-three, lived in Texas, had little history past a dozen years ago, and managed an electrical engineering company.

"Maybe," Joey said. "Not sure our guy would turn to management, though. It's hard to show how smart you are when you're not doing the visible work."

"All right." I scrolled down to the next one. "I like this one a little more." Fifty-two-year-old Kieran O'Ceallaigh was as Irish as allowed by law, lived in Vegas, and ran a gambling consulting business. "Look at the last name. Take O'Kelly, add a few shamrocks, and you get his."

"Was our guy a bettor?" T.J. said.

"Let's find out." I texted Tara, asking if her father wagered on sports, played the ponies, or anything which could lead to Kieran O'Ceallaigh's current gig. She responded a few minutes later. *He loved to play poker. Pretty sure he bet on sports, too. My mom talked about it a few times when we'd watch football.* I showed the message to Joey and T.J.

"Could be our guy," Joey agreed. "I wonder who he consults for."

"I'm not sure it matters," I said. "Gambling is a zillion-dollar business now. There's money to be made anywhere you look." I thought back to my old acquaintance Vinny Serrano. He ran an old-fashioned sportsbook when we were in high school and college. It ended up not being enough for him, and his ambition put him on my radar during the first case I worked. Vinny ended up in jail for ordering a man murdered so the life insurance money going to the widow would pay his gambling debts.

"I like him for it," T.J. said.

Joey put up his hand. "Let's review the other names before we crown this guy." We went through them quickly. Most could be disqualified within fifteen seconds or so. A half-hour later, we'd settled on Kieran O'Ceallaigh as the most likely suspect. "Now what?" my secretary asked.

"I go to Vegas," I said. I glanced at Joey. "You up for a trip to Sin City? I might be able to use some backup."

"I'll pack a bag," he said.

CHAPTER 11

T.J. FOUND us flights to Vegas leaving in three and a half hours. Joey and I each went home to pack while she worked on a hotel reservation. Gloria wasn't there when I walked in. I loaded some clothes into a roller and stuffed my laptop into my trusty bookbag. Before I left, I considered moving the ring. Gloria rarely used my home office, and I doubted she would encounter a locked drawer and yearn to know its contents. I called her as I drove to pick up Joey. "I'm heading out of town," I said when she answered.

"Oh. That's sudden."

"Yeah. We got a line on the dad in Vegas, so Joey and I are flying there soon."

Gloria chuckled. "The two of you traveling together. It's funny. If you were driving, it might make a good road trip movie."

"It would also take three days," I said. I paused and imagined Gloria frowning. "Keep your eye out for a green Mustang. One almost barreled into Joey as he drove, someone slashed my parents' tires and escaped in one, and I almost got run over a few mornings ago walking back from the park."

"Oh, my god. Why didn't you tell me?"

"It was the first thing to happen. I figured it was some asshole driver. Look, I'm not a big believer in coincidences, so something is going on. I don't know what it could be or who's involved. Maybe someone just wanted to scare us." I considered this unlikely, but the idea of the threat being over might put Gloria's mind at ease. "I don't think anything will happen while we're gone. Just be careful, all right? Call Rich if something looks suspicious."

"You be careful out there, too," Gloria said.

"I'll win enough at the tables to get a bodyguard."

She chuckled again, and it was good to hear. "Whatever you do, I need you to make sure you come back in one piece."

"I will. Love you."

"Love you, too," she said, "even though you're a pain in the ass sometimes."

"It's all part of my charm," I said. I curbed the S4 in front of Joey's house a few minutes later. He came out with a large rolling bag and set it in the trunk.

"If we wrap this up quickly, maybe we can enter a poker tournament," he said as he buckled his seatbelt.

"I'd win."

Joey scoffed. "You think you're a better player than me?"

"I think you'd get hungry as the day wore on," I said. "The visions of mozzarella sticks dancing in your head would cause you to make some mistakes."

"Maybe just a cash game, then."

I drove to BWI Airport and parked in the daily garage. A bus pulled in a couple minutes later. We climbed on with our bags and got off at the near end of the terminal. Joey and I each had tickets on our phones. We got through the initial check-in quickly before bogging down in the TSA line. Plenty of time remained before our flight, so I wasn't worried we would miss it. Still, I hated getting delayed for security theater which comprised much of the ridiculous procedure involved with actually getting on a plane.

The line moved quickly enough. I took my shoes and belt off on command and collected them a couple uneventful minutes later. Joey walked away from the checkpoint behind me and caught up. "You see the short woman there?" he asked. "The blonde?"

"Yeah."

"I thought about making a joke when she told me to take my shoes and belt off. Quickly reconsidered."

"Good call," I said.

"You would've bailed me out, right?"

"Sure . . . after I got back. These are non-refundable tickets."

Joey grinned and shook his head. As we approached our gate, the number of restaurants grew more plentiful. If I listened closely, I probably could've heard Joey's stomach rumbling. "You're buying the food, right?"

"You know there's a size limit to a carry-on bag?" I said.

"It'll be a struggle." Despite an abundance of fast-food or fast-casual options, Joey walked into Captain Jim's Seafood, an actual restaurant. Two carry-out orders later—one normal-sized and the other fit for a famished family of four—we sat in uncomfortable chairs at our gate. After about thirty minutes, an agent announced we would begin boarding soon. Joey and I lined up, got onto the plane, and found our assigned numbers. T.J. was smart enough to book me an aisle. Joey frowned at his window seat across the lane.

"Wanna switch?" he said.

"Not a chance." I plopped down, slid my bookbag under the chair in front of me, and kept my take-out bag on my lap. Joey grumbled and shuffled sideways to sit. The plane filled up quickly. A slender husband and wife sat next to Joey, while a mother and her daughter took the other two spots in my row. While I've always considered myself outgoing, I've never been a fan of talking to someone because circumstances tossed us together. The two people next to me buried their faces in iPads and headphones right away. Always nice to meet a couple kindred spirits.

After a flight attendant finished reviewing the safety procedures no one listened to, I texted T.J. *We're about to take off. See if you can find any more about our guy . . . like clients he might've had. Want to know more before we chase him down.*

She responded a couple minutes later. *On it, boss. Hope your plane doesn't go down in a big ball of fire.* Another text followed. *Dibs on your car if it does.*

At least she was consistent.

———

Harry Reid Airport let you know you landed in Vegas as soon as you set foot inside. I didn't have any interest in playing slot machines the moment I stepped off the plane—or ever, really. As Joey and I waited for our rental car, I checked my phone. T.J. texted while we were in the air. *Found one person who used O'Kelly's service. Willy Chen. He was a high-stakes player with a big following. Not so much anymore, but he's often hanging around poker rooms. Still has his schedule online from when he used to be popular. You can find him tonight at Caesar's.* I showed the message to Joey. "We're staying more or less across the street," he said.

I texted back. *Thanks. We'll check it out.*

A reply came quickly. *You're not dead. I knew you'd make it there in one piece.*

A few minutes later, we were the proud temporary users of a Dodge Charger. Joey grabbed the keys even though the reservation was in my name. He set off for the Planet Hollywood hotel and casino. I insisted on staying on the Strip. There's not much point to Vegas if you don't. I've enjoyed the downtown area, but it's always been a different vibe. Joey and I walked in, and the clerk told us we were sharing a two-queens room. I plastered a smile on my face, accepted the keys, and headed for the elevator. "I need to have a long talk with my secretary," I said as the doors closed.

Joey chuckled. "She's probably just trying to save you a little money."

"The client came from my parents' foundation."

"You're working with them again?"

"We floated a trial balloon. The point is when someone else is paying the tab, you don't skimp on the accommodations. I need to make sure she knows."

"It's like you're running a real business," Joey said with an amused smile. "Next, you'll have to write an employee handbook."

"Piss off," I grumbled. "It'll be worth it to have future rooms to myself." The image of Joey's persistent silly smile in the mirrored wall made me shake my head and grin. The elevator dinged for our floor, and we walked down the hall to our room. The inside was nice enough. Everything looked new or newish. The Hollywood vibe came mostly from pictures on the walls. Ours were adorned with stills of Marilyn Monroe, Al Pacino, and Vin Diesel. I tossed my bag onto the bed closer to the window.

"How do you know I didn't want it?" Joey said.

"I'm not getting in the way if you have to make a dash to the bathroom at two AM."

"You hungry? We have some time until the guy shows up at Caesar's."

"A little," I said. "You must be starving by now. You've only eaten four meals so far."

"If your folks are picking up the bill, I'm sure they won't

mind if we order room service." Joey picked up a book on the nightstand between the two beds.

"If my mother faints at the expense report, I'm throwing you under the bus."

"Only fair," he said. We made a few choices of generic American fare, and someone knocked on the door twenty minutes later. To my surprise, Joey only ordered a burger and fries. Maybe he didn't want my mother to faint, after all. Once we'd eaten and put nicer clothes on, we headed to Caesar's. The garish Roman theme dominated the exterior and interior from the famous fountains to the underground shops. Extra vigilance for knife-wielding men would be required.

The poker room lay past an array of blackjack tables. Willy Chen was easy enough to find. He was a tall half-Asian man with long, stringy black hair, and he wore aviator sunglasses. Three other players joined him at the limit Hold-em table with $25 and $50 bets. I'd played for smaller stakes in my day. Good thing I brought a decent amount of cash. No one sat on either side of Chen, so Joey and I plopped down and exchanged money for chips with the dealer, a pleasant-looking middle-aged woman.

I folded my first few hands, and no one at the table seemed eager to engage in conversation. Then, Chen raised, I called, and we ended up as the only two players in the pot. A few more bets later, my nines beat his eights. "Nice hand," he muttered as the dealer shoved the chips in my direction.

"Thanks." He still enjoyed a nice stack, and so did I after winning the hand. No need to push too hard for now. About fifteen minutes later, we showed down another hand, and this time, his straight beat mine. I offered a reciprocal, "Nice hand," to which Chen grunted and nodded. I wondered if he enjoyed playing poker. No aspect of his demeanor indicated a whit of joy. His movements were all perfunctory. Even when he won a hand, he seemed to be in no rush to collect his chips. This made him stand out from everyone else at the table. Dark glasses made his eyes impossible to see—useful to stop tells but also to hide a general malaise. Maybe Chen's status as a has-been caught up to him.

A few minutes later, Joey raised, and Chen and I both called. The three of us stayed in the hand the whole time. Joey's three Jacks took it down. Chen said, "Nice hand" to him in the exact same tone he used with me.

I figured now was as good a time as any to start in on Chen. "We learned a little bit from Kieran O'Ceallaigh," I said. Chen offered no reaction, though his glasses did their job in limiting my ability to read his expression. "You know him?"

"Nope," he said right away.

"Funny. You both have said the opposite in the past."

"What are you, a reporter?"

"No," I said. "Just someone interested in talking to O'Ceallaigh."

"Can't help you." He turned his shoulders to angle himself away from me as much as possible in the chair.

The dealer slid cards to each of us in turn. Chen—first to act—looked at his. I let mine sit. "If you don't want people to talk to you, maybe you shouldn't post your schedule on your website."

"Whatever. Raise." He put his chips in the pot with more vigor than I'd ever seen him use.

Maybe it was a tell. I looked at my two cards. The eight and five of diamonds. Not a hand I'd normally be eager to play, but I might have gotten under Chen's skin enough to put him on tilt. "Call," I said. The table folded around to Joey, who took a few seconds before surrendering his cards as well.

The dealer tossed one card in the muck and flipped over

three. King of clubs, ten of hearts, and the five of spades. I'd made bottom pair. Chen reached for a chip right away and tossed it into the pot. "You here to talk or play?"

"Raise." I slid a fifty-dollar chip across the table. Chen shook his head and called.

The next card came—a five of hearts. Now, I had three fives. If Chen kept two hearts, he'd be on a flush draw, but his immediate bet made me think he had a king among his two hole cards. He bet right away again. I called. The last card was the three of clubs. Chen pushed a fifty out there, and I did the same. We turned up our cards. He showed the King and Queen of diamonds. When he saw my lowly five, he let out an exasperated sigh. "It's all good," I said as I collected my winnings. "I'm sure Kieran O'Ceallaigh will be happy to work with you again." I swept my arm at the emptiness around our table. "You really draw a crowd."

"You think I can't have you thrown out of here?" Chen said, turning toward me.

I shrugged. "I think it doesn't matter. You're avoiding a simple question."

Chen flagged down a passing floor worker. The man wore a nice suit and looked like he could have picked up the table and tossed it clear across the casino in the event of an emergency. "This guy's harassing me." He jerked his thumb in my direction. "I want him gone."

The burly man raised his eyebrows. I put on my best smile. "I'm just happy to meet a player I recognize from TV," I said.

"Piss off, Willy," the worker said. "You don't want to meet people, fine. Stop telling them you'll be here." He walked away.

"That went well," I said when he'd left the area.

"Color me up," Chen demanded, pushing his chips toward the dealer. She frowned but counted his stack.

I leaned a little closer to Chen and lowered my voice. "Kieran O'Ceallaigh. Why are you so desperate not to talk about him?"

The dealer handed Chen a smaller stack of chips he could quickly exchange with a cashier. He shoved them in his pocket. "If you're smart," he said, "you'll stop asking. Me. Anyone else." Chen stood and stormed away from the table.

Joey smirked. "You really have a way with people."

CHAPTER 12

BACK IN THE HOTEL ROOM, I texted Gloria to see if she was still awake. The time difference would make it about one AM back home. She replied a minute later and said she was in bed and tired but still awake. Capitalizing on Joey getting in the shower, I called her. "How's Vegas?" she asked.

"Haven't seen much of it this trip. I did win a couple hundred dollars playing poker, though."

"How's the case going?"

"Slowly," I said. "The guy I beat at the table was supposed to be a client of the missing dad. Didn't want to talk about him, though, and basically said we shouldn't keep asking."

"Of course, you're going to keep asking."

"I do like the Socratic method. Must be the philosophy classes I took."

Gloria chuckled, and the weariness in her voice provided an alluring husk to her tone. "Try not to piss anyone off too badly. I'd like you to make it home in one piece."

"I'll survive," I said. "Joey's out here to keep an eye on me . . . when he's not enjoying a buffet."

"That's good," she said. "Just don't meet some floozy and get married by Elvis."

"I'm all shook up by your accusation."

"Are you staying at the Heartbreak Hotel?"

"I think I might like a little less conversation," I said.

An airy laugh sounded in my ear, and I smiled. "We're reaching the limit of my knowledge of Elvis songs," Gloria said.

"It's just as well. Any more, and I'd be tempted to launch into a bad impression." I paused. What prompted Gloria to joke about an Elvis-officiated wedding? Was she dropping a hint about proposing? I didn't know, but I ran with it. "If I do get married, I'd like it to be in Baltimore. Not Vegas."

"Is that so?"

"Yeah. A casino just isn't my venue of choice."

"You have anyone in mind for this wedding?" Gloria said.

"Maybe," I said when I couldn't think of anything else.

"You should ask her, then. She might say yes."

My throat went dry. Gloria practically told me I should pop the question, and I was two thousand miles away in a hotel room thanks to my current case. When I got back, I wouldn't waste any time. "I'm glad to hear it," I said, again at a loss for words. I was normally good at talking to people, especially Gloria. Proposing would make things a lot easier.

She yawned on the phone. "It's late here. You're probably tired, too."

"I still need to count my winnings," I said. "Might be up a while."

"Don't skimp on sleep," Gloria said. "I wouldn't want you to forget any questions you might want to ask."

"I'm on it," I said. "Get some rest. Hopefully, I'll see you in a couple days. Love you."

"Love you, too. Good night." We hung up, and Joey came out of the bathroom a minute later.

"Were you talking to Gloria?" he said.

"Yeah. I think she's figured out I want to propose."

He snickered. "Of course she did. She's smarter than you. Did you really think you could surprise her?"

It had been my hope, but I always considered the possibility it fell into the foolish and vain category. "I suppose not," I admitted.

————

The next morning, I woke up too late to intercept Joey before he found the closest breakfast buffet. The pictures he sent me compelled me to walk down the Strip and join him. While we ate, I tried to stay productive by texting T.J. *First meeting was a dud. Chen didn't want to talk. Did you find anyone else?* After a mere three plates crammed with pastries, eggs, potatoes, and an array of other foods, Joey tapped out. As we returned to our hotel and rode the elevator, T.J. sent me another name.

I called the man and told him what I wanted to know. He suggested in the strongest possible terms I should perform a biologically impossible action and broke the connection. "No one wants to talk about this guy," I said.

"Maybe he's mobbed up," Joey suggested. When I frowned, he added, "Let's not pretend the Irish don't have gangsters."

"It's just not every day the Italian with the sketchy job accuses someone else of having mob contacts."

Joey shrugged. "It's a possibility."

"I guess. Seems like a bit of a long shot, though."

"You want to do anymore background work on this guy?"

"No," I said. "No one wants to talk about him. I'll get his address, and we can pay him a visit."

"You're aware we're unarmed," Joey pointed out.

"I know. Let's avoid situations we'd need to shoot our way out of. We're only going to see what's going on." I took my laptop from its bag, spent a few minutes making sure I used a secure and anonymous connection to the Internet, and got to work. O'Kelly, or whatever the hell he called himself now, lived in a large house. It was registered in the name of his business instead of to him personally, but this merely took a few more seconds to untangle. The place looked bigger than Gloria's, and a black fence surrounded it. He lived about ten minutes off the Strip.

I called ahead for our rental car, and the valet pulled it up to the curb as we walked outside. After tipping the young man a five, I grabbed the keys, and we left the commercial area of Vegas for a ritzy residential section. Gloria lived in Brooklandville, a posh part of Baltimore County. Apart from the differences in tree coverage caused by being in the desert, O'Kelly's neighborhood looked pretty similar. Large houses. Long, winding driveways. Lots of privacy fences—and one forbidding black metal version.

As we drove around the block again to scout the area, my phone rang. T.J. I set it on the console and put it on speaker. "Tara wants an update," she said.

"And I want a Porsche on my parking pad."

"You buying one?"

I snorted. "Is she there now?"

"No. She called a little while ago. I told her I'd ask you and get back to her."

"Did you tell her where we were?" I asked.

"No," T.J. said.

"Good. Don't. I'd rather not get her hopes up. Or encourage her to fly out here and see what's going on."

"What should I tell her, then?"

Before I could answer, Joey interjected. "Tell her C.T. is

with a very good-looking and capable friend. The situation is well in hand."

"All right," T.J. said.

"No, don't tell her—" The line went dead. Joey chuckled. "Has anyone ever told you how annoying you are?"

"Sure," he said. "When they pay for my flight, hotel, and meals, though, I tend to forget about it."

I made the left onto O'Ceallaigh's street. Each house sat on a generous lot. This wasn't a gated community, but the residents could afford a security patrol. We'd deal with them if they showed up. I drove a couple houses past his, turned around, and curbed the car across the street.

"Now what?" Joey said.

"We see what develops."

Not much did. Joey and I talked a lot about Tara's case recently. I needed to catch him up on recent developments. "I bought an engagement ring."

He turned to regard me with wide eyes. "No shit?"

"No shit."

"Wow. I'll try not to be offended you didn't ask me to shop with you. We Italians are natural appraisers."

"I took Rich," I said. "If only I'd known about your ethnic bonus."

"Shoulda asked," he said. "You give it to Gloria yet?"

"No. Waiting for the right time . . . hasn't come up yet."

"The perfect moment doesn't exist. When it feels like a good time, you should just do it."

I chuckled. "You're drawing on your vast experience getting down on one knee?"

"We Italians might be natural appraisers," Joey said with a smile, "but we really shine in matters of the heart. Listen to me, and you'll be engaged in no time."

"I'd rather be engaged at the right time." Joey didn't have

a clever retort or another attribute he derived from his heritage. At least he knew now.

A few minutes later, he said, "This isn't a very exciting part of the job."

"Feel free to pay for your own hotel and meals, then."

Joey smiled. "Let's not get crazy."

———

We waited a while longer. Even in fall, the desert heat forced us to fire up the engine periodically and run the air conditioner for a few minutes at a time. "We even know if this prick is home?" Joey asked as cool air filled the cabin.

"Nope."

"So we might be sitting out here for nothing."

"Yep," I said.

He shook his head. "You have a weird job sometimes."

"Welcome to doing stake-outs. T.J. checked his calendar. At least according to what's available online, he had no plans for the day and should be here in his house."

"Maybe we oughta walk up and knock," Joey said.

"Sure. People who disappear for twelve years are always delighted to meet strangers who want to dredge up their previous lives. He'll probably offer us some iced tea and finger sandwiches."

Joey grunted. With the interior at an agreeable temperature, I killed the engine again. We were able to leave it off for about fifteen minutes before discomfort required colder air. Someone looking from the house might see the exhaust while we ran the motor, but it wouldn't be continuous. Short of waiting for a cool day which wasn't in the forecast for months, it was our best bet. After another cycle of hot and cool, I opened the driver's door. "I'm going to take a closer look at things."

"You might draw some attention," Joey said.

I shrugged. "I'll try not to, but it may be inevitable. Not exactly a lot happening here at the moment. You take over behind the wheel. If shit goes south, we'll need a quick getaway."

He climbed out. We each shut the car doors as quietly as we could. I stayed low and moved across the street. While most homes featured fences, O'Ceallaigh's was the only one made of black metal and the only one which encircled the entire property. As I drew closer, I saw a small camera mounted atop a post. Anyone trying to climb over would alert whatever security detail a man like O'Ceallaigh employed. I preferred not to find out.

The black barrier did a poor job of hiding anything behind it. From the neighbor's front porch, I could see the entirety of the house in question. To keep up appearances, I rang the doorbell and reviewed my options for what I might say if someone responded. No one did. I pushed the button again as I kept an eye on the O'Ceallaigh compound. When the second buzz went unanswered, I crouched and scooted as far down the porch as I could.

As houses went, O'Ceallaigh's was nice and pretty large. I'd seen and been in bigger residences. My vantage point allowed me a look inside three first-floor windows. No one milled about inside. I saw enough of the furniture to presume a decorator ordered it under the guise of some unified vision for the decor. I'd seen this at my parents' place. All it did was add twenty percent to the cost of shopping out of the ritzy catalog.

A few minutes passed. No one seemed to take notice of me. I remained low and moved back toward the steps. I crouched near the edge of the neighbor's house. My phone vibrated in my pocket. Joey texted. *No signs of movement.* I waited a couple minutes before standing and approaching the property line. O'Ceallaigh's fence didn't break in the front. I saw a gate but no way to open it from the outside. Visitors needed to pass muster and get buzzed in.

I moved to the side of the house and stopped at a window. It was one I saw into before. Nothing changed. I prepared to move along and stopped when a large man approached from the rear. I turned and an equally massive fellow walked toward me from the front. Considering how secretive—and probably paranoid—O'Ceallaigh was, I figured someone would spot me sooner or later.

On the whole, I would've preferred later.

CHAPTER 13

TO THEIR CREDIT, both men wore white shirts with black suits despite the heat. Their lone concession to the elements came in each omitting a tie. Both were bigger and broader than me. While I could probably outrun them, the black fence on my left limited my available terrain. They slowed as they drew close, each stopping about five feet from my front and rear. I spread my hands. "Is this the site of the Gamblers Anonymous protest?" Neither said anything. "We're trying to hit all the highly-paid consultants. I'd hate to miss one."

"This is private property, sir," the one standing between me and the road said. His long blond mullet belied the serious nature of his job, and his accent identified him as a recent transplant from Texas.

"You need to move along," the other added. He had darker hair and wore it in a less ridiculous style.

I didn't really want to get into a tangle with these two in a residential neighborhood. Someone could have been watching. "Fine," I said. "The movement will continue elsewhere." I headed for the street, and the long-haired goon put a hand on my chest to stop me. "I'm getting some mixed messages here. If you want me to go, you should let me."

"Maybe you should answer some questions first."

"If I thought the two of you could ask a good one, I might consent."

He glared and leaned closer. I felt the one behind me take a step forward. Usually, I favored a defensive fighting style. I didn't want either of these lummoxes getting their hands on me, so I went on offense right away. While Captain Mullet held his face close to mine, I drove my forehead into his face above his nose. It hurt me a little, but he grunted and staggered back a step. The guy to my rear surged forward.

Odds were high he was right-handed, so I ducked and pivoted to my left. Sure enough, his meaty right fist swung toward my former position in a fast and violent arc. It connected with his compatriot, and the poor blond fellow got blasted from his feet and landed with an undignified thud in the grass. He didn't move.

I faced the remaining guard. He recovered from the surprise of knocking out his partner and glowered at me. "I hope O'Ceallaigh isn't paying you idiots too much."

"You'll regret coming here today," he growled. I dodged his first punch and blocked the next two. My arms stung from the force. This guy wasn't holding back. He aimed to drop me to the ground with a single swing. While his punches were strong, injecting maximum power made them slow. I stepped forward as I blocked another. While the goon drew his fist back, I hit him with two quick shots in the solar plexus. His arm dropped to his side as he sucked wind.

Through the window, I saw another black-suited muscleman take an interest in the skirmish. I needed to leave before the reinforcement arrived. With my foe still stunned, I elbowed him in the face, grabbed him by the neck, and rammed his head into an unforgiving black fence post. His eyes swam, but he didn't go down. I did it again, and this time, he sagged to the grass. Once he fell, I sprinted to the front of the house. Joey already had the car ready. One man emerged from the front door and ran toward the gate.

I didn't bother going around to the passenger's side. Instead, I opened the rear door and climbed in behind Joey. He took off with screeching tires before I even got it closed.

The Charger didn't come with GPS, so Joey used his phone to get us out of the neighborhood while I climbed back up front. He took a circuitous return route to the heart of Vegas. We didn't see a tail anywhere. "I was careful," I said when we turned onto the Strip. "They had a chance to see me, but the response came really quick."

"Maybe too quick," Joey said. "There was nothing going on, and all of a sudden, I saw a guy come out of the house."

"Another one from the back."

"I think they knew we were coming."

It made sense. I didn't see any cameras looking into the neighbor's yard. If someone detected me, they did so manually—and I also didn't notice any goons peering from a window. "We got ratted out," I said. "The only person who makes sense is Chen."

"Son of a bitch gave us up," Joey muttered.

"He didn't seem eager to talk about O'Ceallaigh." Joey drove past our hotel, made a U-turn, and then swung a quick left into the garage. No one followed us through his maneuver. "Maybe he's in debt to the guy, and this is his way of paying some of it off."

"Or he didn't like you beating him in a couple showdowns."

"I wouldn't have needed to if you'd played a few hands."

Joey parked the car and shrugged. "I got shit for cards. The couple times I had something good, I got beat on the flop." He paused to look in the mirrors. "What do you want to do?"

"I think we need to check out and go somewhere else," I said. "Let's assume Chen gave us up. He probably described us, too, and O'Ceallaigh's men got a first-hand look at me just now. If our guy has any friends in the casino, he's probably circulated our faces around. These places are all their own businesses, but they cooperate against people who try to screw them and anyone they don't like."

"Off the Strip, then."

"I think we have to. Some place like the Rio is too obvious."

"I have a spot in mind," Joey said. We left the car, took the elevator to our room, packed our stuff, and checked out. A few minutes later, we climbed back into the Charger and headed away from Planet Hollywood.

"You going downtown?" I said as Joey navigated us back to the main drag.

"Yeah. Always wanted to stay at the Four Queens. I loved their cheap blackjack tables when I was younger."

Both of us remained vigilant for any miscreants following us. Sure enough, I spotted someone a couple blocks down the road. "Gray SUV behind us. Picked us up just after we left the garage."

Joey got over one lane to the right. A few seconds later, the other vehicle mirrored the movement. "Yep. We got a tail." It was too early for traffic to be heavy, so the trailing SUV was easy to spot. As the light ahead turned yellow, Joey got on the gas and drove through the intersection.

Our pursuers sped through and followed.

CHAPTER 14

.

"I KINDA HOPED we'd lose them there," Joey said.

"Would it be wrong to say I wanted someone to T-bone them?" I checked the mirror. The gray SUV was closer than ever. The driver abandoned any pretense of not following us.

"I wish this car were faster." Joey changed lanes again. The other vehicle remained where it was for now. "My BMW would do a lot better."

"At more than twice the price, I should hope so. Not a lot of Five Series sedans at the Hertz counter, though."

Joey grunted and glanced at his phone. His car featured built-in navigation on a large screen. Still, he made the best of the situation. Traffic grew a little heavier as we drove along. The light we approached flipped to yellow. Joey swung a hard left in front of two oncoming cars. I held onto the oh-shit handle with a white-knuckle grip as the first sped by the rear bumper with a blaring horn. The SUV behind us couldn't make the turn immediately. Joey went right, going the wrong direction on a one-way street. He got to the next intersection before a few cars came toward us.

With this buffer—and thanks to a few more turns—Joey lost the SUV chasing us. He puttered around off the main road for a while, but we didn't see the gray vehicle again. A few minutes later, we parked at the Four Queens. I paid cash for a room, and Joey used a convincing fake ID for himself in the name of Floyd Rayford. "An Orioles backup from before we were born," he told me on the elevator ride to our room.

The accommodations here were much like they were at Planet Hollywood. The motif of the room owed no allegiance to the film industry, and a discerning reviewer would probably note one star's worth of difference when crafting the ratings. It would work quite nicely for what we needed, however. I unpacked my laptop and set it up for secure and anonymous browsing. We still needed to corral Kieran O'Ceallaigh, and I didn't think we'd get another chance at his house.

"He runs a gambling consulting company," I said. "He must have an office."

"Not necessarily." Joey tossed his bag down and stretched out on the bed closer to the door. "It's something he could do from home."

"It is, but I don't think he does. He works with some bettors, but a lot of his testimonials are from casino employees. They're going to expect someone to keep an actual office and not just a spare bedroom in their house."

"I guess."

I opened Signal and found T.J. online. *We got made at the house. Changed hotels. Going to look for a business address.*

She answered a moment later. *Couldn't find one in his name, but maybe you'll have better luck.*

O'Ceallaigh set his company up under KOC Wagering and Consulting. No corresponding business under this name existed in the registry, however. This would be the dead-end T.J. hit. A few more minutes and some time unwinding a couple LLCs told me KOC Wagering and Consulting existed as a wholly-owned subsidiary of a company called Double K Enterprises.

Double K maintained an office just off the Strip.

———

We'd been on a good run with him behind the wheel, so Joey drove toward the offices of Double K. He took a winding route before getting onto Las Vegas Boulevard, which became the Strip once the casinos came into view, and the scent of money filled the air. My phone vibrated in my pocket. I was surprised to see Rich calling. "If you want me to ring shop with you," I said, "you'll have to wait a couple days."

"Not why I'm calling," he said. His voice sounded serious, even for my straight-laced cousin.

"What's going on?"

"My house got shot at earlier this morning. The ones on either side of it, too."

"Were you home?"

"No, I was at work. Uniforms told me about it, so I came back."

"Anybody hurt?"

"No," Rich said. "The guy on the left side was home, but he was upstairs at the time. Bullets only hit the lower level. Same at my place. A few holes in the siding and one broken window. I guess I got off easy."

I didn't like this one bit. First, I almost got flattened walking back to my house. Then, someone slashed my parents' tires, and maybe the same someone nearly T-boned Joey in an intersection. Now, a mystery shooter sprayed Rich's house with bullets. I tried not to take it all personally, but it felt like someone targeted me and those close to me. I would need to check on Gloria and T.J. after talking to Rich. "I'm going to guess no one saw anything."

"Nope. Shots didn't even get reported right away."

"Any of your neighbors have a doorbell camera?" I said.

"The couple to the right. Their walkway is too long, though. The street's not in view."

"I'm surprised you don't have something."

"Maybe I do." The line went silent except for Rich's footsteps on a wooden floor. "Remember the new pole lights I installed near my driveway?"

I didn't remember or care about Rich's yard projects, but I still said, "Sure."

"One of them has a camera mounted on top," he said. "It's a lot closer to the road. Could've picked up something."

"Worth a try." Joey frowned at me. I shook my head and mouthed I would tell him later. We passed the Luxor casino on the right. Joey's phone showed a few more turns and five minutes remaining.

"I'm checking on my computer now," Rich said.

"You know there's probably an app," I pointed out. "You could put me on speaker and just look on your phone."

"Easier to see on my monitor." He paused, and I didn't press the point. Rich would be forty in a couple years. If he needed a larger screen, he should use it. There would be plenty of chances for mockery later. "All right . . . I think I have something. The whole street's not in the shot. I might need to move the camera a little."

"You see anything?"

"A car comes up . . . muzzle flashes . . . it drives off."

"Any guess as to the make or model?" I asked.

"Hard to tell. Going by the shape, I'm pretty sure it's a sports car." My mouth went dry. "If I had to guess, I'd say a Mustang."

I blew out a deep breath. "Does your setup record in color?"

"Yeah. It's green."

Shit. "Rich, you need to know a few things."

"Am I going to like this conversation?" he said.

"Probably not," I admitted. "A few days ago, I very nearly got run over walking back home after running around the park. Later, my parents' tires all got slashed while they were at the foundation. Then, Joey almost got T-boned going up Eastern Avenue leaving my office."

"So?"

"Now, someone ventilated your house. Want to guess what ties all these together?"

"Besides you looking for some deeper meaning?" He paused a beat. "The green Mustang?"

"Bingo. So far, no one's been hurt, but this is the fourth time something happened. The same kind of car has been involved every time. I know you don't believe much in coincidences."

"I don't," he said. "You working a case where someone might come after people you know?"

"Unlikely. When I almost got hit, I hadn't even started my current gig. The timing doesn't line up."

"As much as I don't like it when you try to make things about yourself, you do seem to be the common factor here. Anyone hate you enough to do all this?"

"Anyone who's still in prison because I helped put them there," I said. "It's a sizable list."

"It'll take a while to go through, but it's a start."

"Do me a favor? Check in on Gloria and T.J. I'm two thousand miles away, or I'd do it myself."

"Wilco."

"Thanks," I said, and we ended the call.

"Everything all right?" Joey wanted to know. I filled him in on what happened. "We'd better wrap this up out here. Someone seems to have it in for you."

"Yeah." I frowned and looked out the window. "The question is, who?"

———

Double K Enterprises would not be hosting high-end clients.

Their office lay in what looked like an industrial strip mall. I expected painting stores and a sketchy car repair shop to be in the neighboring buildings. It turned out they were both vacant. The area was full of long one-story buildings broken up into separate units. While the ones on either side of Double K went unused, the rest of the complex seemed to be doing OK. People constantly walked in and out of the tile store three doors down. We parked near it and kept Double K in sight.

Joey took out his camera. Despite both our phones taking fine photos, he brought an actual 35-millimeter model with an add-on lens. "Rich has his boomer stereo system," I said. "You have your camera."

"I enjoyed photography class in college," Joey said. "Even dated one of the girls I met there."

If I thought of the right person, she was a blonde airhead who loved to take pictures of dying flowers. She and Joey didn't last long. I didn't belabor the point. "You should've taken swing dancing, then."

"We Italians don't need classes to help our rhythm."

I snorted but let him have his little victory. Besides, I met a couple Italian girls in the classes, and they were probably the best dancers there. They were certainly the best lovers. We went back to watching the business. Rich's house getting shot up by the green Mustang still bothered me. He said he would check in on Gloria and T.J. What kind of almost-fiancé would I be if I left my future wife unaware? I sent her a text. *Hi. Just want you to keep an eye out for a green Mustang. The same car was there when my parents' tires were cut, Joey almost got T-boned, and Rich's house got shot at.* I left out the part about me nearly turning into road pizza. Gloria would be sufficiently worried already.

Sure enough, she replied a minute later. *OMG! You didn't tell me there was a suspect in your parents' situation.*

Just found out before I left. Today, Rich told me about the bullets hitting his house. He's going to check in, but I want you to be careful. If you see the car, call him and drive somewhere safe. Your rocket can outrun a Mustang.

I know . . . you've done it! :) I knew the emoji at the end of her response belied her nerves.

"She pissed you didn't mention it earlier?" Joey said, leaning closer to read my text thread.

I turned my screen away. "I think she's more worried about the same car turning up at all these different things. Kind of like I am."

"You'll figure it out."

"Being most of the way across the country ramps up the difficulty," I said. "Even for me."

Joey pointed to his left. Two guys walked out of Double K. One looked like he could have ripped the door from its hinges if it got stuck. The other was a smaller middle-aged guy losing his hair on the top. Joey aimed his camera toward them. He snapped a few pictures before they got into a large SUV and drove away. We remained in our parking spot. "I think I got a couple good ones," he said. "I'll send them to you."

He did so from the camera's native menu. "You must have gotten a newer model," I said as I saw the images pop up on my phone.

"Yeah. Wi-Fi and everything. It's using my phone as a hotspot now."

"Rich and his stereo stand alone, then."

Joey grinned. "Maybe your cousin is a secret vinyl-loving hipster."

I shook my head. "No. He doesn't have a beard, and I've heard of most of the bands he listens to. Those factors disqualify him right away." I saved the best of the pictures Joey sent me. It featured a head-on look at the former Kevin O'Kelly. "Let's do a comparison." I opened a remote connection to my server in Maryland and used it to access the BPD's facial recognition tool. On my first case, Rich committed the cardinal sin of leaving me alone at his computer. Ever since, I've been able to get the network to accept mine as one of its own.

I uploaded a photo of O'Kelly from a couple years before his disappearance and the one from today. The system crunched its algorithm for a second before spitting out a result. I showed the screen to Joey.

99.3% LIKELY MATCH.

CHAPTER 15

WE PULLED out in pursuit of the SUV after a moment. It was easy enough to find in the complex. Kieran O'Ceallaigh and his goon stopped for lunch at a deli five minutes away. From there, they drove back to the office. Joey and I headed back to our downtown hotel. "Looks like he's not spooked," I said.

"You thought he might be?"

I nodded. "If I'd moved two thousand miles away and created an entirely new life, I think someone staking out my house would raise the alarm."

"He seems to be well-known enough in gambling circles," Joey said. "Maybe people who followed his advice and lost have come to his place before."

"Maybe. At least I can let Tara know we found him." I took out my phone and called the client. "Good news," I said when she picked up. "We located your dad."

Silence persisted as the only response for several seconds. Eventually, Tara said, "You really did?" in a quiet voice.

"Yes. I'm sure it's him."

"Where are you?"

"Pretty far away," I said.

"You don't want to tell me?"

"I don't want you flying out here in the hopes of a cheery reunion."

"I gave up on the chance of that years ago," she said.

"Unfortunately, it was probably for the best. We found him, though. Is there anything else you want me to do?"

"Can you get close to him?"

Trying again at his house would be a poor idea. The two goons I tangled with weren't hurt badly. They'd both be back on duty, and O'Ceallaigh might have beefed up his security. Getting to him at work would be simpler—probably not easy but doable for a couple of guys like Joey and me. "I'm pretty sure we can."

"Good. Ask him why he left." Tara's voice cracked. "I want to know. Why did he leave us all of a sudden and with no money? Tell him what's happened. Tell him his ex-wife ended up in psychiatric hospital." She paused and cried for a moment. I stayed quiet. "You make sure he knows," she said through tears. "Make sure he knows how hard this has been for us."

I wondered if O'Ceallaigh would even care at this point. He'd carved out a nice life out here, and his old one was a dozen years in the rearview. If Tara wanted me to unload it all on him, I would. "All right," I said. "I'll tell him."

"Thank you, C.T." She sniffed a few times. "Let me know what he says . . . the bastard." She ended the call.

"I'd wanna know, too," Joey offered.

I bobbed my head. "I think it's natural to."

"What's our next move?"

"I want to have T.J. do a little more research. Business partners, smaller clients . . . those kinds of things. In the meantime, you and I need to stay on him and see where we might be able to get to him."

"I don't think we should try the house again," Joey said.

"Me, either," I said. "Which leaves the office . . . or somewhere between the two. Let's settle on a good spot."

————

"I'm not sure what else I can find," T.J. said over the phone. Joey and I had returned to our hotel. "You're out there. You might have better luck."

"Time to earn your bonus," I said. In reality, I could have done a lot of the research myself. I'd done a ton in the past. Being local would help with some of it—or not, as our encounter with Willy Chen showed. I didn't need anyone else selling us out to Kieran O'Ceallaigh. T.J. soaked up knowledge and techniques like a sponge. I wanted to give her a chance. "Besides, I'll be busy keeping Joey out of the buffet lines."

"I can overpower you," my friend said.

T.J. snickered at the exchange. "He's right, you know."

"Can we get back to the part where you're doing your job?" I said.

"Yeah, yeah." Her keyboard clattered in my ear. "The businesses are his alone. Both KOC Wagering and Consulting and Double K. No partners or outside investors."

"Maybe he's working on his *Shark Tank* pitch."

"Could be," my secretary said. "His online calendar doesn't have a lot of availability."

"Doesn't mean anything. He might not have made many dates and times available. It creates false scarcity and entices people to make an appointment . . . which they presumably will need to pay for."

"We could try the same thing."

"Let's discuss our business model when we're both in the same room," I said.

"OK, boomer."

Joey chortled. I didn't have the call on speaker, but T.J.'s voice was loud enough to carry. "I want to know who his clients are. We talked to Chen, and I'm pretty sure he dimed us out. O'Ceallaigh's probably on alert now, though we saw him coming out of his office. He didn't seem to notice we were there."

"You get any pictures?" T.J. wanted to know.

"Yeah," I said. "Joey brought an actual camera and got a few photos. I used the BPD to compare it to one we had of Kevin O'Kelly. They're the same guy." Before T.J. could ask the obvious question, I continued. "Tara knows. I already talked to her."

"How did she take it?"

"In stride, I guess. She suspected he was alive. Getting actual confirmation instead of just probabilities makes a difference. She gave me a couple questions to ask when I see him."

"Good." She typed some more. "Looks like he meets with reps from a few different casinos. I don't know what the big ones are out there. Binion's, the Four Queens, Paris . . . Treasure Island. I don't see any others in the last six months."

"None of them are titans," I said, "but they're still decent feathers in his cap. A lot of smart guys can't get on a casino's radar at all. He must be doing something right." I figured O'Ceallaigh ingratiated himself with the players first. Guys like Willy Chen who mattered in the poker world at some point, maybe a well-known sharp bettor or two. If they dropped a name on the floor, it would get recorded and eventually make its way up the chain. Even a second-tier Vegas operation could outspend one gambler.

"His calendar looks full for the next couple days, actually," T.J. said. "I'm using the backdoor you taught me."

"See? You're earning your bonus already."

"He'll need to be at his office by nine-thirty for meetings."

On some level, I liked a man who didn't believe in an early start to the day. "He'll wrap up by four."

"All right," I said. "Thanks. We'll figure out the best way to try and get to him." We ended the call. "You hear the end?"

"Yeah," Joey said. "We scoped out the office a little today. I think we need to follow him to and from. See if there's something we can take advantage of."

"Sounds good. Let's do it tomorrow morning."

"Great." Joey patted his midsection. "Now, let's find a buffet."

———

The next morning, Joey and I got up early enough to head to O'Ceallaigh's neighborhood before he would leave for the office. Joey wasn't eager to wake up so early, and we still stopped for breakfast en route. O'Ceallaigh enjoyed a fairly short commute, however, so we were in position in plenty of time. After getting caught snooping near his fence, I didn't want to get too close. We curbed the car around the corner from his house.

If his first meeting started at nine-thirty, he'd probably want to be there early. Nine-fifteen or so. The clock in our rental struck nine o'clock. A few seconds later, two dark SUVs rolled down O'Ceallaigh's street and made the right turn at the stop sign. Both drove past us without a second glance. I spied our target in the back seat of the lead vehicle. Joey waited for the mini convoy to make the next left before firing up the Charger and driving after them.

We knew the route they would likely take, so letting them get a little bit ahead didn't matter. The drivers weren't in a hurry. They stuck to residential streets as long as they could, and both obeyed the speed limit. "Looks like two guys in the second Blazer," Joey said.

"O'Ceallaigh must be pinching pennies," I said. "I'm kind of surprised he doesn't have a pair of Yukons. Most other rich assholes do."

"It's kind of the official car of people who only want to be seen as important. The Land Rover CEO must be furious."

I shrugged. "Enough soccer moms buy them."

Joey let a Prius merge between us and the pair of SUVs. It never hurt to have a buffer. Everything I knew about following another car I learned from Rich and a bunch of spy movies. I figured Joey had the same pedigree. O'Ceallaigh likely employed his goons for their fighting prowess. The odds of any being wizards at defensive driving were small. Still, we played it safe.

A few blocks from the office, a light changed to yellow. The lead Blazer zoomed through. The second didn't risk it, however. Joey and I glanced at each other as the car stopped. "One driver is more gas-happy than the other," I said.

"They're close to his building, so maybe they don't see it as a problem."

"It's a vulnerability, though. It's one we can use."

The signal went green. "You want to grab him on the way in?" Joey asked.

"I think I'd like to be at the office ahead of time. Then, you can play Mario Andretti out here on the Strip and leave me with just one goon to deal with."

"Thanks for naming an Italian driver."

"It was him or Danica Patrick," I said, "and you're not pretty enough."

We didn't need to get spotted near the office again, so Joey kept going after the SUVs turned. We did a 180 a few blocks up and headed back to the hotel. "I don't like the idea of doing this unarmed," Joey said. "Those guys are gonna be packing."

"We're not licensed to carry out here." I wasn't even sure if Joey carried legally in Maryland.

"I'll find us a couple guns later."

"You just going to stroll into a black market pistol exchange?" I said.

He grinned. "I know people who know people. Leave it to me. I do this, you're springing for the buffet tonight."

"I'd better hope the poker and blackjack tables are kind to me, then."

CHAPTER 16

I DID ALL RIGHT at the tables. Not great but enough to treat my friend to another all-you-can-eat dinner without cringing at the receipt. After indulging in the very enjoyable sin of gluttony, I went upstairs while Joey hit the streets of Vegas to get us some weapons. I hoped he knew what he was doing— or at least had the contacts he claimed to. He returned a couple hours later carrying a small bag. In it were a Beretta .380 semiautomatic for me and a long-barreled .357 revolver for him. Each came with extra ammo.

"Looks like the kind of Walther PPK James Bond might carry," I said as I turned the weapon over in my hand.

"Don't bother," Joey said. "You don't like martinis."

"No trouble getting these?"

He shook his head. "Cost me a little more than I've won at the tables so far, but it's fine. They'll more than pay for themselves even if we don't need to use them tomorrow."

We went to sleep soon after. I woke up early the next morning. Maybe it stemmed from being on unfamiliar turf, but I felt amped up about going after O'Ceallaigh. I'd been slacking on my workouts since coming to Vegas, so I headed to the fitness center, where I ran three miles on a treadmill and worked over the heavy bag for fifteen minutes. Confident I could outrun and outkick any goons we encountered, I returned to the room for a much-needed shower. Joey still snored when I finished, so I lingered in the bathroom, closed the door, and called Gloria. "How are things out there," my soon-to-be-fiancee wanted to know.

"Moving along. We should wrap it up today if all goes well."

"Wow. That's good. It'll be nice to have you back."

"I know," I said. "You haven't traveled for tennis in a while, so neither of us has really been out of town. I miss you."

"I miss you, too."

"I guess I'm used to coming home and seeing you there."

"Me, too. It's easy to get used to."

We danced around the topic of proposing and marriage again. I didn't want to push it too far while I was most of the way across the country, but this was a positive sign. "I could even get used to your place," I said. "So long as the neighborhood watch doesn't mind a lowly private eye."

She chuckled. "I'd be glad to have you. So would the neighbors."

Another positive step. Gloria didn't blanch at the idea of living in one house together. I didn't want to give up my Federal Hill digs, but considering her place could swallow mine twice over and have room remaining for a swanky shed, it wasn't much of an argument. "Joey's snoring away out there." Even the closed bedroom door couldn't completely mute the sounds of him sawing wood. "You think I'm bad, you should hear him."

"You in the bathroom?" Gloria said.

"Yeah. I just showered. Now, you're picturing me naked."

"Something I do several times a day already."

"I knew I loved you for a reason," I said.

"More than one, I hope. Oh, I had an appointment with the orthopedist yesterday. Everything is healing well, but I'll still need two more weeks in a cast. A little smaller now, at least. I don't look like I'm about to club people."

"At least the end is in sight."

"It is," she said. "It's almost ten-thirty here. I need to get some work done. Let me know how things go. I'd love to give you a proper welcome later tonight."

"Can't wait," I said. We exchanged I-love-yous, and I ended the call. When I walked out of the bathroom fully dressed a moment later, Joey still snored.

"Wake up." I slapped him on the shoulder, and he grunted and stirred. "We need to get a move on."

"What time is it?" he mumbled.

"Seven-thirty. I want to be at O'Ceallaigh's office way before he is."

Joey sat up in bed and wiped sleep from his eyes. "We'll need breakfast on the way. If I'm going to back you up, I can't do it on an empty stomach."

"Can you do *anything* on an empty stomach?" I asked.

"No," Joey said.

At least our time in the drive-through line was brief. I munched a breakfast sandwich and drank mediocre coffee as Joey drove to O'Ceallaigh's office. The whole complex looked empty. We were still pretty early. Employees whose businesses which opened at nine and didn't require a lot of prep or setup in advance wouldn't need to unlock the doors for another half-hour. "I'm going to wait inside," I said. "Let me know when I can expect company."

"Sure." Joey nodded. "I'll keep the guys in the second car occupied."

"Try not to get shot."

"Aww, you're getting sentimental on me," he said as he devoured half a hash brown in a single bite.

"No . . . just contemplating the logistics of your coffin in the cargo hold of our return flight."

Joey chuckled and shook his head. "Piss off. Go do your thing." I climbed out of the Charger. It wasn't really possible to bring an item like a snap gun on a plane without attracting the wrong sort of attention. I kept some old-fashioned burglar's tools on a special keyring, however, and no one scrutinized them at a security checkpoint. I checked the front door for alarm sensors, found none, and got to work.

A minute later, I popped the lock and walked in. Joey waved and drove away. I kept the lights off. The sun coming in the left half of the large front window was enough. O'Ceallaigh's office looked completely unremarkable. The front half served as a waiting room, with a couch in need of new upholstery, a nice coffee table, and a selection of magazines. It made me recall many a trip to the doctor or dentist. His selection of periodicals was no better.

The back half held a large desk with a massive executive chair I would've been proud to sit in. Three guest chairs lined the other side. Two monitors sat atop the main desk, along with a single screen on the smaller one to the side. Each held a large tower computer. A small table on the side served as the coffee station. As much as I wanted another cup, I didn't turn it on. I plopped down in O'Ceallaigh's fancy chair and turned away so only the massive back could be seen from the door.

Then, it was time to wait.

It's a common thing with my job. I've gotten good at it

over time. Few people in Maryland can count ceiling tiles as quickly or thoroughly as me. I glanced at my watch. Still too early. I spun back around and looked at the keyboard. A quick tap of the space bar brought up the Windows login screen. My faint hope O'Ceallaigh didn't bother with a password got dashed. I checked the desk for a paper or sticky note where he might have written his credentials down. It happened often enough to make the search a good use of time.

Sure enough, a small piece of paper was taped to the bottom side of the mousepad. *TheGambl3r!,* it read. Not a bad password but not great, either. I typed it, pressed enter, and gained access. O'Ceallaigh kept a super clean desktop. The Recycle Bin was the only icon. I explored the file system. His sense of organization produced a logical structure. I didn't bring a flash drive. Instead, I opened a command prompt, noted the hostname, IP, and physical address of his computer, and logged off. If I needed to, I could access it remotely from the hotel.

A few minutes later, my phone vibrated. Joey texted. *They're headed in. Should be a big enough gap between SUVs for me to stop the second one.* I pivoted back around in the chair and told him I was ready. He called, I popped an earpiece in, and we kept the line open. Soon, an engine rumbled outside and then cut off. The lock spun and opened. Two pairs of footsteps walked in. I turned around and faced the room. Two pairs of eyes widened. "Good morning, Kieran," I said. "Or would you rather I called you Kevin?"

"Boss, who the hell is this guy?" The tall blond goon glanced between me and the man who signed his checks. "Want me to throw him out?"

"Yes," O'Ceallaigh said.

The enforcer advanced. I stood to meet him.

I took a defensive stance. The goon rushed through his last couple steps and threw a wild punch. Once his fist went back, I rocked on my heel and leaned away from it. He followed with another. I blocked and gave him a short jab in the solar plexus. He gasped but didn't back off. His punches were powerful even though he sucked wind. I turned them aside and looked for another opening.

The muscleman surprised me with a side kick. I got my arm down but not in time to blunt it completely. His foot took me in the right hip and drove me back a step. He closed the gap and tied off a strong punch. I grabbed his forearm, spun sharply, and flipped him onto his back. He landed on the tiled floor with a hard thud. I leaned down and punched him in the face. His head bounced off the ceramic, and he lay still. A gun peeked out from his light sportcoat at the side, so I grabbed it and stuffed it into my waistband.

"Like I was saying . . . would you rather go by Kieran or Kevin?"

"Who the hell are you?" O'Ceallaigh demanded.

"Someone who saw through your little ruse," I said.

In my ear, brakes screeched. A door thunked. "Stay in the car," Joey said. "Keep your hands where I can see them." A pause. "No, I ain't a cop. My friend and I have some questions for your boss." He went silent again. "Nice and slow, toss your guns out the windows one at a time. You twitch, I fire."

"I have more men," O'Ceallaigh said. "They're probably here now."

"I know," I said. "My friend is with them." He frowned. "We came prepared."

"What do you want?"

I sat back in his chair, and O'Ceallaigh scowled. "You're

not in charge here, Kevin." I gestured to one of the guest spots. "Have a seat." He did. "Your daughter hired me. She was convinced you were still alive somewhere, and it turned out she was right."

"How is Tara?"

"Don't say her name. You haven't earned the right. You forfeited it when you abandoned your family."

"So you found me," he said. "Now what?"

"It's really up to her. She told me to ask you a couple things, but it's probably better if she hears the answers right from you, don't you think?"

O'Ceallaigh put his hands up. "I don't know if I'm ready."

"You've had twelve fucking years," I said. "Tough shit." In reality, I didn't mind him stalling. It allowed me to keep the line open with Joey and know what went on outside. It sounded like he managed to disarm both guys in the second SUV. I couldn't count on the situation staying good for the visiting team forever, though. There were two of them, and they could have another weapon stashed in their vehicle somewhere. Or the driver could ram Joey. "First, I want you to call off the guys outside. Tell them to go have breakfast somewhere."

"What if I don't?" O'Ceallaigh crossed his arms.

I took the unconscious man's gun from my pants and pointed it at his prone form. "Then, you get to put a *Help Wanted* sign in the window."

"You wouldn't."

"You don't know me," I said. "I flew two thousand miles out here to find you. The businesses around you aren't open yet. I could put two in his chest right now." He stared at me. I stared back.

"You wouldn't," he said again.

"You're the gambling consultant. I could be bluffing. Let's

do the downside math. If I'm not trying to put one over on you, Bobby here—"

"Fred."

"Whatever. Fred here gets to bleed out on your floor. How many times do you recommend people push all their chips in when they're drawing to an inside straight?" I leaned down a little and moved the gun closer. "I could close my eyes and hit him at this range."

"Wait, wait." O'Ceallaigh slipped his phone out of his pocket.

"Show me the number you call." He did. It was local, and a man answered a moment later. "Take off. It's fine. I . . . need to talk to these men."

"But boss—"

"No, Jake. Go. Have breakfast or something. I'll be all right. It's . . . something you don't need to be involved in. Don't worry. Come back in an hour."

"I don't like this."

"I pay you enough to do things you don't like," O'Ceallaigh said. "Get out of here."

"Fine." The line went dead. Tires squealed a few seconds later.

"They're gone," Joey said. "I'll stay out here."

"Thanks," I said and broke the connection.

"You're welcome," O'Ceallaigh said, laboring under the delusion I talked to him.

"Let's talk to your daughter now."

"What's she going to want?"

"You abandoned her and her mother and left them to rot," I said. "They've had a pretty rough go of things in more ways than one. Don't expect a teary reunion." I inclined my head toward his desk drawers. "Might want to have the checkbook ready."

O'Ceallaigh grimaced. "She's after money?"

"I don't know, really." I shrugged. "We didn't go over every nuance before I came out here. In her spot, though, after what you did . . . I'd want to bleed you dry." O'Ceallaigh continued to wear a sour expression. I called Tara. She picked up on the second ring.

CHAPTER 17

"TARA, I HAVE YOUR FATHER HERE." I said. Silence hung in the air. I expected a reaction of some sort, and getting nothing felt anticlimactic. Then, her halting breaths came on the line. "You all right?"

"I don't know," she said through obvious tears. "I imagined this moment a lot of times." Tara cleared her throat, and her voice became more certain. "It's different in the moment."

"You're doing great. Your father wants to say hi." O'Ceallaigh remained quiet, so I punched him in the arm hard enough to draw a deep frown.

"Hi, Tara," he said.

"You son of a bitch," she said. The venom in her tone made me smile. "You walk out on your family and start over two thousand miles away. What kind of man does shit like that?"

"A weak one," I chimed in when O'Ceallaigh couldn't find his voice.

"He's right," the man confirmed. "I was weak." His voice cracked, and his eyes welled. "Things between your mother and me . . . weren't great. You probably remember. I wasn't sure what to do about it."

"Normal people go to counseling, Kevin," she said, practically spitting his original first name at him. "You want to know what they don't do? They don't disappear, turn up on the other side of the country, and start a new life!"

"I could say I'm sorry, but I don't think it would matter."

"It doesn't, but it's nice to hear it. Let's call it a promising start."

I felt a bit like a spectator who watches an argument as a captive audience. Still, I couldn't leave. I needed to make sure my client got what she wanted, even if I didn't know what it was. O'Ceallaigh wiped his eyes. "It's easy to say I should've done something different," he said. "Everything is simple with hindsight. I don't know. I felt . . . trapped, I guess. Your mom and I weren't in a good place, and my job started going to shit. So I squirreled a bunch of money away for a while. Didn't really have an idea in mind, but I figured it would be useful if I needed to do something."

"You could have worked it out with Mom," Tara said. "She's really struggled. She blamed herself for years. How could she not? You left us. She told me you died, but I was old enough to know it was bullshit. Even when we had you declared legally dead, I knew you were out there. I didn't want to push it, though. Mom was so fragile." She choked up and lapsed into silence for a few seconds. "She's been in a hospital for a while now. Had a breakdown. A decade of living with what you did was finally too much for her." She snorted. "Like you give a shit."

A tear slid down O'Ceallaigh's cheek. "I'm sorry about what happened to Katherine. I never intended for something so bad to—"

"Yeah, well, it did. What did you think would happen when you just up and vanished?"

"I had no idea," O'Ceallaigh said in a small voice. "Look, I know a lot of time has passed, and I . . . well, I did a lot of bad things to the family we used to be. I wanted to reach out to you lots of times over the years."

"Why didn't you?"

"I'd created a new life and identity out here. The casino guys . . . they're not the mobsters you might hear about, but I didn't want to get on their bad sides. I wanted to keep Kieran O'Ceallaigh separate from Kevin O'Kelly."

"*That's* the name you picked?" Tara said. "Jesus. Why not just wear a shirt with your birth name on it?"

"You'd be surprised how unwilling people are to make obvious connections," he said. "Put a few facts counter to their assumptions in the way, and they don't pursue anything. It's something I've talked about in my business, only I'm usually relating it to playing cards."

"I don't care about any of that." Tara sighed. "You screwed Mom and me when you left."

"I know. I . . . wish I could do something to make it right."

"You can get part of the way there. Mom's hospital isn't cheap. I don't think she'll be there much longer, but it's drained all her money and then some. I'm paying what I can, but I have student loans and bills of my own."

O'Ceallaigh looked at me. I shrugged and rubbed my thumb and first two fingers together in the universal sign for money. "Of course. If I'd been there, it all would've unfolded differently. Your mother wouldn't have gone to the hospital, and I would've paid for your college. How much do you need?"

"To clear all the debt?" Tara said. "About two hundred grand."

"All right," O'Ceallaigh said, though he winced at the figure. "Here's what I'll do. I have an account with about half what you need in it. I'll add you to it, and you can withdraw everything. Then, I'll liquidate a couple things and make a new account for you." He paused. "I'm sorry. I know this is very transactional, and it's not how I imagined getting back into your life, but I'd like to . . . if you're willing."

"I don't know yet. There's a lot of water under the bridge."

He nodded. "I understand. Would you be OK if the man you hired leaves your phone number with me?"

Tara was silent for a few seconds. Then, she said, "No, but he can bring me yours."

"All right. I'm logging into my bank now." O'Ceallaigh pulled up the page and authenticated. He owned several accounts, but only one held the balance he needed. A couple of clicks later, he modified the basics. "I'm adding you now."

"I can confirm he's doing it," I said. "I'll also watch him set up the other account." O'Ceallaigh frowned but didn't protest.

On my watch, I read Joey's incoming text. *All quiet out here, but our hour is running short.*

Got it, I tapped back. Once Tara's name appeared on the details page, I added, "Part one is finished, Tara."

"All right," she said. "I don't really want to stay on the line. This has been a pretty exhausting call. C.T., can you take care of the rest?"

"I'm on it. I'll talk to you later."

"All right."

"Bye, Tara," O'Ceallaigh said.

"Goodbye, Kevin," she said and ended the call.

"Tell your goons to keep waiting," I said. "I don't want them storming the place when the hour is up." As if on cue, Fred stirred, rolled over, and looked around in confusion.

"It's all right, Fred," O'Ceallaigh told his lackey. "Sorry. I should've let you know what's going on. You can wait in the lobby. This man and I have business. He also has a friend outside."

Fred rubbed his head, nodded, and staggered off toward the front of the building. I watched as O'Ceallaigh texted the goon patrol and ordered them to stay away for another hour. Jake didn't seem happy about it, but the chain of command carried the day. I pointed at the screen. "One more account, and then I'm out of your hair."

"I really ought to hate you for this," O'Ceallaigh said. "I don't. On some level, I know I didn't do right by Tara and her mom."

"'Didn't do right' is carrying a heavy load there," I said.

"Fine." O'Ceallaigh waved a hand. "I ruined their lives. I didn't know how to fix whatever was wrong, so I split." He sighed. "I should've reached out. I could've tried to make this right sooner." His eyes welled again.

"Save the sob story for your girlfriend. You have another account to create for your daughter."

O'Ceallaigh bobbed his head and got to work. He sold off a couple investments and moved the proceeds to his bank. A few minutes later, he called to confirm the money was available, authenticated to the online portal again, and created the additional account. Tara had access to all the money he'd promised her.

"I hope she'll let me be involved in her life," O'Ceallaigh said. He handed me a business card.

"It's up to her." I put the card in my wallet.

"Do you think she'll ask you for advice?"

"I don't know."

"What will you say if she does?" O'Ceallaigh wanted to know.

"Honestly," I said, "I hope she tells you to fuck off." I stood. "You deserve it." I walked outside. Joey and I climbed back into the Charger and drove away.

On our ride back downtown, I filled Joey in on how things went down in the office. "Most things come down to money," he said. "Seems a pretty poor substitute for having your dad in your life."

Joey—who lost both his parents to a car accident in our senior year of high school—knew something of what he spoke. I didn't want to press the point and come across as insensitive. "Her mother's stay in the psych hospital is killing their finances," I said. "It probably wouldn't have happened if he didn't abandon them twelve years ago."

"I guess. Just seems kind of . . ."

"Transactional?"

"Yeah."

"I guess it is." I shrugged. "In Tara's place, I don't know what I'd do or say. Pretty sure I'd take a pile of money, though."

"It usually helps," Joey said.

We parked at the Four Queens. With the O'C situation resolved, we didn't need to keep looking for tails on the road and goons around every corner. Joey insisted on getting lunch--and further insisted I pay, of course, which I did--and then we headed downstairs to the casino. I spent a half-hour breaking even at the fifteen-dollar blackjack table before moving on to poker. A two-table tournament was about to start, so I paid my entry fee and sat among nine strangers.

Within an hour, we'd condensed to eight players. Only the top two got paid, and while I had many more chips in front of me than when I started, my stack looked below average. Joey walked by to be a railbird a few times before moving on to something else.

When we were six-handed, I picked up pocket queens. A good raise represented a quarter of my stack, so I did it. A man in sunglasses who'd barely said a word the whole time raised behind me. I didn't think I'd see many better hands, so I went all-in, and he called. I flipped up my red ladies, and he turned over the Ace of clubs and a king of spades. The first three cards the dealer turned up were all low and of various suits. The fourth was a king, however, and I now faced long odds to win. The final card turned out to be an ace, adding a little insult to the injury. I offered a rote, "Nice hand" as I walked away.

The man who now owned my chips remained silent. I found Joey a few minutes later. He'd moved on to a roulette table. I declined to play, but I watched my friend win some money. "Blackjack again?" he said as he stood and walked away from the wheel.

"Sure. I busted out of the poker tournament. Need to win a few hands if I'm paying for dinner tonight."

Joey grinned. "What do you mean 'if?'"

As luck would have it, I went on a good run, doubled down a few times, and walked away a hundred dollars in the black about an hour later. I texted T.J. to check our flights and see if she could get us on one tonight or in the morning. She said there was nothing else headed to Baltimore tonight, but we could leave before seven o'clock local time tomorrow. "Looks like we have one more evening in Sin City," I said as we rode the elevator up to the room.

"I'm sure there's a buffet we haven't been to yet."

I patted my wallet. "Good thing I won some money, then."

———

I relaxed in the hotel room later when my phone rang. My dad called. "Don't tell me Mom wants a souvenir from Vegas," I said.

"We got rear-ended," he said.

"What?" I sat up. Joey glanced at me and frowned. "You guys all right?"

"Your mother is insisting we get checked out, so we will despite both of us feeling fine."

"What happened?"

"We were at a red light," he said. "I didn't see it until it was too late . . . couldn't have done anything either way. A car came up on us and plowed into the back. Then, it backed up, moved over a lane, and zoomed off."

I checked my watch. It would be early evening in Baltimore. Depending on where my parents were, traffic could have been light. It would be a requirement to pull off a maneuver like this. "You sure you're all right?"

"I doubt the doc will tell us anything different. Maybe a little stiff, but we'll be fine. Could have been worse."

"You call the cops?" I asked.

"Sure did. They just left. Paramedics are checking your mother out now. They're going to give us a ride to Saint Joe's."

I flashed back to the green Mustang nearly running me down as I walked back to my house. The same car almost T-boned Joey. I caught it on camera fleeing the scene after my parents' tires were slashed. The shooting at Rich's house saw a green sports car of indeterminate make and model. "What kind of car was it?"

"Mustang, I think," he said. "Green. I tried to look for a plate, but it didn't have one."

I took a deep breath. We'd resolved the O'Ceallaigh situation. I doubted he was behind these events to begin with. Unless he harbored a grudge after the fact, he remained an unlikely culprit. Someone else targeted me and those close to me. I didn't know who or why. A lot of guys went to jail because of work I did—usually with the BPD—since beginning my career. They ran the gamut from my former acquaintance Vinny Serrano to failed financial whiz Aaron Ritter. Any of them could have wanted revenge. A few might have been able to do something about it.

I couldn't solve this from a Vegas hotel room.

"I'm going to be home soon, Dad," I said. "Let me know how things go."

"What's going on, son? First, we get our tires cut, and now this. It's like someone has it in for us."

"I wish I could tell you it was all a coincidence. Someone might be coming after me and going after my loved ones. For now, only go out when you need to and be careful when you do. I'm going to figure out what's happening."

"All right," my father said. "I'll tell your mother it was just bad luck for now. She'll get nervous if I divulge more."

I agreed, and we ended the call. I dialed T.J. Even though it was late enough for her to be off the clock, she picked up. "What's up, boss?"

"My parents just got rear-ended."

"Oh, my gosh! Are they all right?"

"They seem to be," I said. Joey frowned, but I kept talking to T.J. "Remember the green Mustang I told you about?"

"Yeah," she said, dread creeping into her tone.

"You see one?"

"Nope."

"All right. Something's going on. People I know are getting targeted. I need to get ahead of this and figure out who's behind it."

"What can I do?" my eager secretary asked.

"Get me home sooner," I said. "I'll take a late-night flight, a red-eye . . . whatever. I can't be two thousand miles away while this shit goes on."

"I'm not sure what's going to be available. You might need to take a different airline altogether."

"Fine. Whatever. Just get me home."

"Me, too," Joey added.

"You don't need to fly back tonight," I told him.

"I'm flying with you," he said.

"All right, looks like you need to change both tickets."

"I'll see what I can do," T.J. said.

"Thanks. I know it's after hours."

"I gotta earn that bonus you gave me."

I grinned. "Email me the tickets if you're able to get us something tonight."

"I will," she said and clicked off.

"This can't still be related to O'Ceallaigh," Joey said.

"Agreed," I said. "He's had plenty of chances to come after us since we left his office."

"What the hell is going on in Baltimore, then?"

I shook my head. "I don't know, but I'm going home to puzzle it out."

CHAPTER 18

T.J. CAME THROUGH FOR US. Joey and I would have separate seats on an American Airlines flight leaving Vegas at ten o'clock local time. We'd arrive in Baltimore before dawn after the nonstop trek. "I'll buy some Dramamine at the airport," I said as we packed our bags.

Joey zipped his roller and set it on the bed. "You don't get motion sick."

"No, but I'll need to sleep. I can't lose hours tomorrow being tired. I'll be zonked out for the food service. I guess you'll have to eat enough for both of us."

"Consider it done," Joey said with a pat of his belly.

We made good time going back to Harry Reid Airport. I again declined to play any slot machines. Gambling on getting some shut-eye on a plane zooming through the sky at five hundred miles per hour was enough of a risk. I downed the two pills while we waited to board and felt drowsiness creep in by the time we took our seats. I had a window near the wing. Joey plopped down somewhere behind me on the other side.

Shortly after takeoff, I lost the battle against my eyelids closing. I awoke to the announcement of the plane making its final descent into BWI. The suited man sitting next to me frowned as if I offended him by sleeping during the journey. I checked myself for drool, found none, and ignored him. We deplaned a few minutes later and waited for our luggage at baggage claim. I fought to remain awake. Thankfully, restaurants were starting to open. Once we'd retrieved our rollers, I ordered the largest cup of coffee I could find.

We retrieved the S4, and I dropped Joey off at his house. From there, I went home. Gloria's car was missing. A note in the kitchen confirmed she'd gone home until I got back. It was probably better. Maybe her neighborhood watch received an alert every time a non-luxury car neared the neighborhood, and they could stop the Mustang before it caused a problem.

The coffee didn't have much effect, so I napped upstairs for about an hour. After a quick shower, I texted Gloria and drove to work to find T.J. already there. She ran forward and hugged me. "I'm glad you guys made it back."

"Me, too," I said. Once she sat at her desk again, I poured another cup of java.

"Tara's coming in soon," she said. "Once you resolved everything with her dad yesterday, she wanted to settle up."

"Which means my parents' foundation gets the bill." I kicked my feet onto my desk. "Were the tickets back to BWI expensive?"

"It's not cheap to get two nonstops flights for the same night."

"They were going to the hospital when we last spoke." I glanced at my watch. "I'll call them soon and see how they are. Make sure they have clean bills of health before we hit them with a big invoice."

"You have any idea whose green Mustang is causing all these problems?" T.J. wanted to know.

"I wish I did," I said. "Once Tara leaves, we're going to need to solve it."

———

Tara arrived about a half-hour later. T.J. freshened the coffee and served a cup to the client. I cleared my throat and stared, and she eventually got the hint. A steaming mug appeared on my desk, too. It was my third, and I already felt like I would need a fourth. Maybe before Tara left. "Thanks so much for all you did," she said as T.J. wheeled her chair to us. "I can't believe you were able to find him."

I took the business card out of my wallet and slid it across the desk. "He wanted you to have this in case you decide to reach out."

She frowned at the card before picking it up. "God, it really says Kieran O'Ceallaigh."

"Yeah," I said. "As similar as we find it, it's different enough to fool people at first blush. Resurfacing two thousand miles away in a totally different profession probably helps."

"I can't get over how he set himself up as a gambling consultant."

"It's big business now. Always has been in Vegas, but with so many states legalizing various forms, there are billions of dollars to be made."

"Did you have any problems out there?" Tara asked.

"Not really," I said. "Got caught snooping by his goon squad once. We watched him go to and from his office to see how the process went." I shrugged. "Found something we could exploit, and it worked."

"I still think it's awful he did what he did. At least he sort of seems sorry."

"Probably because he got caught. If you hadn't come

here, and I didn't find him, I wonder how often he would've thought about you and your mother."

She snorted. "Not often enough, I'm sure."

"Have you told your mom yet?" T.J. said.

"No," Tara said, "but I will. She's a little delicate. I'm sure she'd be happy I found him, but I also don't want her to have a setback because she's thinking about him and what might've been."

"The doctor seems like he cares about her," I said. "Maybe discuss it with him first."

"I will." She paused to blow out a deep breath. "I'm not sure how the rest of this works. Your parents' foundation referred me, C.T., so I'm afraid I'm not paying you today."

"I know. I still think we should review my time and expenses so they're getting an accurate accounting of everything." I pointed at T.J. "Make sure the food column in the spreadsheet is set to handle four digits. Joey loves buffets."

"All right," Tara said. "I've never done this sort of thing before, but let's give it a go." T.J. went over the basics with her. This mostly covered my hourly rate. On her advice, we established one for individual clients and a higher figure for corporations. Tara—through my parents' charitable arm—got my time at the lower amount. I provided some estimates, and the two of them hashed out a total.

"Don't forget Joey," I said. "Even ignoring his lunches and dinners, he contributed, too. I probably couldn't have done this without him. Put him down as a consultant. Half my time and half the hourly rate."

"Won't he be offended?" T.J. said with a grin.

"What he doesn't know won't hurt him."

"I'll tell him how indispensable he was."

"You're fired," I said.

"We have to add in the cost of tickets," T.J. continued unperturbed. "And your hotel stays."

I handed my secretary two pieces of paper. "I actually got printed receipts from each place. I felt like I was a hundred years old asking for them."

"You look pretty good for your age," Tara said.

"Working with people who secretly plot your demise is the key to staying young," I said.

"He's so dramatic," T.J. whispered to Tara, and the two enjoyed a few good snickers. She added everything and came up with a total bill. It might make my parents' eyes water, but we could prove it all, and they entered into the arrangement. I would wait until the green Mustang situation was over before giving them the invoice, but I wouldn't go easy on the expenses just because their foundation would write the check.

"Are you going to talk to your father at some point?" T.J. asked our client.

Tara spread her hands. "I don't know. He really screwed over our family. It was also a long time ago, and he seems contrite now. Maybe. After a little time has passed and my mom is out of the hospital."

She thanked us again, and we bid her adieu. "Another one in the books," T.J. said as she returned her chair to its normal place. "And the first one involving your folks."

"Yeah . . . I'm not sure how I feel about it yet. Let's see how they react when they get the bill."

"You think they'll push back?"

"No," I said. "They paid me a flat rate before. Now, we're itemizing. This will show us how committed they are to the new arrangement. My guess is it'll turn out to be an occasional thing."

"That's good, right? It means they don't have a lot of people who could use your services."

"I guess so."

"Excellent." T.J. cracked her knuckles. "Let's move on to the Mustang situation."

"Yes." I downed my now-lukewarm coffee in three gulps. "Let's."

———

The Mustang search proved pointless and tedious. No one had seen a plate on the car, so we couldn't even presume the owner registered it in Maryland. Add in the likelihood of the car being stolen—no missing green pony cars were on file in the state—and the whole thing felt like looking for the proverbial needle in a haystack. We confined our search to Maryland because almost all my cases involved local people.

Even narrowing our parameters to models from the last ten years produced too many results to sift through easily. "Any of the registered names jump out at you?" T.J. asked as we reviewed the list.

"No. We can't presume any of these people are involved. The car might well be stolen."

"I'm not so sure." When I frowned, she continued. "Think about it. This has been going on for days. How many people keep the same stolen car so long?"

"Good point," I said. "It makes whoever is after me dumb or brazen. Given the choice, I prefer dumb."

"Me, too," my secretary said.

We kept going through lunch. By the end of the workday, I felt tired from the time zone change, sleeping on the plane, and everything we'd done. My eyes hurt, too. We'd hit a wall on the green muscle-car angle, and I didn't see a way past it at the moment. The shop downstairs had gotten quiet, too. Manny sometimes started and wrapped up early. It seemed like an excellent idea. "I'll walk you to your car," I said. "Too many attacks on people I care about."

"And here I thought you just tolerated me for my scheduling skills."

"They help." We left the office, locked up, and walked down the metal stairs. With Manny and the crew's workday over, fewer vehicles remained in the lot. T.J.'s car sat next to mine. We crossed the asphalt. Tires squealed from our right. A green car sped down Eastern Avenue and slowed on approach. The passenger's window lowered. "Get down!" I grabbed T.J.'s arm and pulled her to the ground with me. Gunshots barked. I covered her as bullets whizzed past us, tearing into one of the old junkers remaining onsite.

I flashed back to the harbor. Out for a run. A man emerged from behind one of the pavilions. He raised a pistol, and my life changed forever. While I'd mostly recovered from getting shot twice and nearly drowning in the water, situations like this provided unwelcome reminders of what I'd been through. I'd worked on this. Lots of conversations with Doctor Parrish plus some time at the range. A couple deep breaths, and I was fine again.

Another screech of rubber, and the car zoomed away.

T.J. sucked in short, rapid gulps of air below me. I moved to the side. "The car's gone. We're not hit. You're all right."

She sat up and stared at me with wide eyes. "They shot at us." Her breathing slowed, but her expression remained fixed. "They shot at us."

I grabbed her hand. "You're all right. The shooter hit some old heap across the lot." T.J. bobbed her head, and I sat with her while she calmed down.

"We calling the cops?" she asked.

"It's not even five o'clock," I said. "Someone probably did already." No one stopped to check on us. I wasn't surprised. Sirens grew near. "I think they're coming." I watched cars go by on Eastern Avenue as I went to the sidewalk. The green car—it had to be the Mustang, but I didn't notice before the shooting started—slowed before the gun came out. I knew where it was on the street. Based on its position and where the junker sat, the bullets missed us by a good ten feet to the right.

Either whoever held the gun was an awful shot, or he missed on purpose.

"You look like you're thinking about something," T.J. said.

"I am. We'll talk about it later." The sirens grew louder. "Let's tell the cops what happened and go home." If our mystery gunman did, in fact, whiff deliberately, he must have done so under orders.

Which meant someone didn't want us dead. Yet.

CHAPTER 19

THE COPS ROLLED up a couple minutes later. I didn't know either officer who approached us. Two more cruisers stopped at the curb. The older uniform—a middle-aged black woman named Carter—asked most of the questions while her large Hispanic male partner Benitez took notes. "You don't know what kind of car it was?" she asked not for the first time.

"It was green," I said. "I lost the rest of the details in trying not to get shot."

"People shoot at you a lot?"

"My popularity waxes and wanes."

Benitez chuckled, but he stopped when Carter glowered at him. "This is serious, Mister Ferguson," she said. "I don't need to tell you how many people have been shot in Baltimore this month, do I?" When I didn't answer, she turned to T.J. "Did you get a good look at the car?"

"I can tell you it was green," T.J. said. "I don't think I even saw it. We were leaving the office, C.T. yelled at me to get down, and then he pulled me to the asphalt. Right after, a few bullets flew at us."

I declined to point out my theory about their trajectory.

Let the police bring their own ballistics people and draw independent conclusions. "What about the shooter?" Carter pressed.

"A hand and arm with a gun," I said. "I didn't get much chance to stand around and gape into the car. The whole dodging bullets thing again."

"Neither of you are particularly helpful."

"Officer Carter, did you notice the make and model of the cars near you as you stopped?"

"Not really," she said.

"Note I'm not standing here casting aspersions on you," I said. "Now, imagine trying to do it while someone is shooting at you."

"I think we have all we need for now," Bentiez said. Carter's expression indicated agreement and a frequent diet of lemons, but she didn't say anything. "Thanks for your time. Let us know if anything else comes to you."

We said we would, and a bunch of officers milled about the scene. A crime scene van arrived and parked in the lot. T.J. and I both left before they closed the area off. I offered to follow her home, but she declined. I made the short drive back to Federal Hill. Gloria's coupe sat on the parking pad. I left the S4 beside it and walked into my house. She came into the kitchen and wrapped me in a tight hug. "I missed you."

"I missed you, too," I said, and I almost didn't get to finish talking because she kissed me. She didn't appear interested in stopping, and neither was I. I tossed my backpack on the counter, and we dashed upstairs. "I need to leave town more often."

Gloria pulled her shirt over her head and grinned. "Shut up and get in bed."

I decided not to argue.

Later, Gloria rested her head on my chest, and we talked about the Vegas trip. "I'm glad you were able to find that girl's father. Maybe they'll get to have an actual relationship someday."

"Maybe," I said. "I'm not sure she wants it yet."

"You dove back into things right away."

"Yeah." I sighed. "It's not all sunshine and puppies."

My beautiful girlfriend raised her head. "What do you mean?"

"Someone shot at T.J. and me as we left the office today."

Gloria wrapped her arms around me again. "I worry about you. What the heck is going on?"

"I don't know," I said. "It can't be connected to Vegas. Someone has it in for me. Rich's house got fired upon, too, and somebody rear-ended my parents' car yesterday. It's always a green Mustang."

"Know anybody who drives one?"

"I wish. This would be easy if I did."

"What are you going to do now?" she said.

"Get to the bottom of it," I said. "Not much else I can do. I want you to be careful. No one's gone after you yet. Doesn't mean they won't."

"I will."

"Good." I thought about popping the question. Lying in bed with Gloria counted as a good moment. With this mess hanging over my head, however, I didn't feel it was the right time. I needed to puzzle out who came after me and my loved ones. I couldn't stand to lose any of them . . . especially not Gloria.

———

As usual, I got up before Gloria the next morning. I debated going out for a run. While I needed one, I had no desire to be steamrolled while I walked back home. I also had no desire to live in fear, so I put my exercise attire on and headed for

Federal Hill Park. A few other joggers enjoyed the morning, and no one fell in behind me to try and kill me. No suspicious cars roamed the streets, either. It was a perfectly normal morning in Baltimore.

About a half-hour later, I made my way back up Riverside Avenue. I scanned for the green Mustang every chance I could. I looked for it in rows of parked cars. As I approached cross streets, I stopped to see if any vehicles sped toward me or darted away from a curb. Nothing. I made it back home without incident. Gloria remained asleep while I showered and dressed, and only the brewing coffee could rouse her from her slumber.

After a quick breakfast of scrambled eggs and toast, I kissed Gloria goodbye and headed to the car. She implored me to be careful, and I promised I would. Nothing registered as unusual as I backed into the alley and started my commute. Despite my increased vigilance, traffic was heavy enough for one car to hide. I noticed a dearth of both green vehicles and Mustangs—the only one I saw was a convertible model dating from the 'nineties.

The lot at Manny's looked like it did before the shooting started last night. No crime scene tape or other evidence of police activity remained. They'd gotten as much as they could. I saw the second Mustang of the morning as T.J.'s occupied its usual spot. I parked next to it. As I approached the main door, Manny walked out to intercept me. He was about my height but thicker, and every shirt he wore carried a grease stain somewhere. "What the hell happened yesterday?"

"There are moments my popularity wanes," I said.

"Anybody hurt?" he asked in a voice carrying only the hint of an accent.

"No. We're fine. The shots didn't really come close. I think they were designed to scare us more than anything."

"Did it work?"

"My secretary was pretty rattled," I said. "I was, too, in the moment. Kind of hard not to be." I didn't have the best memories when it came to bullets flying in my direction, but Manny didn't need to know all my secrets. "We got down right away."

"Look, I know you do good work," he said, "and I'm really thankful for the computer help you've given me. I can't have people shooting up my place, though. What if they fire inside while one of the guys is still here?"

"I don't think they would."

"But you don't know." I shook my head. "OK. They didn't hit anything besides the old junker I never get around to doing anything with. No harm there. This time. I don't want there to be a next time."

"Me, either," I said.

"Good." One of Manny's crew appeared in the doorway, The boss told him to get back to work in colorful Spanish. I headed upstairs. In addition to all the other reasons I needed to get a handle on what the hell was going on, not getting the boot from an office I liked joined the list. Great.

————

My secretary leaned forward in her chair and stared at her monitor. She didn't even throw me a glance when I entered. I closed the door with more force than required. Still nothing. I dropped my bag off at my desk and walked to the coffee pot. Only half remained. She'd never brew less than a full pot in the mornings. "How long have you been here?"

"What?" She looked at me in surprise. "When the hell did you walk in?"

"Just now." I picked up the carafe. "Looks like you've been hitting it hard. How long have you been here?"

"I don't know." She looked at her phone. "About an hour and a half, I guess."

"Pretty early." T.J. didn't answer. I poured myself a mug of coffee and joined her at her desk. "Almost an hour before you normally come in. What's going on?"

"Just wanted to get an early start," she said without so much as glancing away from her screen. She'd called up the city's traffic cameras. Clearly, T.J. paid attention when I told her how to make use of resources we weren't supposed to access.

"Bullshit," I said, and she stopped working. "I know you take this job seriously, but you've never come in at the crack of dawn before. And it's the morning after we got shot at. Probably not a coincidence. Clue me in."

It took a few seconds before she said, "I'm scared."

"No shame in it. I don't enjoy getting shot at . . . believe me. Lots of bad memories."

Her head bobbed slightly. "I didn't have it easy before Melinda. Never did. My old life was pretty violent. Took a beating here and there, and not just from an asshole john." My hands clenched into fists, and I hoped T.J.'s old pimp met a gruesome fate. "But through it all, I never got shot at."

"Now you have something to brag about at parties," I said.

She offered a small, polite smile. "I live with a friend. Never really came out and said it because I didn't want to drag her into anything. I couldn't go back home. Melinda's not really setup to be a residence hall. So I found a friend from grade school. She . . . knows how my life went off the rails, and she was nice enough to give me a place to stay. I don't want to bring shit like this to her door. I won't."

"You shouldn't have to." I jutted my chin toward her screen. "Trying to get a line on our shooters?"

"Yeah."

"Anything?"

"Not really. The car first appears on a camera about a mile south . . . does a couple loops of the neighborhood . . ."

"Waiting for us to come out," I said.

"Yeah. You can see there was some traffic then but not enough to stop what they had planned. After the gunshots, the Mustang heads north for another mile, then turns off on side streets, and I lose it. No traffic cameras wherever it headed."

"And wherever it came from. Someone knows the limitations of the city's system."

"Along with the fact that we'd be looking," T.J. added.

She raised a good point. If someone were targeting me and the people I cared about, our mystery man would know enough to presume I'd do things like check the traffic camera system. Appearing and disappearing using blind spots would be a good countermeasure. "I wonder if it shows up anywhere else later," I said. "Gaps in the coverage are only so big."

"It might." T.J. shrugged. "I'll try looking later. It seems this car either has no plates or stolen ones, so I'm not sure how effective finding it would be. If someone knows the system, they're not going to keep the damn thing where it could be seen."

"True." If the electric eyes always began tracking it at the same point, however, it could tell us something. T.J. probably knew this. I would tell her later if she didn't arrive at it on her own. For now, she probably needed a break from looking at her screen and worrying about bringing gunshots home to her friend. "I went ring shopping."

"What?"

"When Tara first came in. My appointment you were so curious about."

She grinned, and it was good to see. "You weren't trying to get a blonde growth removed?"

"I don't think my insurance covers cosmetic surgery."

"Ring shopping." T.J. leaned back in her chair. "You pop the question yet?"

"No," I said. "I'm trying to find the right moment. Doing so in the aftermath of coming back to town and getting shot at seemed poor."

"Probably. Even so . . . good for you."

"Thanks. I'm just not sure when I want to do it. Gloria's smart, so she'll sniff out a basic attempt. I want to surprise her, but I also don't want to worry about it while someone is shooting at me and my loved ones."

"We don't control the future," T.J. said. "We can only make the best of the present."

"You taking philosophy classes now?"

"It's something Melinda taught us. A lot of girls don't want to leave the street because they're worried about what's going to happen. She encouraged us to make our lives better today. Propose to Gloria. You've done this a lot longer than me, so you know what all can happen. Don't wait for the perfect moment. It probably doesn't exist."

She was right, of course, and I guess I needed to hear someone else say it. I expected it to be Rich or even Joey, but it's hard to quibble with the source of an epiphany. "When did you get so wise and fatalistic beyond your years?"

T.J. flipped her blonde ponytail. "I've always been this way."

"Don't show up the boss," I said.

CHAPTER 20

"AREN'T you glad I made you file these paper copies?" I asked.

T.J. glowered at me from the black metal cabinet. When we couldn't track the green Mustang, we decided to review my old cases. This created almost four years of material to sift through, though my note-taking in the early days could charitably be called spartan and accurately called nonexistent. "Come a little closer," she said. "I want to see if I can tip this over on you."

"Getting the damn thing up the stairs was enough for me, thanks."

"Have I mentioned how shitty your record keeping was when you started?" T.J. joined me at her desk.

"Not today," I said, "until now."

"Remind me later, and I'll tell you again." She slammed a stack of manila folders down. Each held maybe a page or two which served as my official writeup for the cases. "I guess the upside is we'll get through these quickly."

"I guess."

She leafed through the collection. "They're not even in date order."

"I blame the girl who did the filing," I said. "She didn't seem very into it."

T.J. smirked but didn't answer. It was probably for the best. "All right, let's just start with the top." She opened the folder. "Chinese sex traffickers . . . The Zhang family."

"Rich and I busted up one of their operations with help from the state police."

"Could they be coming after you now?"

"Maybe," I said, "but they'd probably be more direct. They explicitly tried to kill me at least once. Didn't bother with the rest." I paused. "Hmm. Working this case is what introduced me to Rollins. I wanted a bodyguard, and he came recommended."

"You might need him again," T.J. said. I'd already thought about it. She set the file aside. "They seem unlikely." She scanned another set of notes. "Holy shit, you went after the mayor? Melinda's dad?"

"He wasn't the mayor then. Just another rich asshole with a shady family history."

Another tan-colored jacket. "What about the pedo ring in Cecil County?"

"I hope they're all still behind bars," I said. "Even if anyone got out, they're small-time. No reach."

She set another aside and opened the next. "What about Vinny Serrano?" She snickered. "He's named after a pepper."

"He was pretty dangerous. Ambition got the better of him. He wanted to be more than just a bookie so he got into loan-sharking. My first client came to me over him. Vinny's goons murdered her husband over a gambling debt to try and trigger a life insurance payout."

"Wow." T.J. frowned at the two pages of notes I wrote. "Could he be doing all this?"

"I'd be surprised," I said. "Vinny's still in jail. He'll be there until we're at least fifty."

She closed the folder. "Could he be pulling strings from the inside?"

"Doubt it. Vinny . . . well, let's say he didn't inspire a lot of loyalty in the people he employed. They all flipped on him for whatever they could get. He doesn't have the people to pull something like this off."

"We're running out of ideas." T.J. leafed through several more files. "A bunch of these people are dead."

"Pretty sure we can eliminate them," I offered.

"Great. Thanks for your contribution." We went over each folder at least twice. It took a while, but at the end, we'd come up with no good suspects. "We're right back where we started," T.J. said as she slammed the cabinet shut. "This sucks."

"Welcome to the PI world."

"We need to solve this."

"I think we will," I said, "but it may not be today. You have to get used to a certain level of disappointment."

T.J.'s only reply was a grunt. I didn't want her to get used to any such thing. It sounded like she didn't, either.

———

As the clock struck two, I said, "I'm going out for lunch. I'll bring you something."

"Fine."

Maybe my Italian leftovers would cheer up poor T.J. I hoofed it to Little Italy, keeping an eye out for green Mustangs. None made themselves obvious. About fifteen minutes after I set out, I walked in the front door of Rizzo's. Gabriella and I enjoyed something of an uneasy truce after she chose to interrogate me about her father's death. I didn't want to see her, and I imagined she felt the same, but I needed to know if she'd decided to come after me. We had a long history, and she'd be straight with me.

When her father Tony ran the place, he sat in a table by the fireplace on the first floor. Like many restaurants in the area, Rizzo's occupied a rowhouse. Gabriella carved out a space for herself on the second floor. I walked up the creaky wooden stairs. The renovations spread up here. The floors were newly polished and darker. Fake brick paper covered the rear interior wall. Tony never would've used so much even if it did evoke a Brooklyn bistro. Gabriella stared at me as I approached her table, and the two enforcers with her stood. I didn't recognize either of them. She'd broomed most of her dad's crew out the door and started over. "I didn't think we were dropping in on each other yet."

"We're probably not," I admitted. "Something bad is going down, though, and I need to talk to you about it."

"Fine." She held a hand out toward the opposite chair, and I sat. Gabriella Rizzo was a few weeks older than me, beautiful, and ruthless. In addition to the restaurant, she inherited the city's organized crime operation when Tony ate a bullet. Despite the fact we'd known each other for two decades or more, she ordered me abducted and beaten as she tried to come to terms with how her father left this world. The pair of goons took their seats again after I did. "What's going on?"

"Is our truce still in effect?"

"Why wouldn't it be?"

"I've become a target recently," I said. "Someone tried to run me over a few days ago, and a person in the same car took shots at my secretary and me yesterday." Gabriella didn't say anything. "It's not me alone. My parents' tires got slashed, and someone rear-ended their car. A gunman shot up Rich's house and the two near it."

"You think I did all this?" Gabriella glared and crossed her arms. I tried to avoid looking at the lift this provided her breasts.

"Whether you did or not, I want to hear it from you."

A waiter approached. Gabriella shook her head, and the man scampered away. Her hard expression softened just a little. "I'm sorry all this is happening to you. I'm not behind it."

"My first guess. Heard anything about who might be?"

She shook her head. "Not a peep. Wasn't even aware."

I believed her. She held my gaze as we talked, and Gabriella had little reason to lie. If she wanted to cap me, either of the men sitting beside her could make the attempt. When she wanted information from me, she came after me directly. Cat-and-mouse games weren't like her. "All right. Thanks."

"Anything else?"

"I'll order some takeout," I said.

"Do it downstairs . . . and pay for your goddamn meal. My father always gave you a free lunch. Those days are over."

"Discount for an old friend and fellow business owner?"

She stared ahead. "Oh, well. A shame our truce is so limited." I swore the corner of Gabriella's mouth turned up a fraction. "See you around." I walked downstairs, ordered a couple entrees, and waited. No green Mustangs drove by.

———

As dinner time approached, Gloria busied herself on her laptop. Even with half her left arm still in a cast, she balanced the machine well and didn't seem to suffer any ill effects. "How's your venue coming along?" I said.

She didn't look up from her screen. "I think we're in the homestretch."

"Good." I looked at my watch as my stomach growled. The end of my conversation with T.J. played in my head. *Propose to Gloria*, she told me. *Don't wait for the perfect moment. It probably doesn't exist.* "How about we get some dinner?"

"Sure." Gloria smiled and closed her laptop. "Where do you want to go?"

"You pick."

She chose the Capital Grille. We each changed into nicer clothes, and while Gloria finished getting ready, I grabbed the ring box and slipped it into my jacket pocket. The drive to Pratt Street only took a few minutes. Inside, the restaurant wasn't very crowded yet. Maroon carpet yielded to dark cherry wood. Color and brightness came from the white ceiling and tablecloths as well as the triangular chandeliers. Large oil paintings hung on the walls, and I felt glad our table sat a good distance from them. I didn't need giant eyes staring at me as I struggled to ask my girlfriend what should have been a simple question.

Once our water glasses were full, we opted for the calamari appetizer. Despite being in a steakhouse, Gloria decided on the roasted chicken entree. I maintained tradition by ordering a filet mignon, and we selected asparagus and brussels sprouts to share. The waiter complimented us on our selections—he probably never criticized any—before heading toward the kitchen. "I haven't been here in a while," Gloria said.

"Me, either."

"I've come to appreciate pubs and places like that, but it's hard to beat a nice restaurant." She grabbed and squeezed my hand. "Thanks for taking me out tonight."

"My pleasure," I said. Gloria turned in her chair and took in the place. I capitalized by palming the ring box and sliding it into my pants pocket. After dinner, I would ask her to marry me. Gloria smiled, and I knew I wanted to see her happy expression for the rest of my days. I drank some water to cover my suddenly dry throat.

Our fried calamari came out a moment later, further sparing me. Gloria actually cut her pieces of squid. I simply speared them on my fork. I finished long before she did. Her pace allowed our entrees to arrive while she finished the appetizer. I closed my eyes and inhaled the aromas of my meal. Seared beef. Butter. Peppercorns. Who could ask for more? I sliced into it and saw a ribbon of pink inside. A perfect medium.

I moderated my eating. Gloria cut her chicken into tiny pieces. Ever since she got serious about tennis and fitness, she'd sliced her meals microscopically and eaten slower than before. It worked for her on the court, but it meant I finished before she would get a third of the way through something. No matter tonight. I needed to wait for her to finish, anyway, to pop the question. My filet was delicious, and the sides accompanied it very well.

Even going slower, I still pushed my plate in well before Gloria. She finally moved across the finish line, and a busboy collected our stuff. I dropped my hand to my pocket and felt the outline of the ring box. "We've been dating a long time," I began, "and more or less living together for . . . at least a couple years now."

Gloria smiled. "Very true."

"I could get used to it."

She chuckled. "I think we've already gotten used to it."

This was going swimmingly. I'd left room for her to offer sensible rebuttals to my intro. Maybe I should've paid more attention during my brief tenure on the high school speech and debate team. "I guess you're right. What I'm saying is . . . I'd like to keep it going. I—" My phone vibrated. Rich's name flashed on my smartwatch.

"You need to get that?" Gloria asked.

"No." I took my phone out, declined the call, and set it face-down on the table. My throat felt dry again, so I drank more water. Gloria smiled at me. I got the impression she knew where I was headed, and she was determined not to offer me a lifeline. Fair enough. I needed to ask the question without being rescued. "Anyway, I love you, and I love waking up next to you every morning."

"Me, too."

My hand closed on the hard plastic box. Before I could say anything else, my phone went off, and it was Rich again. I declined his call a second time. What the hell was so urgent? The interruption threw me off. "Uh . . . where was I?"

"Telling me how much you loved waking up next to me," Gloria said with a grin. She definitely knew.

"How could I not?" I said, trying to cover my nerves. "I was hoping you'd like to keep it—" My cell buzzed again. For the third time, it was my cousin.

Gloria nodded toward my phone. "You might need to take his call."

"Dammit." I answered this time. "What the hell is so important?"

"Remember Margaret Madison?" Rich said. I met her on my first case. She was a bet-taker and enforcer for my old acquaintance Vinny Serrano. When he went to jail, she took over the gambling part of his operation.

"What's wrong . . . she not offering you good odds this weekend?"

"She's dead."

I couldn't find any words for a second. "What? How?"

"Come to her house and see for yourself." Rich ended the call.

Gloria signaled for the check. "It seems like we need to go."

"Yeah."

"What happened?" she said.

"Someone I've come across a few times is dead. Rich wants me to head to the scene for some reason."

"Is it far from here?"

"She lives . . . lived . . . in Canton."

"Might as well go right there, then. I'll get an Uber."

"No," I said. "No, I'll drop you off. It's no big deal."

"All right. I'll never say no to a ride from my boyfriend." It sounded like Gloria emphasized the final word as if to tell me she knew why we came to the Capital Grille this evening. Normally, I might have said something about her double entendre.

Not tonight.

———

I waited for Gloria to walk inside before pulling away. As I left our neighborhood, I scanned the area for the green Mustang. No sign of it. I even did a loop around the block and looked again. The drive to Margaret Madison's house in Canton wouldn't take long. The lights cooperated, and my lead foot helped, too. I slowed as I steered down Linwood Avenue. A phalanx of police cruisers lined both sides of the street, and a white medical examiner's van had already joined the fray. A uniformed officer tried to stop me at the barrier of yellow tape, but a familiar voice said, "He's fine. Let him through."

Sergeant Paul King did not use his promotion to improve his hair or grooming. His mop of dirty blond hair and stubbly chin made him look like a mid-thirties bar band singer who could never quite give up on the dream. He wore a suit, but it was a hideous off-the-rack model which needed a few adjustments to fit him properly. His appearance belied his skill. Maybe he aspired to be Columbo. "Thanks . . . Sergeant."

"Yeah, yeah."

"I said I'd be on your side against Rich when you were a detective," I said.

"Something about lieutenants being tools of the system."

"Sergeants may not be far behind them."

"I'll do my best to soldier on without your support," King said. He led me toward the house. The front door remained open as cops came and went. "Caught a bad one here. Rich tells me you know the deceased."

"Listen to you . . . 'the deceased.' You learn this fancy talk in sergeant school?"

"These are more progressive times. We can't talk about dead broads who caught a chest full of slugs anymore."

I grimaced and braced myself for what I might see. We walked in to Margaret's living room. A short man in a white medical suit crouched near the form of a prone woman. Rich jerked his head to beckon me over. I joined the crowd. Someone beat Margaret's once-pretty face into a barely-recognizable mass of blood and bruises. Her final expression looked pained, perhaps accentuated by the many missing teeth. Bullet holes dotted her torso and midsection, and most of the blood in her body was either on her face or seeping into the wooden floor under her corpse. "Jesus," I whispered. "Looks like someone emptied the clip into her."

"Pretty much," Rich said. "We're not sure, but the ME thinks she was beaten for a while first."

"Margaret could take care of herself. This was no garden-variety goon."

"Can you think of anyone who would have it in for her? You know her."

"We're acquainted," I said. "I wouldn't go any further."

Rich shrugged. "My original question still stands."

"I can't think of anyone besides Vinny, and he's in jail."

"All right," my cousin said. "You can stay if you want, but try not to get in the way."

I've played things fast and loose with the police many times over the years, from withholding little details to telling outright lies. I'd been honest with Rich, however. While I'd met the late Margaret Madison a couple times, I wouldn't say I knew her, and I couldn't think of anyone who hated her enough to have her beaten to a pulp before shooting her a bunch of times. Except Vinny, her former employer and my former lacrosse teammate and almost-friend. Twenty years remained on his sentence.

Challenge your assumptions, the rational part of my brain chided me.

I dialed Liz Fleming, a former public defender who recently struck out on her own. "I'm usually the one calling you," she said.

"I need to know something. I could probably look it up, but I think you could get it faster."

"All right . . . what's up?"

"Can you tell me if someone who went to prison almost four years ago is still inside?"

"Pretty easily. Name?"

"Vincent Serrano," I said, "like the pepper."

"All right," Liz said. "I'm logging in now. Give me a minute or two." I carefully left the living room and moved into the far less crowded kitchen at the rear of the house. Liz's keystrokes clattered in my ear. "Huh."

"What?"

"I'll have to do a little more digging and read the full

report, but there's a note about testimony against another inmate."

My stomach churned. I had an idea of the implications but needed to know for certain. "Meaning?"

"He's out, C.T.," Liz said.

CHAPTER 21

I STARED AHEAD at Margaret's oven, which she would never get to use again thanks to Vinny Serrano and his improbable release from a long prison sentence. Now, it all made sense. He went after me because he was delusional enough to blame me for his downfall and arrest. Ditto Rich, the officer who arrested him. My parents caught blame for bringing me into the world. Vinny knew Joey from our time together at school, and he must've presumed I had help in the investigation.

The only person he hadn't gone after yet is Gloria.

I barely knew her when the mess with Vinny went down. We'd met at a gala, enjoyed some overpriced wine, and talked a couple times. For his long list of faults, however, Vinny was smart, and he'd be sure to bring people into his orbit who could learn about Gloria. I couldn't presume she'd be safe. While I pondered these depressing ideas, Liz texted me and said she could get the scoop on what happened with Vinny's release. I asked her to come to my office, and she agreed.

"Where are you going?" Rich called after me as I left.

"Talk later," I said, and I hoofed it out of the house and back to my car. Shortly afterward, I unlocked the office, flipped on the lights, and set a half-pot of coffee to brew. I knew I would need some. Light footsteps came up the stairs. Someone knocked on the door a few minutes later. My hand closed on the grip of my .45.

Liz opened the door and poked her head in. "Good, you're already here." She walked in and sniffed the air. "And you brewed coffee."

"I have something to add to it," I said, taking a mostly-full bottle of bourbon from a desk drawer. "Seems appropriate tonight."

"It does." Liz and I worked together a few times before she left the public defender's office. She was a tall brunette, pretty, and good at her job. In her professional capacity, she favored skirts which showcased her terrific legs. We'd flirted in the past, and even if I were a single man, I would've harbored zero interest in it tonight. Well after normal work hours, she wore a sensible sweater and a pair of jeans. I felt overdressed in my button-down shirt and khakis.

"What the hell happened, Liz?" The coffee machine beeped, and I poured us each a mug. I added some whiskey to mine. Liz nodded when I held the bottle up, so I livened hers up, too.

"I still have some contacts in the PD office," she said. "They know people." Liz opened her laptop. "I can't access some of the resources I used before, but a colleague sent me a screenshot." She turned the machine around to show me an official-looking PDF. "It seems Vinny was a cooperating witness inside. He turned state's evidence and got out nine days ago."

I sighed and took a long drink of the coffee. "How does this happen? Vinny was in jail for his role in multiple assaults and murders, at least two kidnappings . . . not to mention his illegal gambling operation. Who the hell was his cellmate, Stalin?"

"No one I've heard of. A multiple murderer from southern Maryland. Cops suspected he did more and worse. Apparently, Vinny got him to open up."

"Ridiculous." I shook my head. "I get the idea of rewarding someone for coming forward. Setting a murderer free twenty years early strikes me as way beyond the pale, though."

"It's . . . unusual," Liz agreed. "Normally, someone in Vinny's situation would get a few years lopped off his sentence or maybe moved to a lower-security facility."

"Then, I'm back to wondering how this happens," I said. "He wasn't well-connected. The cops assembled a strong case against him even without the evidence I gathered."

"I don't know." Liz spread her hands. "My contact didn't have that info, either. It's unusual but not unheard of. Sometimes, prosecutors pull out all the stops to land a big fish."

"And they set a goddamn shark free in the process." I refreshed my java and bourbon. Liz declined a second cup. "So Vinny's just free to go? No restrictions? No one keeping an eye on him?"

"He's technically on parole," Liz said. "He'll need to check in with a PO and all the usual stuff."

I waved a dismissive hand. "Easy for him to get to one meeting a week. He can spend the rest of his time planning revenge against the people he thinks put him in jail."

"Namely you."

"Yeah," I said. "Thanks, Liz. I have to see what the hell I can do about this mess."

"Good luck," she said.

I knew I would need it.

I stewed on the problem after Liz left. Vinny enjoyed a nine-day head start on me and anyone else he might target. While he'd never been great with people—driven home by his crew turning on him *en masse* almost four years earlier—he probably still had access to money. In addition to the green Mustang driver, other mercenaries and goons could be in his ranks.

This was too big for me alone. Rich made a nice resource, but he also held down a busy and important full-time job. Joey could help, but I wanted someone with more direct expertise. I called Rollins. In the three years since I first hired him as a bodyguard, he'd helped me off the books with a few cases. He always seemed on call and ready to go, to the point I wondered if he ever slept. As usual, he picked up quickly. "What's going on?"

"How long you got?"

"*Reader's Digest* version would be nice."

"All right," I said. "In my first case, I took down a guy I went to school with. He was supposed to get twenty-five to life. Now, he's out. I've seen two attempts on my life, my parents have been targeted, Rich's house got shot up . . . I can't cover it all on my own."

"Damn," he said. "Normally, I'd be all over it."

My heart sank. "Normally?"

"I'm out of town. Can't exactly come back at the drop of a hat." On some level, I understood Rollins hired himself out to people, and he earned a good living doing it. This did little to quell my disappointment. "Sounds like you're in a bad way, though. Let me call you back in a few minutes. I might be able to get you someone."

"Is he as good as you?"

"Is anyone?" Rollins said and broke the connection. I waited. A lot of former military folks lived in Maryland. Rollins was one of them. I'd never met anyone as stealthy as him. I didn't know who he would recommend, but the person would have some big shoes to fill. A few minutes later, he called back. "I found someone."

"Great," I said. "Who is it?"

"Remember John Tyler?"

"Who?"

"A few months ago," he said, "you helped us with a cartel problem."

I remembered. Tyler and I never met in person, but we talked over the phone a few times. "All right. Hopefully, I won't need him for more than a couple days."

"The two of you can hammer those details out. Can you be in your office at nine?"

"Sure," I said.

"I mean at nine. Don't be late. Tyler won't be."

"T.J. and I will be there."

"All right," Rollins said. "If this shit goes on more than a few days, I can probably be back and help you out."

"I want to wrap it up as quickly as possible."

"Tyler's your guy, then. Remember—nine o'clock."

"Yeah, yeah," I said. "Thanks." I ended the call. I wondered what Rollins meant about John Tyler being the guy to help resolve this in as little time as we could. I didn't want some loose cannon who would just murder everyone in Vinny's crew. The more I thought about it, the more the description fit someone who would take on a cartel. There was a saying about beggars and choosers, however, and I would see what arrangements Tyler and I could come to in the morning.

For now, I still had other things to do.

———

A few hours before, I'd planned to have a pleasant conversation with Gloria. We would talk over dinner and dessert in the restaurant. Then, I would get down to business —and on one knee—and ask the question which had lingered over me for days. She would say yes, we would come home, and after a vigorous round or two of sexual revelry, we would start talking about a wedding.

Vinny's early release scuttled it all.

"What do you mean you want me to get out of town?" Gloria said with her hands on her hips.

"Just for a few days."

"How dangerous is this guy?"

"He's not a serial killer," I said, "but he does blame me for his arrest. I think this ties everything together, including Joey's near-accident, my parents getting their tires slashed and then rear-ended, and Rich's house getting shot at."

"Plus someone firing at you and T.J."

"All of it."

"Why don't you come with me?" she said. "Tell Rich what's going on. Let the cops handle it."

I shook my head. "Not how I'm wired. Vinny wants to come at me, fine. I'll deal with him. I don't want to have to worry about anyone else."

Gloria crossed her arms under her chest. "Who else are you sending away?"

"You're the first. I love you, but I kind of hope the rest of these conversations are easier."

"Who else?"

"My parents. T.J. Joey. I'll ask Rich, but we both know he'll just tell me to piss off."

"Did you call Rollins?" Gloria asked.

"He's out of town. Referred someone else to me. I'm going to talk to him in the morning."

"I don't like this."

"Me, either," I said. "There's no way I can look after everyone, though. Vinny wants revenge on me. He's not going to chase someone down four hundred miles away."

"What the hell do I do, then?"

"Pack a bag. I have some cash I can give you. If you need an ATM, use it before you leave, and then make sure wherever you're going is in the opposite direction. I think you should be at least one state away. I'll follow you for a while to make sure no one else is there."

"I don't like this," she said again. A small smile danced on her lips. "Your parents are going to hate it. Imagine your mother trying to pack for a trip without a reservation and itinerary."

"I know." I grinned. "She'll first be upset I'm calling after nine-thirty. By the time my father herds her out the door, she'll be shrieking at the clouds."

"All right." Gloria sighed. "Let me throw a few days' worth of stuff into a bag or two." I fully expected her to need six pieces of luggage even for a short stay. Any smaller amount would surprise me. Gloria's bags-to-days ratio was the inverse of basically everyone else I knew.

"I'll make some other calls while you do." I walked into the next bedroom while Gloria looked through her portion of the closet. What began as a few clothes here and there for when she slept over morphed into her using as much square footage as I did. If she ever added the rest of her wardrobe, I would be in serious trouble. While I pondered this, I called my parents' house. My father picked up.

"Little late to be calling, son."

"It's ten-thirty. Let's not pretend I woke you up in the middle of the night."

"What's going on?"

"I know how everything ties together," I said, "including what happened to you twice. Remember Vinny Serrano?"

"Didn't he go to jail?" my father said.

"Yep. And he managed to get out way early. He still blames me for what happened, so he's lashing out."

"Wow." He blew out a deep breath. "What can we do?"

"Leave town for a few days."

"Your mother isn't going to like it."

In the background, I heard her ask, "Is that Coningsby? What am I not going to like?"

"She'll get over it," I said. "The important thing is keeping you safe. You have a stash of cash on hand?"

"We do."

"Good. Use it. Go somewhere at least one state away. Don't use your cards or your phones. Buy one somewhere. Do you still have a rental car?"

"For a few more days, yes," he said.

"Even better. I know this will throw Mom for a huge loop, but you need to leave tonight. I don't think Vinny is aware I know he's doing all this, so I want to stay ahead of him."

"All right. I'll handle it. Be careful, son. Vinny sounds dangerous this time."

He was before, as well, but my father didn't need to know this at the moment. "I will, Dad. I'll give you the all-clear when it's safe to return."

We hung up, and I tried T.J. next. "You stay, I stay," she told me. I tried to persuade her for a couple minutes to no avail. "You're stuck with me, remember?"

"How could I forget?" I said.

I dialed Joey next. He declined to leave town, though he offered to accompany Gloria on her mini-trip. "Remember, I called dibs on her in the event you get brutally murdered," he said.

"I'm sure it would be a great comfort." I clicked off and

moved on to calling Rich. Sure enough, I got the reaction I expected.

"Screw him," my cousin said. "I'm not leaving town."

"Did you know he'd gotten out?"

"No idea. We generally don't hear these kinds of things. Who told you?"

"Liz Fleming," I said. "I called her. She still knows people in the PD office."

"I'm sticking it out," Rich said. "If I ran away every time some asshole with a grudge against me resurfaced, I'd live out of a suitcase."

"I figured you'd stay. Just be careful. Vinny's clearly OK to spread out the misery."

"I will." Rich ended the call. I thought about warning Melinda, but I had no idea she even existed when Vinny went down. My only connection to her was through T.J., so it was indirect. I texted my secretary and asked her to warn Melinda if she thought it was worthwhile. When I walked back into the bedroom, Gloria finished packing her third and final bag.

"I don't think I've ever gotten ready so fast," she said.

"Hopefully, you won't need to be gone more than a couple days."

"Is there . . . anything else you wanted to talk about?"

My throat went dry. "What do you mean?"

"I don't know. I feel like you've been trying to have a certain conversation with me for a while." She smiled. "Maybe even ask me something . . . but you keep getting interrupted."

I opened my arms, and we shared a tight, lingering embrace. "It'll keep until you get back," I whispered. "Let's get through this mess first."

"All right." We kissed. She grabbed my face, and we kissed again. I surprised myself by pulling away.

"You need to get on the road."

"All right. I'll meet you downstairs." Gloria picked up the smallest of her bags. "Can you bring the other two?"

"Sure." I carried the other two downstairs and left them outside the office door. When I bought the house and knew which room I would work out of, I paid a contractor to cover about two-thirds of the closet opening. A large bookcase sat in front of it. I slid it to the side, crouched, and moved inside the hidden cubby. In here, I kept a backup laptop, a couple burner phones, some flash drives, and emergency cash. Armed with a thousand dollars and one of the mobiles, I buttoned everything back up and took the luggage to Gloria's car.

Her coupe featured a decent trunk considering it was built for escape velocity. She stood outside the car, and we shared a final embrace. "Be careful," she said. "It seems we need to have a conversation when we get back. I'd hate to miss it."

The cast made it a little awkward, but I rubbed her left ring finger a couple times. "You be careful, too. Take my burner. Don't use your own phone. I know the number, so I can call you on it."

"All right."

"I'll follow you out of the city and make sure no one else is taking an interest in us." I loaded the bags into the cargo hold, and we both climbed into our respective cars. Thirty minutes later, I honked at Gloria a couple times as I got off I-95 to turn around and head back to Baltimore.

She would be safe. Vinny could come after me all he wanted, but I wouldn't let him hurt anyone I cared about.

CHAPTER 22

I MADE sure to be up in time to arrive at the office by nine. Arranging last-minute travel for people tired me out more than I expected, and I felt groggy as I brewed coffee and fixed a quick breakfast in my kitchen. I drove to the office hoping T.J. came in early and more java would be waiting for me. Her yellow Mustang sat in its usual spot. I pulled in beside it. As I walked to the building, a loud engine rumbled, and a dark green muscle car swung onto the lot. I looked at my watch—eight-fifty-five.

"We have a guest coming," I told T.J. as I walked in. "Rollins is out of town, so he asked someone else to stop by. His name is John Tyler."

"You work with him before?"

"Sort of." I poured a cup of coffee. "I helped him and Rollins with something a few months ago."

A moment later, footsteps rang out on the stairs, and the door opened. A man walked in. He wore jeans, sensible black shoes, a T-shirt, and a leather jacket. His salt-and-pepper hair was cut short in the classic former military look. Dark eyes scanned T.J. and me in turn. The newcomer wasn't big— probably five-ten—but he looked compact and solid. His loose movements told everyone he knew how to take care of himself and would have no problem proving it.

"Mister Tyler?" my secretary asked.

He nodded. "Just Tyler is fine."

"Coffee?"

"Sure. Black, please."

I sat behind my desk, and Tyler approached. Rollins was in his early forties. Tyler looked about a decade older. Still, he'd played a significant role in taking down the Maryland operation of a Mexican drug cartel. Middle age must not have taken much off his fastball. "Nice to meet you in the flesh," I said.

"Likewise." We shook hands, and Tyler stared at my guest chairs. He pivoted one so I would be on his left and the door would be visible on his right. Interesting. T.J. handed him a paper cup before wheeling her own chair to us. "Rollins tells me you're fairly jammed up, but he didn't go into a lot of specifics."

"Close to four years ago, I worked a case where my old acquaintance from college came under suspicion. His name is Vinny. He turned out to be behind a lot of stuff, and he got sent away for a long time. Recently, though, he turned state's evidence and got a surprise early release."

"And now he wants to make your life hell." It wasn't a question.

"Speaking from experience?" I said.

Tyler shrugged. "Not hard to imagine. Revenge is one of the world's oldest motivations."

"Yeah, he's coming after me. Already started. The problem is he's targeting people I care about, too. I sent my girlfriend and parents out of town last night. My cousin refused to go, but he's a cop. I figured he'd say no."

"Your cousin's a cop?" Tyler said. "Ferguson . . ." He paused. "Rich?"

"He's the one. You've met him?"

"A couple times." Tyler sipped some coffee to hide a smirk. "I'm pretty sure he thinks I'm a loose cannon, and I definitely think he has a stick shoved pretty far up his ass."

T.J. snorted. I smiled and bobbed my head. "You're not wrong." In reality, Tyler knowing of my cousin didn't represent a positive development. It meant he'd left some bodies behind him. I hoped we could avoid a lot of bloodshed.

"What kind of outfit does Vinny run?"

"I don't know yet." When Tyler frowned, I clarified. "I literally found out he'd been cut loose late last night. My focus then was getting people to safety."

"How about before?" Tyler asked.

"Not applicable. His main goon is in jail—I checked—another got deported, and he killed the woman who used to work for him."

"Sounds like a real charmer. Also sounds like you need to gather some intel. What's my role in all this?"

"I want someone to stick with me and T.J.," I said, "especially if one of us is out during the day." I went over all the attempts on people's lives starting with me almost getting run over near my house. "So far, they've all come from a green late-model Mustang, but I don't want to presume we'll always see the same car."

"All right." Tyler imbibed some more caffeine. "I'm not a trained investigator, so I don't want to step on your toes. The PI stuff is all yours. I'm a mechanic, door-kicker, and shooter."

"I'd prefer we not shoot anyone if we can help it."

"If we can help it," he said, and I imagined we would apply this standard differently. "What's your next move?"

"I have a feeling Vinny reached out to someone who used to work for him," I said. "I think I'll pay him a visit in jail."

"You want me to tag along?"

"What's your availability?" I said.

"Open," he said. "I own a car shop, but a couple guys there can get by without me."

"All right. I appreciate it." Tyler nodded. "For now, I'd rather you stick with T.J. Jails are secure enough. She'll give you my number. Shoot me a text so I have yours."

"Roger that." He looked at the coffee pot. "We're making more, right?"

"Absolutely," T.J. said.

"I'll see what I can learn about any new crew Vinny might be using." I shrugged into a jacket and headed for the door.

———

I stopped at home and retrieved a couple of security cameras. One already kept an eye on the front door. Now, I mounted one at the back of the house and another on the side. Connecting them to my existing system only took a few seconds once they were in place. I wanted to install two more at work, but Manny owned the building. His existing setup contained a small number of blind spots. The calculus changed when protecting people instead of old cars became the priority.

From Federal Hill, I drove to the prison in Jessup where Sal resided ever since he flipped on Vinny. Salvador LaRocca was a beefy Italian with dyed blond hair the last time I saw him. We tangled a couple times, and the encounters didn't go well for him. I expected him to be indifferent today, maybe even hostile. He didn't have any reason to talk to me. The state's attorney already cut him a deal. Five years remained on his sentence, and he could probably get out in three for good behavior—if he had it in him not to be an asshole.

After checking in and waiting in a stale room begging for fresh air and paint, a guard led me down a corridor. We veered off into a long, narrow room. Partitions of plexiglass separated one side from the other. Thanks to a set of small holes in the barrier, inmates and guests could talk without the need for a phone. The guard told me to wait in the eighth spot, and I did. The stalls on either side of me remained empty. Maybe no one wanted to sit on the hard, ugly metal chairs.

A couple minutes later, Sal approached. He'd lost about fifteen pounds but he looked brawnier than ever. He'd even kept his hair color though he wore it shorter these days. He scowled when he saw me and dropped onto the chair. "The fuck do you want?"

"It's so nice to be remembered," I said.

"What are you doing here? You got what you wanted. Vinny went down."

"He did. He also got out way early."

Sal stared ahead and then shrugged. "Really?"

I couldn't get a good read on him. If I found out Sal remained in jail, Vinny would be able to, as well. There would be no reason for him to visit, but Sal could've found out another way. "Really. State's evidence."

"Good for him," Sal said. "Why do I care?"

"Because he's going scorched earth," I said. "Vinny made his own choices, but he blames me for everything. I don't care if he comes after me, but he's had people go after friends and family, too."

Sal mimed wiping tears from his eyes. "Boo hoo. So what?"

"You know anyone he might've brought into the fold to replace you?"

Sal glanced to the side before answering. "Nope."

It was a lie, but I'd come back to it. "Here's the thing, Sal. You know Vinny. He's pretty bright, and he probably pays well, but he does himself in. His entire organization flipped on him before, and history just might repeat itself. I doubt the son of a bitch got any nicer in jail."

He spread his large hands. "Again . . . don't see why I give a shit."

"Because if you know someone who's thrown in with him, the story won't have a happy ending."

"You think you can take him down again?"

"Sure," I said. "I'm smarter than he is. Always have been. Vinny will ultimately sabotage himself because he doesn't do well with people. He's going back inside."

"I ain't convinced," the former goon said. "You might be smarter, but Vinny ain't no fool. He's not going to lose the same way. We done here?"

I needed something else. If Sal had any useful knowledge, I didn't want to leave here without it. Time to play my best card. "Margaret's dead."

He recoiled and frowned. "What?"

"Yeah. Found in her home. Somebody beat the shit out of her and then emptied a clip into her chest." I shrugged. "Only one person I can think of would hate her so much. But hey . . . you don't know anyone working for Vinny now. I guess it's all good." I pushed my chair back and started to stand.

"Wait." He held up a hand.

I sat again. "This chair sucks. Talk fast."

"All right. My kid brother came to see me a few days ago. Says this guy talked to him about joining a crew. Not the usual strong-arm stuff. This was scaring people and getting revenge."

"Vinny."

"He didn't drop a name," Sal said, "but yeah. I told him to be careful. He probably didn't listen."

"You think your brother killed Margaret?" I said.

"Doubt it." Sal shook his head. "Mikey don't mind beating people up, but he's not a killer."

"All right. Like I told you, Vinny's going scorched earth. I'm not going to let him hurt someone I love. He's going down. I'll try to go easy on your brother . . . if he lets me."

"I get it." He snorted. "Damn kid. I wish he listened to me."

"Maybe you'll be cellmates soon," I offered. "Plenty of time to offer some pearls of wisdom."

"Fuck you," Sal said.

"I can see why he doesn't listen to you much." I got up from the horrible chair. A thought occurred to me. "What's your brother drive?"

"Huh?"

"What kind of car?"

"I ain't exactly seen him out in the world for a few years," Sal said. "Last time I did, he had some old Toyota. A Camry, I think. Why?"

"Just curious," I said. "If your brother comes by in the next day or two, try hard to convince him to ditch Vinny."

"I'll do my best." Sal called for a guard, and a massive Latino man came to escort him back to his cell. I collected my belongings and left the prison. The security app on my phone showed no suspicious activity on the cameras.

———

I arrived back at the office to see T.J. and Tyler laughing it up over pizza. "Didn't know we were having a party," I said as I closed the door.

"It's all good," my secretary said. "You paid for the pizza."

"Learn anything?" Tyler asked.

"Sal's brother Mikey is part of Vinny's new crew. He doesn't know any other names."

"Being an asshole runs in the family."

"Usually does," I said.

"What's next, boss?" T.J. wanted to know.

"I'm going to join the pizza party." I grabbed a plate and put a slice each of pepperoni and cheese onto it. "You're going to look up known associates for Michael LaRocca."

She nodded and got to work. Tyler dropped onto one of my guest chairs when I sat behind my desk. "Having fun?" I said around a mouthful of pizza. I couldn't put a place to the taste.

"My daughter's nineteen and in college. She's thinking about going for a criminal justice degree. T.J. said you could probably find an internship spot here for her if she did."

"And I thought I was generous by buying lunch."

Tyler put up his hands. "I wasn't trying to impose. She offered."

"It's fine. I didn't learn much besides Sal's brother's name and likely affiliation. Mikey drove a Camry last his brother saw, by the way." I called to T.J. "Check what kind of car he drives, too. I wonder if he's upgraded his ride."

"You need me to stick around?"

"Probably not. What part of the city are you in?"

"I live in Mount Washington," Tyler said. "If I'm at work, my shop is basically at the corner of Northern Parkway and Harford Road."

"Straight shot, at least," I said.

"Yeah. You from Baltimore?"

"Born and raised. You?"

"Born. Raised . . . in a bunch of places. My dad was in the navy."

"But you went into the army?"

Tyler grinned. "I get seasick. You have my number?" I nodded. "All right. Let me know if you need anything."

"Thanks." He left. His loud car rumbled to life a minute

later. I looked out the window. Manny walked up, and the two had a conversation. Probably about the classic ride. I saw the numbers 4-4-2 on the back, but they didn't mean much. My appreciation of cars started with a more modern era. I liked creature comforts.

A little while later, T.J. said, "I have a few known associates for Mikey LaRocca. Looks like he still drives a Toyota, so no help there."

"Maybe one of his friends is into sportier cars," I said.

"I'll look. Mikey lives right across the street from a Seven-Eleven. They have cameras on the outside." She smiled. "I did what you told me. I used Shodan, I found a couple devices, and I checked for default credentials."

"And you got in."

"I got in. It's hard to believe how easy it is."

"As much as it benefits people like you and me," I said, "There are times I wish it were a lot more difficult. Anything going on?"

"Nothing at the moment," she said. "No car in his driveway or in front of the house."

"OK. Keep an eye on it."

She told me she would. While I ate some now-lukewarm pizza, Rich called. "Your parents got rear-ended, right?" he said when I picked up.

I didn't like the start of this conversation. "Yeah, why?"

"Someone tried to run me off the road. Maybe I can take my car to the same body shop."

"You all right?" I said.

"Fine. I did say they *tried* to run me off the road. Didn't succeed."

"But whoever it is got away?"

"Yes," Rich said.

"Green Mustang?"

"No. Different car this time. And unlike before . . . I got a plate."

"Talk about burying the lede," I said.

"Meet me downtown," my cousin said. "You, King, and I will look into this."

"See you there."

CHAPTER 23

AT BPD HEADQUARTERS, King took over Rich's old desk.
The one opposite him sat unused. A few plainclothes cops
milled about, and the occasional uniform joined them. Rich
walked out of his office as I approached. "Ready to get to
work?"

"Sure," I said. "Good thing you got a plate."

"They took off the rear one. I managed to get ahead of the
car at one point. Saw the front tag in the mirror." He paused.
"Before you ask . . . yes, I can read backwards." He sat at the
desk opposite King, who smirked.

"Excuse me, Lieutenant. My *current* partner sits there."

"Your partner's in court," Rich said. "You'll have to make
do with me."

"I'm not sure I can manage," King said.

Rich ignored him and logged in to the workstation. He
entered a few keystrokes and turned the monitor around.
"This is the car. It's an old Honda registered to a man named
Charles Phillips." King took his turn working the keyboard.

"Got a rap sheet," the sergeant said. "Usual stuff. Assault,
robbery. Got out of jail about six months ago."

"Can you see if he overlapped with another prisoner?" I asked. "Vincent Serrano."

King ran another search. "He did. They were on the same cell block for about a year."

"There's one member of his new crew. Pretty dumb to use his own car."

Rich shrugged. "Nobody said these guys were geniuses."

"What about the green Mustang we saw so often?"

"I checked it out earlier," Rich said. "Stolen." He ran his report again. "Reported about a week ago. I'm surprised you didn't look."

I mentally kicked myself for the oversight. "I guess I didn't think they'd keep using a stolen car. Everything they did was spread out over days, and some of their shit happened in broad daylight."

"Unusual for sure."

An idea popped into my head. "Who wants to be logged in when I do some searches of questionable legality?"

"I just got promoted," King said. "They're probably not gonna bust me back down right away. What did you have in mind?"

"I want to look at traffic cameras. If they used a stolen car over a period of days, they must be stashing it somewhere. A garage or something."

"All right." King stood, and I took his place in the chair. It provided nominal comfort. I couldn't imagine sitting in it for any significant length of time. "The date and time the owner reported the theft is there."

I ran with the information. The 9-1-1 call came in during the morning rush hour. This meant the owner noticed it then, probably on her way out the door. The real theft happened hours earlier. The best time would be overnight. The combination of darkness and fewer people around to see anything made this likely. I started my search for cameras in the area at eleven the prior night.

We watched a bunch of nothing for a while. Traffic slowed to a trickle after midnight. At around two in the morning, we saw the green pony car leaving the neighborhood. "There it is," Rich said. "Try using some cameras nearby. Let's see if we can figure out where it goes."

"What would we do without your sage guidance?" I said as I already worked on doing what my cousin suggested.

"I shudder to think."

About two miles away and fifteen minutes later, the Mustang stopped in another neighborhood. It ended up far enough away from the intersection for us to lose sight of it. "It might be better if I did the rest of this on my phone," I said. Rich sighed but nodded. I used my cell to open a secure connection to my main computer. The car's last known location was a street which would have been busy during daylight hours. I hoped this meant some homes and businesses would have security cameras we could borrow.

My search found a small auto parts store which could offer us a view. I found the specs on their system, hunted for its default credentials, and attempted a remote login using them. It worked. "Damn," King said. "You make this look easy."

"A combination of natural brilliance and people not doing the basics. Leaning toward the former, of course."

"Of course," he said while Rich snorted.

"The question now," I said, "is how this place stores their old footage. If it's local, I can probably access what we want. If the system sends it to the cloud, we might be out of luck." I poked around the limited archives which were available. "Based on the age of this setup, I'm going to guess they keep things in-house. Looks like they don't hold onto old data for very long."

"Long enough?" Rich said.

"Yes." I found the date I wanted, and I entered a time range starting shortly before the Mustang rolled up. We watched the empty street. My phone didn't make the best viewing medium, but the image was clear enough. The driver remained in the car. Two men got out the passenger's side. They looked around for a moment before pointing at another car. The camera captured the trunk half of it. One fellow removed the rear license plate while the other kept watch. They then moved out of frame, where I presumed they repeated the process in the front.

A moment later, they jogged back into view. The one who kept an eye out before did so again, this time while his friend replaced the Mustang's tags with the ones they just stole. When they were finished, they climbed back into the Mustang. The driver checked for traffic before he pulled away, giving us a good shot of his face. I rewound a couple seconds, paused, and took a screenshot. "This was the only clear look we got at them," I said.

"I don't think he was the guy driving the car which came after me," Rich said. "Hard to tell on this video, but it was probably one of the other two."

"I'll send this picture to the two of you."

"We just watched you access someone's camera illegally." Rich frowned. "This would be inadmissible. I know you want to take Vinny down, but we need to make a case against him."

"Rich, go back to your office."

"What?"

"King," I said, "close your eyes."

"All right," he said, and he did.

I deepened my voice a bit. "Sergeant, I'd like to make an anonymous tip."

"Thank you, citizen I've never met."

Rich shook his head and returned to his office. I used a

temporary email address to send the screencap to King. I wheeled around to his side while he opened the file and plugged it into the facial recognition system. We got a match a moment later.

"Meet Quincy Weeks," King said. "He goes by Quinn because bullies beat the shit out of kids named Quincy. Decent rap sheet. Probably appealing to this Vinny guy you're going after."

Rich rejoined us and looked at the screen. "All right. We don't have enough on the other two yet, but let's get a BOLO out on this guy. Maybe he'll lead us to Vinny. If not, we might be able to get his crew to flip on him like we did before." My cousin smirked at me. "Good thing we got an anonymous tip."

"Good thing," I agreed.

———

I drove away from BPD headquarters. King and Rich put out a BOLO on a henchman and had a plan of action. Good for them. I intended to leave them to it. Let them chase after lackeys. Four years ago, Vinny committed a litany of crimes—including murder—so getting people to roll on him in exchange for lighter sentences was easy. What did he do this time? So far, we couldn't directly tie him to anything. Even so, he'd likely be on the hook for auto theft, property damage, and a few gun crimes.

Nothing there compared to murder.

I stopped about a mile away and picked up coffee from a Royal Farms. In the parking lot, I checked on Vinny's old house. It was where he went down. His hubris compelled him to invite me there under the pretense of me giving up my investigation. In reality, Rich and I turned his people against him and freed the woman he'd kidnapped. The evening did not go at all according to Vinny's plan, and he'd hated me ever since.

Six months after his arrest, his house went on the market, and someone snapped it up. Vinny was probably salty about it, but if he were focused on getting revenge on me, he'd leave it alone. I thought about his other haunts. He used to eat lunch regularly at a place called Donna's, and they even let him conduct his bookmaking business from his usual table. I drove there and parked in the mostly empty lot. This would have been a good time to call John Tyler. The Cross Keys location lay just south of his neighborhood. I was alone here, though, so I made sure to have my pistol under my jacket as I walked in. A few diners ate at tables, but the place looked almost barren. Fixtures and decorations were mostly gone.

I didn't see Vinny. It was odd for people to remain working in the same restaurant for four years. The bartender looked familiar, so I parked myself on a stool. He was tall and thin with long black hair and tattoos up and down his arms. When he approached, I put a fifty-dollar bill on the dark polished wood. "I need an IPA and to test your memory."

He nodded, pocketed the Grant, and filled a glass from a tap. "What do you need to know?"

"You work here long?"

He shrugged. "Over five years. Won't make it to six."

"What do you mean?"

"Look around," he said. "We're closing at the end of the month. For good."

"Sorry to hear," I said despite the fact I'd barely been here before and didn't care. "You remember a guy used to eat at the table over there?" I pointed toward the back end of the restaurant. "His name was Vinny."

He frowned and polished a glass which did not require any further cleaning. "Been a while, but yeah, I remember. What about him?"

"Seen him recently?"

"He's in jail, ain't he?"

I sipped the IPA. Nice and hoppy. If I had a more refined palate, I probably could have picked up on citrus notes or whatever else was supposed to be in there. Mostly, I hated snooty people who could taste all those things. "He was. Got out a little while ago."

"Ain't seem him." The bartender picked up another clean glass and did the same.

"If you do, tell him C.T. stopped by." I took a final draught of the beer. "We . . . have some unfinished business I think he'll want to resolve."

"Sure," he said.

I walked back outside. Donna's was a bust. Vinny hadn't been out of jail long and wouldn't have access to his illicit money from before. He would need to stay somewhere and have a home base for his vendetta.

Where better to start the hunt than with family?

CHAPTER 24

I REMEMBERED Vinny's mother from our days in high school and college together. There weren't many single parents in our circle, so she stood out. She never struck me as a particularly warm or friendly person. I hadn't seen her in a decade or so, and I never knew what she thought about Vinny's arrest and imprisonment. The press tried reaching out to her, and she stonewalled them at every turn. She wasn't hard to find, however, as she still owned and lived in the house where Vinny grew up.

I parked out front. This was technically Roland Park but getting on the outskirts. Houses were a little smaller. Several on the street needed some pretty serious upkeep. Ms. Serrano lived in a Cape Cod with a gray stone front and green door. I checked my pistol, got out, and approached the front door. She answered my first round of knocking and frowned. "You were Vinny's friend."

I didn't see the benefits of debating the finer points of friend versus acquaintance, so I simply said, "I was."

Vinny's mother would be an age peer of my parents, putting her somewhere around sixty. She looked older, though, maybe because of the stress her son the criminal put her through. Silver streaks ran among her mousy brown strands, and worry lines creased her face. "You visit him in jail?"

"Yes." I did—once. It was enough.

She continued to scrutinize me with the door maybe a third of the way open. "You're C.T., right? You played lacrosse with him."

"He liked pointing out how he scored more goals than me," I said.

"You're the one who sent him to prison." She crossed her slender arms. "What the hell do you want now?"

It was time for a dose of reality. "Vinny put himself in jail. I didn't make him do any of the illegal things he got busted for. His notion about me being responsible is a fantasy. He did it to himself."

Silence served as the only reply for a few seconds. "You come here to argue with me?" she said.

"No. I want to know if you've seen Vinny."

Her expression remained neutral. If my question dropped a bombshell about his release, she would've looked surprised. "Vinny's still in jail . . . thanks to you."

"We both know he isn't," I said. "Your son may be a good liar, but he didn't get it from you."

Ms. Serrano snorted. "Probably from my brother. Look, I haven't seen him. Even if I did, I wouldn't lead you to him. You'd put him in jail again."

"He's going after me and people I care about."

"Maybe you should've thought about that before you put him in jail."

"I see the apple didn't fall far from the tree. You can crow about your brother all you want, but from where I stand, Vinny learned how to be an asshole from you."

"Screw you," she said and slammed the door.

No matter. Vinny's mother was unhelpful. On some

level, I should've expected it, but I never knew her well. I'd forgotten about her brother, however. Vinny credited an uncle with getting him hooked on sports, odds, and bookmaking. In the car, I looked him up. Paul Serrano owned a house not far away. His sister probably called him as soon as she locked up. He'd be expecting me. Still, I needed to make the attempt.

The traffic lights cooperated, and my heavy right foot did the rest. This neighborhood represented a step down from the edges of Roland Park. Houses were smaller, usually covered in fading brick or siding and in need of obvious maintenance. A few overgrown yards dotted the street. One home sat in horrible disrepair with a jungle of plants and bushes out front. Probably abandoned. I curbed the S4 about a hundred feet short of Paul Serrano's house.

No one lurked nearby. I climbed from the car and did another check of my surroundings. Everything looked clear. I neared his home and crossed the street. As I did, a sedan a couple hundred feet ahead of me pulled out with screeching tires. The rear window went down, and a pistol pointed at me. I scampered behind a nearby SUV as three shots rent the air and took small chunks out of the asphalt. Then, the car was gone. I barely even got a look at it.

It wasn't a green Mustang, though.

I'd already come this far. Might as well see if the uncle would talk to me. I calmed myself with a few deep breaths and drew my .45 as I approached his front door. He opened up before I could knock or ring the bell. Empty hands hung at his sides. I lowered my pistol. Paul Serrano was tall and portly with a headful of curly hair in transition from black to gray. "He said you'd come," he told me in a voice suggesting he just gargled with a bucket of old gravel.

"I don't suppose you want to tell me where he's going?"

"Eat shit."

"You're not doing him any favors," I said. "Vinny's only going to dig his hole deeper."

Paul took a pack of cigarettes from his pocket. He shook one free. "Maybe." He pulled out a matchbook, which showed a stylized red C on a plain white background. He lit the cigarette and, of course, blew smoke in my face. "If he does, I'm sure you'll be there to shovel the dirt back on top of him."

I didn't give him the satisfaction of coughing or reacting. "He's going after my family. I might pour concrete in the damn hole to keep him there this time."

Vinny's uncle shrugged. "You brought it on yourself."

"As much as I don't like Vinny, I'm starting to realize he never had a chance."

The orange cigarette glow intensified as he sucked in a mouthful of poison. "Whadda ya mean?"

"You and your sister both suck," I said. "You're shitty people. Whatever happens to Vinny is on both of you."

"Get the fuck off of my porch," he said.

Lacking any better options, I did. As I crossed the street, my phone vibrated in my pocket. I checked it when I got in the car. A text showed from an unknown number displayed on the screen. *Nice try, C.T. You always were a step behind me. We'll talk soon.*

I felt sure we would.

———

"Why the hell did you go off by yourself?"

John Tyler posed the question as I sat behind my desk. He and T.J. occupied chairs near hers, and both stared at me. Note to self: don't lead off with a story about chasing down an old adversary and getting shot at next time. "It was a judgment call."

"It was a bad one."

"I didn't know I'd run into Vinny. The plan was to talk to his mother. While I was there, she mentioned his uncle, and it made me remember Vinny talking about him. So I went there, too."

"Vinny shot at you?" T.J. asked.

"I don't know for sure if he pulled the trigger," I said, "but he was in the car."

"What kind of car?" Tyler said.

"The kind with someone shooting at me. I barely got a look at it before the window went down and a gun popped out. Getting to cover seemed more important than standing in the street to get the make, model, and plate."

"Fair enough."

"I don't think whoever fired really tried to hit me. My take was they wanted to scare me."

"A shooter only needs to be lucky, not good," Tyler said.

"Vinny has been going after me and people I know for like a week now," I said. "He's not going to wrap it up by plugging me in the street in front of his uncle's house." I paused. "I don't mean to be rude, but why are you here, anyway?"

"I called him," T.J. said. "I knew we'd be wrapping up soon . . . and I saw a green Mustang drive by when I was heating up lunch."

"Did it come back?" I said.

"No. Might not have been our car, but it spooked me enough to call for reinforcements."

"Good decision." I unlocked my laptop. "Vinny texted me after the car sped away. I'm going to guess it's a burner, and he turned it off after using it, but I'd be remiss if I didn't try to find it." I accessed a triangulation tool of dubious legality. If Vinny left his mobile on for any length of time, I might get to learn where he went after fleeing his uncle's street. I entered the phone number. Sure enough, it had been offline for a while now, and its last tower ping hit the one closest to Paul Serrano's home. "No dice."

"Worth a shot, anyway," Tyler said.

"T.J., why don't you duck out a little early?" I offered.

"You want Tyler to follow me?" she said.

"Maybe we should keep talking about him like he's not in the room. I wonder what he thinks about it."

Tyler chuckled. "It's fine. I'll make sure she gets home safely."

"If you do, you'll actually know where she lives. You'll be one-up on me."

"You should always know where your employees live," Tyler said. "What if she called you with an emergency?"

"I'm sure she could tell me her address."

"You pay her, right?"

"Boys," T.J. said, "as much as I appreciate you fighting over me, it's not necessary. Yes, he pays me, but it's . . . through an agency for now, so it's not direct. Can we go?"

Tyler stood and swept his arm toward the door. "If you need anything later, let me know."

"Is more management advice included?" I said.

He grinned. "For a friend of Rollins? Sure."

They left, and I pondered how else I might try to find Vinnie. His old associates were a dead end—literally in the case of Margaret Madison. I'd get no help from his family. Vinny alienated himself from most of our mutual friends and acquaintances, and I doubt any of them knew he'd been released from jail. Some were probably oblivious to his arrest and incarceration almost four years ago.

I made a few calls and sent a few texts. None of our former lacrosse teammates were in the know, and I couldn't imagine Vinny maintaining friends anywhere else. The idea of going home to an empty house didn't compel me to leave, so I stayed and conducted another hour of fruitless research. I sent Gloria a text lamenting the fact I'd be cooking dinner for one and locked up the office.

On a lark, I drove back toward Roland Park to check out Vinny's mother's neighborhood. Nothing appeared unusual. If I knew for sure what kind of car pulled out and fired at me, my trip might have been more productive. No new bullets flew at me as I drove by, which my expert sleuthing skills told me to take as a good sign. As darkness encroached, I found nothing amiss in Paul Serrano's area and headed home hungrier than before. Maybe I would eschew cooking for the more sensible option of carry-out.

My phone rang a few minutes after I got back on my way. It looked like Vinny's burner number. I answered "What do you want, Vinny?"

"Happy to see me?"

"If I say no, will you turn yourself in?"

"I have a video you'll want to watch," he said.

"This isn't college," I said. "I don't need to see your porn collection."

"I got a feeling you'll want to pay this one some extra attention." Something in his tone bothered me, and a shudder crawled down my back. My phone vibrated as a message came in. "Give it a look. We'll talk later." He hung up before I could say anything else.

I stopped at a red light. What video could Vinny possibly want to show me? Everyone I wanted to leave town did—except for Rich, and Vinny's goons weren't good enough to take him down. I opened the message and tapped on the video. All I saw at first was a sidewalk before a red door with a small window came into focus. The camera showed a woman approaching from the rear. A small purse hung from her right shoulder.

She wore Gloria's blue and gold striped dress.

The hair was the right color. Height and shoes looked right. My stomach clenched. She pushed the door open with her left hand, took a step inside, and backed up suddenly. A masked man followed her, clamped a hand over her mouth, and drove a knife into her midsection again and again. Blood streamed onto the concrete. The killer let the body sag forward before the feed went to black.

I couldn't breathe.

A car horn honked behind me. I shot through the light and pulled into the first parking lot I saw. I grabbed a spot at the back away from anyone else.

My hands shook as I held my phone. I'd watched Gloria pack her bags. I loaded them into her car. She drove off with one of my burner phones. There was no way Vinny and his crew found her.

Was there?

Tears burned my eyes and blurred my vision as I called the number for the temporary phone I gave her.

It went straight to voicemail.

CHAPTER 25

I STARED AT MY PHONE. Breaths came in ragged gulps. I tried the burner number again. Right to voicemail. This must have been a trick. Vinny couldn't have found Gloria. She'd left the state. I watched the video again. The dress fit the woman like it did my girlfriend. It hugged her hips. I'd seen her wearing the same shoes recently. Her hair was in a ponytail—which Gloria almost never wore unless she went casual —but it was the right shade of brown.

Did Vinny find the woman I loved and order her killed?

I played it again looking for any definitive proof of the woman's identity. Whoever filmed the scene did it from the rear. The lady disappeared past the door for less than a second before backing away. She never even gave a profile view to the camera. The knife slammed into her torso. I counted the stabs. Any could have been fatal. Thirteen wounds later, most of her blood spilling onto the pavement, the woman slumped forward.

My heart raced, and my breathing matched. I fought for control and found none. Without even thinking about it, my gun was in my hand. I was going to propose to Gloria. If only I'd found the right moment. Now, she'd never know. The question would go unasked and unanswered. I wasn't sure I wanted to keep going without her. What if I hadn't sent her away? What if I'd put Joey or John Tyler on her? Would she still be alive?

I tossed my phone onto the passenger's seat and wiped my eyes. The rational part of my brain nagged at me. *Watch it again.* I couldn't. Three times proved more than enough. Vinny got his revenge. He won. He murdered the woman I wanted to marry, and I didn't know if I could get out of this parking lot to do anything about it.

Watch it again.

I stared at the .45 in my hand for a few seconds before holstering it. Did I miss something in the video? I picked up my phone and stared at the screen. Going through it again would be torture. I tapped the icon anyway. The playback started. I watched as the lady—Gloria?—approached the door and paused. I couldn't summon any calm, but I knew I needed to take in the details. White stone walls. A fancy red door with black hardware and a card reader off on the right side. This wasn't someone's house.

I resumed. The woman pushed the door open with her left hand and took a step inside. The blackness beyond made her disappear for an instant before she backed out. I stopped it again. Something nagged at me here. Everything about this video was wrong, but some detail definitely wasn't right. What was I missing? I let it play a few seconds more. The masked man could have been anyone of sufficient height and build.

Fifteen seconds back. The woman neared the door. The small window—maybe a foot square—didn't show anything or anyone on the other side. She didn't need to use a card to gain access. Her left hand reached out. I paused again. The dress was sleeveless, and she didn't wear anything on top of it. I could see her entire arm.

There was no cast on it.

I put my hand to my mouth, took a few deep breaths, and cried for a moment. Gloria wasn't dead. Half her left arm would be covered for at least another week or two. Whoever this woman was, she wasn't Gloria Reading. My girlfriend was alive. A stranger, however, was dead. Another body on Vinny's ledger. A body dressed in Gloria's clothes. I backed out of my spot, stomped on the gas as I let out the clutch, and left the parking lot headed for Brooklandville on screeching tires.

With the speedometer over 90 most of the way, I made it to Gloria's swanky neighborhood in record time. She'd given me a key a long time ago. Nothing looked amiss as I pulled into the driveway. I kept one hand on my pistol as I approached the front door. It sat slightly ajar. Chunks of wood were missing from the jamb around it. I drew the .45 and nudged the door open. It didn't make a sound. After checking every room on the main floor, I headed upstairs.

It was empty. Whoever came here got what they were after and left. I saw what they wanted soon enough. The door to Gloria's walk-in closet—large enough to be an extra bedroom in my house—hung open. She always kept it closed. A wire hanger and torn dry cleaning bag lay on the floor. Probably her dress. She'd worn it recently to make the fundraising video. A missing pair of shoes—the ones worn by the unfortunate woman—left an opening on the otherwise packed footwear rack.

I could report the break-in. County police would investigate. Absent any additional information, they were unlikely to find anything unless the thief had been careless. I didn't see the upside, and I also wanted to keep official eyes away from my latest quest to take down Vinny Serrano. He wanted to convince me he'd murdered Gloria. At some point, he would call me again to gloat. I would let him. He needed to think he'd won.

In the meantime, I would figure out who he killed and nail him for it.

————

As I left Brooklandville, I called John Tyler and updated him on what recently went down. "Must've been hard to watch," he said.

"You have no idea."

"I can imagine."

"It took until my fourth time before I picked up on a few things," I said. "I hate to give Vinny and his crew credit, but they made a convincing video."

"This asshole must really hate you," Tyler said.

"Yeah." I shuddered again thinking about watching the video for the first time. Vinny chose someone who could pass for Gloria from behind. Someone who was now dead. "He's blamed me ever since he went to jail. Last time, he kidnapped my client to try and get me to back down. Now, I think he's going to use what I'm supposed to think is Gloria's murder."

"You going to let him believe you're in mourning?"

"Might as well," I said. "I don't see the downside. He'll think he won, and he'll probably leave everyone alone."

"And while he's easing off," Tyler said, "you put the screws to him."

"Starting with figuring out who the woman in the video was. Someone who takes orders from Vinny stabbed the poor girl to death. He needs to answer for it."

"I'm no investigator, but I'll help."

"I just might need you to, especially when I deal with Vinny. Did you follow T.J. home?"

"Left her a few minutes ago," he said. "I waited until she

got inside and locked the door behind her." He paused a beat. "Want to know where she lives?"

In spite of recent events, I smiled. "Later. Right now, I need to get back to work. I'm headed into the city." I zoomed along I-83 South. At this rate, I'd reach the terminus at President Street in about ten minutes. "I'll be at the office again soon. Want to meet me there?"

"All right," Tyler said. "I don't think we should leave T.J. alone . . . just in case. What if Vinny decides one body isn't enough?"

"You're right," I said. "We can probably use her help, too. All hands on deck."

"See you soon." Tyler broke the connection. A few minutes later, I merged onto President Street. Even with the traffic gods smiting me at every intersection, I made it to my office in six more minutes. Manny and his workers were long gone. I opened the outer door, unlocked our part of the building, and tossed my bag down. Before anyone else arrived, I put a pot of coffee on to brew.

We would need it.

———

It didn't take long for Tyler and T.J. to arrive. "You two could leave me at home alone, you know," my secretary complained as she walked inside.

"You're safer here," I said.

She sat at her desk and crossed her arms. "I'm sure the testosterone in the air will keep me safe."

"You don't know what happened?"

"G.I. Joe here isn't really a big talker."

Tyler spread his hands. "She's right. Not one of my strong suits. Besides, I think this is your story to tell, C.T."

"It is." I paused for a deep breath. "Vinny sent me a

video. It showed a woman who looked a lot like Gloria getting murdered behind a building."

T.J. started to say something and stopped. Her mouth hung open before she found any words. "It wasn't Gloria, right?"

"Right. Pretty convincing, though . . . especially when I couldn't reach her after. Took me a few tries to notice." I wanted to play it on a larger screen, and the only choices were our monitors. They'd have to do. "Remind me we need to get a TV at some point."

"Our screens will work."

"Your next bonus is buying us a big-screen," I said. I emailed the video to myself, and everyone gathered around my desk. As I pressed play, my chest tightened. I knew the unfortunate victim wasn't Gloria, but the fakery had been good. Besides, whoever this woman was, she died in a way no one should. Whatever she signed up for when she met Vinny and his goons, it wasn't being stabbed and bleeding out behind an unknown building. I'd never turned the volume up in the car. Here, we heard the very beginning of a scream before a hand muffled her, and then the horrible, wet sound of the knife shredding her body thirteen times.

T.J. walked away shaking her head. She paced the perimeter of the office. "Sorry. I . . . know some girls that almost happened to."

"It's all right," I told her. "We don't need to watch it anymore."

"But we do." She stopped and collected herself with a few deep breaths. "We need to know who she was and where she died."

"You don't need to stand here and take part."

"Where else would I be?"

"Maybe you could go TV shopping?" I said with a grin.

"Piss off," T.J. said, and she chuckled despite her best

attempts to remain stoic. "We never see her face, though. The guy who kills her is in a mask, too."

"I know. I think we need to start with a location."

"Has to be a hotel," Tyler said. "There was a card reader by the door. She didn't use it. Most hotels disable them at side and rear entrances until after dark."

"Good call." I started the playback again. A few seconds in, we got our best look at the building. I didn't know it by sight, and everyone else shrugged when I asked. I took a screenshot and ran a reverse image search. We got a result right away.

Our mystery woman died outside the Cavalier Hotel in Baltimore County. I didn't know the place, but it sat in Essex This would normally be a high-traffic area, but its location was a little off the beaten path, and the back of the place faced nothing but an empty field and some train tracks. Thanks to tree coverage and some barriers near the tracks, anyone who saw the murder would need to be standing close to the hotel—near enough for Vinny's goons to see the person and tick the body count up by one.

"Either of you know this place?" I asked. Both T.J. and Tyler shook their heads.

"Looks like the kind of joint that might rent rooms by the hour," my secretary suggested.

"Maybe." I pondered the idea. "Not sure our victim was a working girl, though."

"Why not?"

I didn't know how much of her background T.J. shared with Tyler during their chats, so I took a cautious approach to mentioning her former profession. "I'm sure there are plenty to choose from in the area. It kind of makes its own vulnerability. You wouldn't want another girl or her pimp to see you go off with some woman you were going to put in a fancy dress and murder."

"Maybe they found her online," Tyler said.

"More likely." I nodded. "Maybe they even placed an ad. Regardless, they found this poor woman and killed her. We know where. Now, we need to know who she was. Vinny and his guys have to go down for this."

"We could turn it over to the cops," T.J. said.

"We can use them," I said, "but I want to keep some control over this. It needs to be on our timeframe . . . not theirs and not Vinny's."

"What are we going to do, then?"

"I'll call Gonzalez, but I'm not sure he'll like what I have to say."

CHAPTER 26

IN MY PAST dealings with the county police, I worked most often with Sergeant Gonzalez in Homicide. I called him, and despite the evening hour, he answered quickly. "I'm off the clock."

"Yet you still picked up," I said. "I'll never question the dedication of public servants again."

He snorted. "What do you need?"

"I have reliable intel about a woman being murdered in your county. In Essex to be specific."

"Recently?"

"Probably within the last few hours."

"No reports came in."

Not surprising considering the lack of visibility of the crime scene. I wondered if Vinny or his crew knew someone at the Cavalier. The chances of a guest happening upon them might be minimal, but a person on the inside could ensure the odds would be zero. "I guess nothing happened, then," I said. "This must be the homicide equivalent of a tree not making any sound if no one is there to hear it fall."

"Hang on," Gonzalez said. "You can't just drop a bombshell like that on me and then try to run away. What happened?"

"A young woman was stabbed to death."

"Where?"

"Essex?"

"Where in Essex?" he demanded.

"I need something from you before we continue," I said. "A man I put away a few years ago is out of jail and trying to get revenge on me. He's already gone after people I care about. The woman was supposed to look like my girlfriend and convince me he'd gotten to her."

"Wait a minute . . . how do you know all this?"

"Like I told you. Reliable intel."

"Bullshit. You said this prick wanted to convince you he'd killed your girlfriend. He must've sent you a video."

I was hoping Gonzalez wouldn't draw this conclusion. He was a smart cop, however, and I should've anticipated it. No matter. I could still work with the situation. "Yes. He sent me a video."

"You need to get it to me."

"I told you I wanted something from you," I said. "Here's what it is . . . twenty-four hours to go after him and put him away . . . for good this time."

"No deal," Gonzalez said.

"All right. Good luck, then." I broke the connection.

T.J. looked horrified, and Tyler grinned. "He'll call back," the former soldier said. "His job demands it."

"You shouldn't jerk him around like that," T.J. said.

Sure enough, the sergeant's number flashed on my caller ID. I answered. "Do we have a deal now?"

"I'll lock you up for obstruction of justice," Gonzalez said. "Interfering with an investigation."

"What investigation? You told me no one was murdered."

He sighed, and it hissed in my ear. "You want the details and the video? Fine. I want twenty-four hours to nail this son of a bitch."

"You got me by the short hairs here."

"I'm aware," I said. "I wouldn't bother if this weren't personal."

"Yeah, yeah." Gonzalez grunted. "Fine. Twenty-four hours and not one damn minute more. Now, where did it happen?"

"The Cavalier Hotel. I'll send the video in a minute. Thanks, Sergeant."

"Don't mention it." I ended the call, found the file, and forwarded it to him.

"All right," I said to my team of two. "We have about a day. I think Gonzalez will err in favor of his department on the exactness of twenty-four hours, and if anyone else happens to report what happened, all bets might be off. He'll have to do something then."

"Let's get out ahead of it, then," T.J. said. "I'll start looking into the girl."

"All right," I agreed. "We'll give Gloria's house another look in case I missed anything. I probably wasn't in the best state of mind to conduct a search. Then, I want to know if anyone in Vinny's family or crew had an in at the hotel."

"You sure we should leave her alone?" Tyler asked.

"I'll have the smell of testosterone to remember you by," she said and smirked.

I took my 9MM out of a drawer and put it on her desk. "Lock the door when we're gone. If anyone you don't know tries to come in, blast them."

"You got it, boss."

As Tyler and I walked to my car, he said, "Is this generally how you work?"

"More or less." I shrugged. "I poke around at things. People get mad. Sometimes, I have to hit them. Then, I find a string to pull until something big unravels." I unlocked the car, and we climbed in.

"Wow. Maybe I can be an investigator, too." Tyler buckled his seat belt. "Even if I'm more likely to shoot people along the way."

"To each his own," I said.

———

We pulled into Gloria's neighborhood. "Why don't you live here?" Tyler asked.

"I like it in Federal Hill."

"Your house would be a shed in a lot of these yards. Mine, too."

"I think I'd miss the city," I said. "It's nice here, but it's a little remote for me."

"At least your Audi fits in. My Four-Four-Two would stick out."

"The neighborhood watch would chase you away," I said as I stopped the S4 in Gloria's driveway. My phone buzzed. It was the burner I gave my girlfriend before she left. "I need to take this before we go in." We hopped out. Tyler headed for the front door, and I lingered near my car to answer the call. "Hey."

"I see you called a few times earlier," Gloria said. "Everything all right?" I fought back tears. A couple hours ago, I thought I'd never get to talk to her again. Even though I knew she wasn't the woman on the video, talking to her was a huge relief. "C.T.? You there?"

"Yeah. Sorry. It's . . . really good to hear your voice."

"I didn't have the right charger for this phone," she said. "Had to go out and buy one. Don't worry. I paid cash."

I smiled. "Glad you got it sorted out."

"Is something going on?"

"I think we're making a lot of headway," I said. "I'll fill you in more once you're back. Hopefully, you won't need to stay away after tomorrow."

"That would be nice. I don't want to keep you from nailing Vinny. Be careful. I love you."

"Love you, too," I said. I released a deep breath as I slipped my phone back into my pocket. After wiping my eyes, I walked toward the door.

"Basic job," Tyler said as he pointed at the door. "You can see an outline here." His finger jabbed at it, and I noticed it.

"Looks like part of a shoe tread."

He nodded. "Someone kicked in the door. I'm surprised your girlfriend doesn't have an alarm system."

"She will after this," I said.

"Whoever did it put the boot in the correct spot. Right under the lock is where you want to be."

"Someone who's done this before, then. Maybe a pro."

"Could be." Tyler shrugged as he pushed the door open and walked inside. "More likely someone who has a narrow set of skills. Your friend just got out of jail. He wouldn't have access to the same resources he enjoyed before. It might force him to shop in the bargain bin."

It was a good point. Vinny was probably smart enough to squirrel some money away where the cops and prosecutors couldn't find it, but his operating budget would be severely curtailed. I led Tyler upstairs, and he checked out the scene in Gloria's bedroom. He pointed out another shoe impression in the thick carpet leading to the closet. I snapped a picture of it in case it became relevant. "Looks big," he said.

I put my foot beside it for comparison. My Nikes were a size 11, and the imprint looked at least an inch longer and a little wider. "Probably a twelve or thirteen," I concurred.

"I don't see much else here. Cops could try dusting for

prints, but even idiots know to wear gloves these days. There might be a random hair or stray fiber we won't see."

"I don't think we'll need to get so granular," I said. "T.J. might be able to find something out about the poor woman in the video. I think we can do some work against Vinny from here."

"You have an office in the house?"

"I keep an older laptop down the hall just in case," I said. "Seems like the perfect time to fire it up."

"This reminds me of the computer my old company gave me," Tyler said as he watched me work. "I don't know how to do much more than turn it on and a couple of basic things. Lucky for me, my daughter's gotten good with it."

"Another reason to pursue computer science," I said. Despite the many cool things I'd configured the machine to do, I began with the basics. In this case, the scene of the crime. The Cavalier's logo was a red stylized C. I stared at it for a few seconds until I remembered where I saw it. Paul Serrano's porch. He used it to light the cigarette whose smoke he blew in my face. Just one more bit of confirmation Paul was an asshole.

He would be the logical person to help his nephew in this case.

Vinny's father split when he was young. It happened long before I knew him, and I remembered him talking about it a couple times. His mother never remarried, and my recent encounters with her led me to believe her personality played a significant part. Her brother Paul tried to help despite his obvious faults. He gave Vinny a desire to seek shortcuts, a love of gambling, and an interest in power.

I needed to tie him in to recent events, so I banged away

at the keyboard. The Cavalier Hotel saw its name change a couple times during its eighty years of operation. Despite a few updates and renovations over time, it lost a lot of luster as newer places with better amenities opened up. The county cops investigated a few times—mainly on the accusation of renting rooms by the hour, as T.J. suggested—but nothing ever came of it. The current owner was a man named Edwin Xavier.

It only took a few seconds to learn he went to high school with Paul Serrano.

They even did a stint in jail together before Xavier went straight and Vinny's uncle kept his crooked activities hidden better. "Here's the connection," I said, pointing at the screen. "Vinny's uncle knows the owner. He must have let them stage the scene."

"I wonder if he knew they'd really murder someone," Tyler said.

"In the end, he's liable either way. I'll let the lawyers figure out intent."

"What are we going to do with this intel, then?"

"Let's add it to the pile." I called T.J. and told her what we learned. She asked the same question Tyler did. "Not our job. We're building a case."

"One you're going to hand over to the cops," my secretary said in a tone suggesting she accused me of something.

"I want to take Vinny down," I said. "He's liable for a lot of things since he got out, and murder is the big one. The cops can pick apart the rest of his organization. He'll probably dime them out once he's in custody, anyway."

"I'm still looking into the victim. Slow going so far. I don't really have much to go on."

"We'll figure it out."

"I'm casting a pretty wide net already," she said. "Might need to make it even bigger. The lady in the video was definitely a grown woman. They didn't hire some underage kid walking the streets. Dress was too filled out. We only got to see her from the rear, though. She could have been beautiful or ugly. College-aged or turning forty."

"Right," I concurred. "She only needed to look convincing when filmed from behind in a dress for twenty seconds. As long as it fit her well, they got what they needed." I recalled my recent time working a case in Frederick where I wore a wig to disguise myself. "The hair might not have been hers. She'd probably hate me saying this, but it's pretty easy to find something to match Gloria's color."

"True." T.J. yawned. "I'll adjust my search."

"Do it tomorrow. You've been at this a while. We'll come back, and Tyler can follow you home again."

"I want to crack this tonight."

"I admire your dedication," I said, but you need some rest. I got twenty-four hours from Gonzalez. Even if the clock ends up shortened, we'll still have time to iron some things out tomorrow."

"All right," T.J. said. "Come on back."

We closed up Gloria's house as best we could considering the damage to the door. I'd call someone for her tomorrow. Tyler and I headed toward the city. Tomorrow, Vinny Serrano would go down for everything he'd done, and his goons and uncle would get a free ride to jail with him. The thought made me give the S4 a little more gas as we sped down I-83.

CHAPTER 27

MY PHONE VIBRATED on the nightstand. I rubbed my eyes and looked at the time. Eight-ten. I didn't have the number stored, but it looked familiar from yesterday. I'd been wondering when he would call. I needed to inject sadness and loss into my voice, and I've never been accused of being a good actor. Thoughts of my late sister Samantha would probably help. I picked up the phone and offered a weak, "Hello?"

"You shoulda left it alone."

"Vinny?"

"Who else would it be?" he said. His voice sounded like he would soon burst with pride. "Who else found your girlfriend, lured her somewhere under the pretense of helping you, and then snuffed her out?"

I attempted a little fake crying. Thinking of my sister might have added some authenticity. It didn't sound great to my ears, but I hoped Vinny bought it. "You're a monster. What did . . . what did she ever do to you?"

"Not a damn thing. You loved her. It's all I needed."

"What do you want, Vinny?" I cleared my throat and added some clarity back into my voice. "Beyond gloating, I mean."

"Gloating's good enough to start with," he said. "Damn, I woulda loved to see your face when you watched the video. When you realized what was about to happen and how powerless you were to do anything about it." He paused, but I didn't say anything. If I let him use the shovel, Vinny would dig his hole deeper. He couldn't help it. "You're probably thinking you want to take me down. I would if I were you."

I sniffed. "I'm just trying to get through today thanks to you."

"Good. I wouldn't want to have to kill anyone else you cared about. Well . . . maybe I would, but it shouldn't be necessary, should it? You didn't learn your lesson a few years ago. This time will be different."

"You won," I said. "Congratulations. Now, go fuck off." I ended the call. It would piss him off. I'd interrupted his gloating and whatever monologue he probably wanted to hit me with. I knew he would call back, and a few seconds later, he proved me right. "What?"

"Hang up on me again, and someone else dies."

I didn't believe him. My parents were out of town. Rich and Joey were up to the challenge of Vinny's crew. T.J. enjoyed the protection of a man who seemed very capable. Still, Vinny didn't need to know any of this. I wanted him to think he'd defeated me. "Fine," I answered in a small voice.

"Say you're sorry."

He was pushing it now, and he probably knew it. Even if I weren't playing along, this would hurt. I took a deep breath and forced myself to get the words out. I'd make him pay later. "I'm sorry."

"Glad to hear it. Now, listen. You were supposed to give up four years ago. I'd kidnapped Alice. I won. Then, I found out you got my boys to roll on me. I guess I got some more scores to settle." He'd already done so with Margaret Madison, but I stayed silent. "This time, no bullshit. You can't find my guys. You ain't flipping them. You're going to surrender to me, and I'll decide if you live or if you join your precious girlfriend."

Anger almost colored my tone, and I swallowed my initial response. Vinny needed to think he enjoyed the upper hand. I injected as much defeat into my voice as my limited experience with it would allow. "I guess I don't have a choice."

"Damn right you don't," he said. "You're gonna meet me tonight. No cops, no friends. Only you."

"Where?"

"Where it all started. Think about Paul Foreman and where you found his body. If you remember, be there tonight at ten. If you don't, be prepared to go to some more funerals." He broke the connection.

I remembered. And I would be ready.

———

"Did you think he would call to rub your nose in it?" T.J. frowned as she worked at her keyboard.

"I was counting on it. Where's Tyler?"

"He took off when I told him you were on the way in. Mentioned he could be available later if we needed him for something."

"Good," I said. "I think we will. What are you working on?"

"Finding who the lady in the video is." Her head shook fractionally side-to-side. "Poor woman. She probably had no idea why she was really there. It made me think about how many times I found myself in a bad spot when I was . . . you know."

"She's lucky to have you fighting for her. Found anything?"

"I think so. Check this out." I stood behind her desk.

"Whoever filmed this was careful to stay in back of her the whole way. She doesn't take a straight path to the building, so the guy with the camera moves with her." The frame made small side-to-side shifts as the doomed woman approached the Cavalier's rear entrance. I'd never noticed before.

"Good catch."

"It's not all," T.J. said. "She's the right height to pass for Gloria, too. A little extra attention to detail, I guess."

"So?"

"So there's a little window in the door."

"I know," I said. "We can't see through it. It seems kind of smoky."

"Maybe it is." T.J. shrugged. "She doesn't approach it directly, but there's a moment when she pushes the door open." T.J. advanced the video. Sure enough, the lady briefly went through the rear entry of the Cavalier, and the playback paused. "Look."

I leaned closer. The side of her face reflected in the glass. "Holy shit. Good work."

"Thanks," she said. "We get a couple other brief looks, but this one is the best. It's not a great one, though, so it makes facial recognition a challenge."

"Sounds like you've already tried."

She nodded. "I got three possible hits right before you came in."

"We'll run them down, then," I said. "This is great work. I probably would've circled back to the video at some point, but I don't know if I would've seen those brief reflections."

"It helps to have young eyes on a project," T.J. said with a grin.

"You're fired. After you send me those names, of course."

"Of course." She sent them my way, and I checked each one. All were in the right age range—in fact, they clustered between 24 and 26—and within an inch of Gloria's five-eight height. None possessed her natural hair color, so Vinny and crew must have provided a wig. All lived in Baltimore County, and while I didn't enjoy the same level of access to their systems as I did the BPD's, none were reported missing yet.

The possibility remained the woman on the video would turn out to be none of these three. For all the great work T.J. did, her facial rec searches were of a woman in a wig reflected in a small pane of glass. Still, it was all we had to go on at the moment, so I started with the first name on the list. Christine Barrett answered the phone, assured me she was alive and unharmed, and she'd never heard of the Cavalier Hotel. I received similar—if much more profane—feedback from Angela Grimes. The remaining woman, Eileen Rhodes, didn't answer her phone.

She was unmarried and between jobs, but her social media told me she lived with a roommate. "I haven't seen her," Linda Skinner told me.

"You don't seem too concerned."

"Eileen's enjoying life."

"Do you know where she went yesterday?" I asked.

"Not specifically, no. She's had an OnlyFans setup for a while. Said someone wanted to do a private shoot with her."

"Has she done this before?"

"Once," Linda said. "I told her she needed to double and triple-check these dudes. I guess she did."

"I'm concerned about her. Can I send you a picture?"

"I don't like the sound of this." She was quiet for a few seconds. "Go ahead."

I forwarded the still T.J. used. "It's a reflection, so it's not the best shot, and the woman in it is wearing a wig."

"Oh, my god. I think that's her. Where is this?"

"A hotel."

"Is she dead?"

"The woman in the video this image came from is, yes," I said.

"Poor Eileen," Linda said, her voice cracking. "What do we do now?"

"I think you'd be better off talking to the police at this point. I hope the woman this happened to isn't your roommate, but in the event it is, I'm sorry." I ended the call.

"Sounds like you narrowed it down," T.J. said.

"Yeah. I'll send her info to Gonzalez. He won't make the connection to Vinny in time. Even if he does, I doubt he's just sitting around waiting for the cops to snatch him up."

"He's got to be somewhere before tonight."

"Doesn't matter," I said. "I'm going to call Tyler and fill him in." He picked up quickly, and I gave him as much information as I could.

"Where are you meeting him?"

"Herring Run Park. You know it?"

"Yeah," he said. "Wow. I don't think I've been there in a decade. My daughter played a couple soccer games there."

"I know Vinny has a specific part of it in mind, but we'll need to cover the ways in and out."

"We'll get there early. I know this is your show, but I've done this sort of thing a lot before."

"I'll defer to your experience," I said.

"Good. We'll get there three hours early. They won't be expecting it. Want me to meet you at your office?"

"No, we can drive separately. I'll see you there." I set my phone back down.

"You're not worried it's going to be a setup?" T.J. said.

"Of course it will be," I said. "We'll be ready, though. Vinny can't have a huge crew."

"You going to bring him in alive?"

"If he lets me."

"And if he doesn't?"

I shrugged. "I guess his mother won't invite me to the funeral."

———

Herring Run Park is a sprawling outdoor environment. It starts at Lake Montebello and extends southeast until it ends at I-895. Trails make up a lot of the square footage. The fields where many Baltimore kids play sports are clustered between and around Harford and Belair Roads.

During my first case, Rich called me to a crime scene. I'd just met Gloria for the first time. We showed up to the same art gallery event, and we broke away from the boredom to share some wine and conversation. Paul Foreman—my client's allegedly unfaithful husband—died in a car crash. His vehicle slammed into a tree in the park near the intersection of Belair Road and Chesterfield Avenue.

This was where I expected to find Vinny later tonight. Tyler and I arrived the prescribed three hours early. Technically, I pulled up two hours and fifty-six minutes ahead of the witching hour. Chesterfield Avenue was crowded with cars thanks to a girls' soccer game in the park. Tyler, leaning against the hood of his green muscle car, fixed me with a neutral expression as I approached. "Traffic," I said before he could make a comment.

"Mm-hmm."

"It's basically your show at this point. What's the plan?"

He jerked his head to the side. "You think Vinny's going to meet you over there?"

"If he's committed to doing it where I found a body almost four years ago, yes."

"Leaves us a lot of ground to cover," Tyler said. "You can wait here." He frowned at the blue Caprice Classic I'd driven tonight. "What's up with the car?"

"Vinny and his new crew wouldn't know about it," I said. "It's . . . a little more interesting than it looks. We can compare horsepower figures later if you want."

Tyler's dark eyes scanned the sedan, and I got the impression he picked up a few details—namely its fortification against small arms fire. The chop shop owner who did it made the work pretty subtle, but someone like Tyler probably knew the signs. "Whatever," he said. "You wait here. Keep an eye on things. The soccer game there can't go much longer. Once everyone clears out, watch for Vinny's guys. My guess is they won't just walk in off a main road."

"Where are you going to be?"

"I'll go toward Harford Road. The trail starts there. Easy to access the rest of the grounds."

"All right." Before Tyler could pad away, I added, "Let's try not to kill anyone tonight." He nodded and moved away. I looked at the soccer game for a moment and turned back. There was no sign of Tyler now. I smiled and climbed back into my car. The game wrapped up in about ten more minutes as dusk settled in. It took another fifteen minutes for athletes, coaches, and especially parents to leave the area. A bunch of cars vacated the street. Once the last one pulled away, I got out of the Caprice and walked onto the grass.

I remembered coming here for my first case. The sea of red and blue lights which greeted me as I pulled up. The police activity. Seeing Rich in plainclothes for the first time. Most of all, I could see Paul Foreman's crumpled car as if it still sat there today. A large hole dominated the windshield, and his body lay some twenty feet in front of the vehicle. I didn't know then the depths Vinny would go to in the interests of his business.

I'd gotten several reminders since.

Keeping low, I moved across the soccer field into the trees bordering the large stream—the eponymous Herring Run.

Trees dotted the landscape as I drew closer to the water, and I parked myself behind one of them. Someone walking down the slope from Chesterfield Avenue would see me, but the thick oak trunk would render me invisible to a muscleman trying to be discreet and approach from the other side.

Early in my illustrious PI career, I learned the value of patience. The lessons didn't always come easily, but they stuck with me now. We still had plenty of time until Vinny was due to make his appearance. I knew he would send his guys to soften me up first. He enjoyed few things more than an unfair fight tipped in his favor.

About an hour before the appointed time, I heard motion in the distance. Someone tried to be quiet, but the wooden bridge across the water didn't cooperate. A moment later, a large man came into view through the trees. If he saw me, he didn't give any indication. Once he cleared the foliage, he stood about fifteen feet from me and kept a vigil on Belair Road and Chesterfield.

I waited some more.

"Where the hell is this asshole?" he muttered a few minutes later.

"We might be on different sides," I said, and he spun around with wide eyes, "but there's no reason for name-calling."

"You." He glared at me. "Vinny wants to see you."

I readied myself for a fight. "Why else do you think I'm here?"

"You don't need to be awake for it." He threw a punch, and even though it came faster than I expected, his long arms gave me time to step back. A left hook followed. I blocked it with my right forearm and fired off a quick jab to my foe's solar plexus. He gasped and took a step back. I kept up the pressure, hitting him with a couple of hard body shots. Despite sucking wind, he grabbed my arm when I went for another punch. Rather than flip me onto my back, he basically flung me away. I stumbled, went into a roll, and came up on one knee.

Because he was still breathing heavily, my adversary didn't close the distance in time. He tried to make up for it with a front kick, but I ducked under it and rocked him with an uppercut into the midsection. A left jab to the face and an elbow to the head put him on the ground. He remained woozy, so I kicked him in the noggin and knocked him out.

He was a large guy and dragging him to the nearest medium-sized tree wasn't easy. I picked a young maple about twenty feet tall and maybe eighteen inches in diameter. I put his arms around the trunk, joined them at the wrists, and zip-tied him in place. Even if he woke up in time for Vinny to arrive, he'd never get free to join the fracas.

I returned to my post behind the oak and waited. No one else approached. I wondered how Tyler fared at the other end of the Harford-Belair corridor. As if on cue, he sent a text. *Two down over here. They have no idea what happened to them. Yes, they're alive.*

I replied. *One here, but he might be big enough to count for two. Have him tied around a tree atm.* Since Tyler was blessed with a young daughter, he'd know what *atm* meant.

A few minutes later, Vinny called. If I answered, he would know I'd dealt with his goons. He'd probably tried them first and could infer what happened when they didn't pick up. Still, he didn't need to hear anything from me directly. We'd have plenty to say to one another soon enough.

I let it go to voicemail.

CHAPTER 28

TEN O'CLOCK LOOMED a few short minutes away. Tyler practiced radio silence since his text a while ago. I didn't even know if he remained in the area, and I didn't want to be distracted by my phone to ask. My guess is he remained. He seemed like the type to see something through to the end. A moment later, he called. "Let's keep the line open," he said. "I put an earpiece in."

I did the same. "All right. Let me know if you see anything."

"Likewise."

Around the appointed time, I heard footsteps coming from the trees and drew my .45. Someone else crossed the bridge over Herring Run. "Movement from the trees," I whispered. I received a quiet confirmation in my ear.

"So this is where it happened." Vinny's voice drifted to me from where he stepped out into the open. He didn't hold a gun, but a bulge under his jacket told me he carried one on his left side. "I've never actually been to the spot before."

"You just let Sal and Chaoxiang do your dirty work."

He shrugged. "Sal got overzealous questioning the guy. These things happen."

"Sure," I said. "Normal people need to stage deaths in a park all the time. I hear this place is booked solid all next month."

"I'm almost surprised you showed up." Vinny moved a little but settled into a spot about fifty feet away. I could plug him easily from this distance. He didn't comment on the gun. The temptation to shoot him gnawed at me. If he'd really murdered Gloria, I would have emptied every magazine I owned into him. Even knowing he murdered a stranger, I felt confident the world would be a better place without Vinny Serrano continuing to use his share of the oxygen. I wasn't a killer, however.

"I told you I would."

"Your girlfriend's dead, though. I'm not gonna lie . . . I kinda hoped you'd eat a bullet and save me the trouble."

"Some of us are made of pretty tough stuff, Vinny."

"The fuck do you know about being tough?" Even in the poor lighting, I could see his face contort into a glower. "I survived prison. Wanna know why?"

"Snitching on the right people?"

"I knew I'd get a chance to settle the score," he said, ignoring my barb. "Didn't expect it to come so soon, but when the opportunity presented itself, I took it. Never fancied myself a snitch, but I always kept the big picture in mind."

"Let me know when you're doing your TED Talk," I said. "Can't wait to watch it live."

He smirked. "How'd you do it? How'd you get over the death of the woman you loved?"

"It was simple. You killed a stranger." All the mirth and braggadocio abandoned his face, leaving a blank expression. "It was a pretty good fake. I'll admit you got me at first. As usual, Vinny, there's always a detail or two you overlook."

"What? What'd I miss?"

"It doesn't matter now. You're not going to get a chance to make another movie. You and your operation are closed. You might be intelligent, but there's a reason I've always thought I'm smarter than you, and it's because I damn well am." He didn't say anything. "You know, if Gloria's phone battery hadn't died, your little video wouldn't have been useful for more than a couple minutes."

He shrugged. "I figured you'd be shocked. Maybe eat a bullet and solve my problem for me."

"Not a chance," I said. "Tried reaching any of your goons recently?"

"If I did?"

"One's tied up not far from where you came in."

"Still leaves two," he said.

I spread my hands—one of which still held the .45. "I guess neither of us came alone tonight."

"Still comes down to you and me. Put the gun away."

I ignored him. "You should know my team and I figured out the identity of the woman your crew stabbed to death. Location, too. I would imagine the cops already rounded up your uncle Paul. Serves him right, the prick." Vinny scowled and reached inside his coat. "Don't do it." He froze. "A lot's happened in the last four years. You got out of jail, and I've had to shoot a few people in the course of doing my job." He retreated a couple steps. "Come on, Vinny. I may not be a marksman, but twenty yards isn't a challenge. Don't make me do it."

"How about we both throw our guns down," he said, "and pummel each other like gentlemen?"

"Sure. You first. Nice and slow."

Vinny went through the process at a deliberate pace. He opened his coat, showed me the pistol holstered under his arm, picked it up in a two-finger grip, and held it at his side.

"I'm going to toss it." He did, and the weapon landed in the grass a good ten yards away.

"All right," I said. "I'll do the same, and then we'll move to my left. Away from the guns." I threw my gun so it landed near his but closer to me. Then, I took a few steps toward the Harford Road side of the park. Vinny mirrored my movements. I took us about a hundred feet away from the pistols before we stopped. "There." I raised my fists. "Do your worst."

Vinny growled and rushed me.

———

We'd played lacrosse together for years, so I knew Vinny wouldn't tire quickly. He was about my height and build, so the added bulk of an enforcer wouldn't slow him down. I didn't know what training he possessed, but he knew I was no amateur. I guessed this would be a fairly even fight. I'm not above getting into a scrape when I have the edge—fair fights are for competitions, after all—but Vinny and I had never thrown down before.

I blocked his opening salvo and gave him a solid right cross to the face. He backed away, rubbed his jaw, and nodded before coming at me again. I blunted three punches before he snuck in a quick kick which took me in the gut. I retreated a couple steps and bobbed my head. Vinny stood in place like he waited for me to make the next move. I favored defense. Perhaps getting under his skin would motivate him. "I thought prison would've made you tougher. Maybe you just enjoyed a little . . . playtime . . . with your cellmates."

"Fuck you," he spat and rushed toward me again. The punches came in quickly, but I blocked them all. My lower left arm stung after I took one just below the elbow. I grabbed Vinny's arm on his next right cross, pulled down hard to flip him, and slammed him to the ground. He grunted but rolled out of the way when I tried to kick him in the head. I followed up with another, but he caught my leg and shoved it away. It didn't put me down, but it unbalanced me enough to allow him time to stand again.

We squared off a second time, circling each other. Our movement caused us to drift a little more toward the Harford Road side. If either dashed for a pistol, they were a good fifty yards away now and probably not easy to find. Vinny threw a kick, backed off when I countered with a punch, and spun behind me. He wrapped his arm around my neck. I struggled to breathe. The maneuver showed his lack of training, however. He left himself open to me grabbing his hair and holding him steady as I drove the back of my head into his face. Something cracked, and he let go. I elbowed him in the gut before turning around to face my old acquaintance again.

Vinny grimaced. Blood ran from his nose. He straightened up to face me. "You could just give up now," I said. "County cops are going to want to talk to you. City, too, for Margaret's murder. You always reach a little too far, Vinny. She didn't need to die. No one did."

He scoffed. "Margaret rolled on me when it counted. She could've kept her mouth shut. When I was gone, she took over a lot of my operation. Did you know?" I did, but I didn't interrupt Vinny to tell him. He spat out a little blood and continued. "Sal was in jail, so I couldn't get to him. Fucking Sam was back in China." His shoulders shrugged. "Margaret was available."

Sam—for "small Asian man"—was Vinny's way of referring to Chaoxiang, who indeed got sent back to China after diming out his former boss. "Was Eileen Rhodes 'available,' too?"

"Who?"

"Of course," I said, "you don't know. The woman your goon stabbed to death on the video."

He snorted. "Some Internet whore who wanted a quick buck. Her job was to be a convincing stand-in for your precious Gloria."

"Don't say her name. You don't deserve to."

Vinny went back on the attack. He came at me with a flurry of punches plus an occasional kick mixed in. After I blocked one of his jabs, he caught me with a backhand. It snapped my head around and forced me a step to my left. Vinny kept the pressure up. After a few crosses didn't land, he went for a front kick. I took it on the hip and pinned his right leg against me with my left arm. An agile person could push off with his back leg and still deliver a blow. Vinny didn't qualify. He tried to wrench his leg free. I kicked him in the side of the left knee and released his trapped foot.

His left leg buckled, and he went down. This time, he couldn't avoid the kick I followed up with, and it snapped his head back. More blood spilled from his nose and mouth. "Stay down," I told him. "You were always smart, Vinny. Don't be an idiot now."

"Go to hell," he said as he got back to his feet, avoiding putting a lot of weight on his left leg.

"You're not going to win."

"Maybe it's not about winning. I might just want to kick your ass."

"Your odds were better two minutes ago," I said. "You were a bookmaker. You get it."

"Upsets happen," he said. His punches lacked some of the power they carried before. I turned them aside without much trouble. Vinny left an opening, so I kicked him hard in the stomach. When he bent over, I drove my knee into his face. This put him on the ground again. He coughed and sputtered as he rolled over on the grass.

"Stay down this time."

Instead, he rose to one knee. His first attempt to regain his feet saw him capsize again. When he tried to get vertical a second time, I moved behind him and put him in the same rear chokehold he used on me. Being seated, Vinny didn't have as much leverage as I did, and I also knew how to keep myself shielded from the obvious counterattacks. He poked at my head a few times but nothing came of it. Next, he grabbed my wrist and tried to pull it away. I maintained the hold.

Another pull did him no good. Finally, he tapped my forearm a few times. I let him go, and he sagged forward, gasping in huge gulps of air. Getting a zip tie around his wrists proved easy at this point. I let him have a minute or two to find his breath again before hauling him back to his feet. "Where do you want to go first, Vinny? We're closer to a city precinct, but the county's already rounding up people who might've helped you. I guess you finally got your wish . . . you're popular."

"Now who's gloating?" he said.

"Did you expect me not to after everything you did?" I gave him a light shove in the back. "Let's go. You can ride with me. If you don't mouth off too much, I won't have to stuff you in the trunk."

"I'll get out again."

"Yeah, yeah."

"I will. Maybe not in four years. It might take me seven . . . or ten . . . or fifteen." Vinny turned to glare at me, and hatred twisted his face. He almost didn't look like himself. "Whatever I have to do, I'll do it. You won't see me coming. The people you love won't see me coming."

"Get moving," I said, pointing toward Chesterfield Avenue. We stood on one of the soccer fields which was in use when I arrived, so we were almost lined up with where I parked. He turned and took a few tentative steps. The street lights didn't help a lot where we were, but I could tell his left knee wasn't good. "I'm not carrying or dragging your sorry ass. You'd better make it on your own."

After another stride, he remained in place and turned again. He stood at my ten o'clock about two paces away. "I didn't get to Gloria this time. Next time, I will. I'll gut her on camera and make sure you see it. Maybe you'll even have kids by then. They're dead, too." The sinister look screwed up his face again. "You hear me? Everyone you love. I'll find a way out, and I'll kill them all."

Before I could respond, two things happened in rapid succession. I couldn't process the order of the events. A loud crack rang out, sounding like it came from all around me. Vinny's body shook, and blood poured from the center of his chest between his throat and heart. Confusion replaced the hatred in his expression as he collapsed to the ground. "Vinny!" I dropped beside him and put pressure on the wound. It only took a few seconds to see the futility in it. More blood poured out than I could stop.

Vinny's head lolled. He stared at his gunshot wound as blood covered my hands and leaked from between my fingers. It was pointless. He was going to bleed out, and there was nothing I could do to stop it. To save him. Vinny's eyes turned glassy, and he struggled to focus on anything. "Hey," I said, grabbing his shoulder. "It wasn't supposed to end up like this."

His head bobbed fractionally before it sagged back to the grass, and his eyes lost focus.

CHAPTER 29

AS I THOUGHT, the line with Tyler was dead. I called 9 1 1. Even if an ambulance made it here in record time, it would be too late to save Vinny. One rolled up about three minutes later, followed by a pair of police cruisers. Four male cops approached, hands on their weapons until they confirmed the threat had passed. I didn't know any of them. A burly Latino with a shaved head walked up to me. His name tag identified him as Alfonso, and he wore sergeant's stripes on his sleeves. We established who Vinny and I were and what I did for a living quickly before he moved on to the meat of why we were all here. "What happened?"

"It's a pretty long story." His expression didn't change. "About four years ago, I was instrumental in building a case against Vinny Serrano. He went to jail, and it was supposed to be for twenty-five years. He ended up turning state's evidence and got out recently."

"Wow," Alfonso said with wide eyes. "Really early release."

"I've never heard of it happening like this," I said. A couple more BPD cars arrived, and uniforms converged on most areas of the park. "Anyway, after he got out, things started happening to me and people I care about. My cousin . . . he's a lieutenant in Homicide . . . got his house shot up while he wasn't there. No one was hurt, but it was obvious someone targeted us."

Alfonso didn't react to me mentioning Rich. I didn't need him to. It planted a seed. "You didn't know it was Serrano?"

"Not at first, no. I only found out later, and then, everything made sense."

"You known him long?"

"Since middle school. We played lacrosse together in high school and college . . . until he got kicked out."

"For what?" Alfonso asked as he jotted down some notes.

"Setting up a gambling ring. It's what he eventually did for a job."

"Why tonight? Why were you two here, and how come my guys have found three men tied to trees?"

"Vinny wanted to meet here," I said. "He wanted me to believe he'd killed my girlfriend. She's fine, but I let him think he did. I knew he wouldn't come alone."

"But you did?"

I recalled John Tyler's text. *They have no idea what happened to them.* He'd come here to help me on a recommendation from Rollins. I couldn't prove he shot Vinny even though I knew he did. Tyler and I could settle this ourselves. I wouldn't jam him up for helping me out even if I disagreed with his methods. "Yes."

"Pretty brazen."

I shrugged. "Vinny hadn't been out long. He didn't have access to a lot of his resources from before. It's not like he could hire anyone good."

"I suppose," Alfonso said. Another cop approached and whispered something in his ear before hurrying off again. "We've recovered two pistols. Neither appears to have been fired recently at first look."

"One's mine. The H and K forty-five."

"Serious gun."

"It's licensed," I said. "Besides, I prefer it when people don't get up after I shoot them. It's very rude of them."

"So you didn't shoot your friend tonight?"

Alfonso let 'friend' do a lot of heavy lifting there, but I didn't need to get into a semantics argument with him. "I was about six feet away to his right and a little behind him. Test my gun. Check me for GSR. You won't find any."

"Who shot him, then?" Alfonso asked.

"No idea."

"You came here alone."

"Right," I said.

"Even though you knew you'd be outnumbered."

"Quantity versus quality, Sergeant."

"You always so confident?" he said.

"Don't know any other way to be."

"Let's presume I believe you. I still want to know who shot this guy."

"I still don't know," I said. "Vinny wasn't the most popular guy around. He'd landed in hot water before, and not limited to me or the police. He didn't exactly make a secret of being out of prison. I'm sure a few people wanted to take a shot at him."

"How many of them knew he'd be here tonight?"

"I couldn't tell you how well Vinny practiced OPSEC." The answer was probably poorly at least when it came to certain things. Vinny was a braggart who wanted to project a certain image. Operational security would have been a secondary concern.

"All right." Alfonso closed his notebook. "Why don't you stick around for a while? We might have some more questions."

"Sure." A crew from the medical examiner's office

arrived during my chat with the sergeant. A tall, lanky woman in a yellow coat covered Vinny's body with a white cloth. A short, compact man helped her load the corpse onto a gurney. They could wheel it across the flatter part of the grounds, though they'd need to carry it up the incline to Chesterfield Avenue. It felt weird to think of Vinny as dead. He'd barely come to my mind between his incarceration and a few days ago. We had a lot of history, and it wasn't all negative. Before ambition consumed and ruined him, he wasn't a bad guy.

I called Gonzalez, who picked up despite the late hour. "Vinny's dead. I don't know who shot him. I'm on the scene with city cops now."

"We'll still build a case against the people who worked with him."

"You'll need to get them out of Central Booking, then. We have three tied up here."

Gonzalez sighed. "You never make things easy for me, do you? Even when you try."

"It's a complicated world," I said and ended the call.

Some things were simple, however—like the matter of who shot and killed Vinny Serrano.

————

It was after midnight when I drove home. Despite the time, I called Gloria. She answered in a sleepy tone. "Is everything all right?"

"More or less," I said. "It's safe for you to come home."

"Thank goodness. I was worried about you."

"It's been an eventful couple days. I should fill you in once you're back. We'll need to get your front door fixed, though."

"What?" she said. "My front door? What happened?"

"I'll tell you when it's not so late. Get some rest. I'll take care of it."

"All right. Can we talk about it in the morning?"

"You bet. Enjoy your last night on the road. Love you."

"Love you, too." She ended the call.

I knew I would be annoying my parents by calling them at this hour. Nine-thirty was pushing it, ten o'clock would get me a lecture and some tsking from my mother, and anything after ten-thirty was grounds for excommunication from the family. Still, they deserved to know. It took a few rings before my father picked up. "What's going on, son?" He spoke quietly and sounded like he stood in a well.

"Where are you? Do I need to send Lassie to find you?"

"I stepped into the bathroom," he said. "The phone didn't wake your mother. I'm trying to let her sleep."

"Probably best for both of us," I said. "The good news is you can come home tomorrow."

"You dealt with Vinny?"

"In a manner of speaking. I was ready to take him to the police when someone shot him."

"Good grief. Are you all right, son?"

"I'm fine. Vinny's dead. Not the way I wanted this to end."

"I'm sure. Wow." He sighed. "I remember some of the parties your team had in high school. He seemed like a decent enough kid."

"He was at one point," I said. "Sometimes, people change. Vinny did, and it wasn't for the better." At least the person who influenced him the most would spend some significant time in prison. All of it came too late for the man I would've called my friend during our early days of high school.

"It's not your fault, son. It sounds like you were trying to do the right thing."

"For all the good it did Vinny and me, yeah. See you tomorrow, Dad." I broke the connection and drove the rest of the way home. It felt good not to worry about green Mustangs. I texted Rich and Joey to let them know what happened. I thought about reaching out to John Tyler. He needed to answer a few questions, but I wasn't in the right frame of mind to pose them. Maybe tomorrow. I settled into bed for my last night alone. Gloria would be back tomorrow, and the world would spin a little more precisely on its axis.

———

The next morning, I ran laps around Federal Hill Park for about thirty minutes. I needed the exercise, and even considering the events of the night before, I felt better as I walked back up Riverside Avenue toward my house. One shower and breakfast later, I headed for the office. En route, I called a company to fix Gloria's front door and locks. If nothing else, we could put in a claim against Vinny's estate—for all the good it would likely do.

T.J. was already at her desk, and the wonderful aroma of fresh coffee greeted me before she could. In the chaos of what went down at Herring Run Park, I'd never told her what happened. A few sips of java in my comfortable chair later, I got down to it.

"Vinny was an asshole," she said when I finished recounting the events. "I wasn't around for his history before, so I only know what he did this time. Still . . . I didn't want him to die."

"Neither did I."

"What do you think happened?"

"I can't prove it," I said, "but Tyler went there with me, dealt with a couple of Vinny's goons, and then disappeared. We kept a line open. When Vinny went on his rant about getting revenge on me no matter what, someone shot him." I spread my hands. "The math seems pretty simple."

"You didn't mention him to the police?"

"No."

"Why not?"

"Like I said, I can't prove anything. Vinny wasn't exactly the most popular man in the city. It's possible someone else could've taken him out."

"But not probable," T.J. said.

"Definitely not," I concurred.

A few minutes later, the door opened, and John Tyler walked into the office. He was dressed much like usual: jeans, a long-sleeved shirt, and a leather jacket. Despite what I relayed to her, T.J. smiled at him. "Morning."

"Good morning," he said with a grin. Like nothing happened. Like he didn't shoot and kill a man the night before.

"T.J., why don't you get us all some coffee?" I said.

"Sure. I just made some."

"Go pick some up." My eyes didn't leave Tyler, who stared back at me. "Take your time. Grab yourself a pastry while you're there."

"Really?" she said, looking from Tyler to me and back again. "The testosterone is getting thick again." T.J. shrugged into her jacket, threw her purse over her shoulder, and headed out the door.

When the last of her footfalls rang against the metal stairs, Tyler dropped into one of my guest chairs. "I figured we should talk about last night."

"What the fuck?" I said. "I had Vinny under control. He lost the fight. I zip-tied him. He was going to get in my car, and the police would take it from there."

"You heard his screed," Tyler said.

"A bunch of words. He was pissed and ranting. None of

it would've mattered. Based on everything he did, Vinny was going away for a long time."

"How long was he supposed to remain in jail the first time?"

"Twenty-five years."

"And how soon was he out?"

I leaned back in my chair. Tyler had a point, even if it was an obvious one. "I get it. He might have managed another early release. It's also possible he would've lived to a ripe old age and then died in prison."

"I served under a colonel," Tyler said, "my last commander in special operations. Name was Braxton. The specifics aren't important, but he got charged with war crimes. I reported him for them. Guess who he blamed?"

"You."

"He was supposed to rot in Leavenworth. The American military has talked about winning hearts and minds for a long time. Problem is you can't measure anything there. The brass loves metrics. You can count dead terrorists, and Braxton was good at delivering them."

"He was popular with the right people, then," I said.

Tyler nodded. "Pretty much. Some of the guys who were his fellow colonels when he got bagged were two-star generals later. He managed to finagle his way out after about nine years. He came for me . . . and for my daughter. Kidnapped her, in fact."

I wouldn't want to deal with anyone in my family being abducted. Tyler's solution was certainly neater, however much I still didn't agree with it. "I presume you got her out."

"She did some of it herself," he said. "Even helped me at the end. The point is you can't count on these assholes to do the time they're supposed to. I learned it the hard way. So did you. Why roll the dice again?"

"Because Vinny didn't need to die," I said.

"He would've been a threat to you and everyone you love. Shooting him was the best solution."

"Not your call."

"It was. I had the rifle. Night-vision scope. You guys were at the end of the effective range until you drifted closer."

"Where the hell did you even go?" I asked.

"There's a Catholic school on the corner of Chesterfield and Harford. Quiet area at night. There's a church behind it. I used the fire escape to get up to the roof."

"Why?"

"You and I took out Vinny's hired hands," Tyler said. "I went up there to lend support in case he got the upper hand."

"I'm better than he is. Was."

"A lot of people died against supposedly inferior opponents. What if he had a revolver strapped to his ankle?"

I hadn't considered something like this. Fighting dirty was certainly in Vinny's wheelhouse, but a hidden gun was a whole different level. "He didn't."

"I get you're upset," Tyler said. "You and Vinny were close once, and you watched him bleed out in front of you. It may not seem like it now, but I did the right thing."

"I'm not sure I can come along for the ride there," I said. "Even if you did, we're not going to agree on the reason."

"Maybe. At the end of the day, we don't have to sit around the campfire and sing songs together. You can disagree all you want. I've seen this before. It doesn't end well. It pretty much can't. I slept well last night, and I will tonight. You should, too."

"How do you know I'm not going to narc on you?"

"It wouldn't matter," Tyler said.

"Why not?"

He grinned, though it didn't look full of humor. "This isn't my first rodeo. The two guys I took out and tied up never got a good look at me. My car is almost as old as I am and doesn't have a GPS. My phone . . ." He held up a flip model, probably a burner . . . "Doesn't have it, either. No one saw me get up on the school's roof or come down." Tyler spread his hands. "How can you say I was there? The cops probably gave you credit for taking out all three guys, didn't they?" I nodded. "They'll conclude the shooter is unknown and investigate for a while. I doubt it'll get anywhere. It sounds like Vinny was an asshole, and he was an ex-con, so no one's going to push for it to get solved."

I couldn't find fault with his reasoning. "I wasn't going to rat you out, anyway." Footsteps came up the stairs, and T.J. walked in. She carried a tan cardboard drink tray with three tall cups and a stuffed white paper bag. "I brought us all some pastries. This company card is great."

"Remind me to apply for a credit line reduction," I said.

CHAPTER 30

GLORIA TEXTED ME AROUND LUNCHTIME. She said she was on her way home and would love it if I met her at her house. I informed T.J. I'd be ducking out early. "You still have the ring?" she asked.

"I hope not to after today," I said, "but I do need to run by my place and get it first." I popped in long enough to retrieve it from my desk drawer before picking up I-83 North and driving to Brooklandville. When I got there, the contractor had already finished. Gloria's front entrance looked as good as new, and they even matched the color of the previous door.

"Not bad," she said as she let me in. We hugged, and I didn't want to let her go. "Wow. I guess I need to go away more often."

"Hopefully not under these circumstances," I said.

We walked into Gloria's spacious living room. Half of my first floor could have fit inside it. If the massive area rug were made of real fur, it would have cost an entire clan of bears their lives. I dropped onto the luxurious sofa. The whole area looked like it got airlifted from a showroom and placed inside Gloria's house. Whatever decorator she paid did a commendable job. "What happened while I was gone?" my girlfriend asked as she sat beside me. "Why did my door need to be fixed?"

"It was tough." I steeled myself with a deep breath. "Vinny found out about you. It must have been after you left town. One of his flunkies broke in and raided your closet. They . . . filmed a woman outside a hotel in the county. She was wearing the blue and gold-striped dress. Looked a lot like you. She got murdered on camera." Gloria's eyes widened, and her hand covered her gaping mouth. "He wanted me to believe he'd murdered you, and it was really convincing."

"Oh, my god."

I gently tapped the cast on her left arm. "This was the only giveaway. She didn't have one on. T.J. and I figured out what the poor woman's name was and who put her behind the hotel to get stabbed to death. It wasn't just Vinny."

"I'm so sorry you had to go through all that," Gloria said.

I nodded. "Vinny called me the next morning to gloat. I let him think I was mourning your death. He wanted me to meet him last night. I . . . took someone with me to help with the goons. Rollins is out of town. I was about to take Vinny to my car when he got shot."

She put a hand on my knee. "I know you two had a complicated relationship. Still, I'm sure you didn't want it to happen."

"No, I didn't."

"Do you know who shot him?"

"It's ultimately not important," I said. "Vinny made a lot of threats against you, our ch . . . other people I love." Even though I thought I covered my error, Gloria raised an eyebrow. I continued. "He'd be looking at a long prison sentence, but the same thing was true almost four years ago."

"Not much is easy in your job," she said.

"Some days, I feel it more than others."

"You want some wine?"

I hadn't expected the question, but her leaving to open a bottle would be a nice transition to the second phase of the conversation. "Yeah. Thanks."

Gloria smiled and left the room. She kept a wine refrigerator in her kitchen, and I couldn't recall seeing it in a state other than full. When she disappeared down the hallway, I slipped the ring box out of my pocket and held it in my left hand. Gloria walked in a couple minutes later carrying two glasses of red on a small tray. "The corkscrew was a bit of an adventure," she said, holding up her left arm, "but I managed."

"I never doubt you," I said as I transferred a glass to the end table beside me. Gloria took her seat and enjoyed a long sip. When she leaned away to set her glass down, I slid off the couch and looked up at her from one knee. She turned back and gasped when she saw me. "I know this is a little unconventional. Weird timing and all. Definitely not how I wanted it to go." I licked my lips and swallowed as my mouth went dry. "You told me you felt I wanted to ask you something before you left, and you were right." I opened the box. Gloria beamed when she saw the ring. "Gloria Reading, will you marry me?"

"Of course," she said. She leapt off the couch and wrapped me in a hug. I wasn't ready to catch her, and the rug did a great job of cushioning my fall as Gloria kissed me. I broke away long enough to slip the ring carefully onto her finger. "It's beautiful." She kissed me again and remained on top. "I have so many ideas. A lot of people I want to invite. I need to hire a wedding planner. There's no way I can do this myself."

"No," I said.

She frowned. "No?"

"I didn't mean will you marry me at some extravagant

ceremony eighteen months in the future. I mean now. Today
. . . tomorrow. Whatever as long as it's soon."

"But our parents . . . "

"They'll get over it," I said. "Besides, it's our day, not
theirs."

She kissed me again. "You got it. I mainly hope we can
pull it off."

"You and I both know the mayor of Baltimore. I'm pretty
sure we can get him to pull a string or two."

"I hadn't thought about that," she said.

"You should be the one to ask him," I said. "He knows I
think he's a prick. Quite rightly, I might point out."

The smile never left my fiancée's face. "I'll call his office
now."

We each needed to talk to a few people and share the news.
Gloria retreated upstairs to spread the mirth, and I remained
in the living room. My first call went to my parents. After he
answered, my father recovered from his shock long enough to
tell me he would put me on speaker. "All right, we're both
here now, son."

"I proposed to Gloria," I said again.

"Coningsby, that's wonderful," my mother said. "Congratulations! Oh, we have so much planning to do. This'll
take at least a year. It's a good thing you're both still young.
I'm sure Gloria would love a few ideas. We could go—"

"Mom. Let me cut you off. We're doing a simple ceremony, and it'll probably be tomorrow."

"Tomorrow!? How am I supposed to get ready on such
short notice?"

"Should I pretend you don't have an entire wall of your
closet set aside for formalwear?"

"Why the rush, son?" my father asked.

"Simple, Dad. I thought I'd lost her recently. The details don't matter now. Chalk it up as another sin on Vinny's ledger. I don't want to wait, and neither does she."

"Let us know when and where as soon as you can."

"I will."

"Congratulations. Your mother might run around like a chicken with her head cut off for the next day, but we're both really happy for you."

"Thanks, Dad." I ended the call and dialed Rich next.

"When were you going to tell me Vinny died?" he asked before I could share the good news.

"Talk about trampling on my *dénouement*," I said.

"You think someone dies in Baltimore, and I don't hear about it?"

"Considering the homicide count so far this year . . . yes. Look, I don't know who killed Vinny, and I didn't call to hash out his demise with you. Gloria and I are getting married."

"Well, it's about time," he said.

"Yeah, yeah. Here's the kicker . . . I want you to be the best man."

"Me? What about Joey?"

"No," I said. "You. We haven't always agreed over the years despite you racking up a lot of commendations off my intellectual labor." Rich snorted, but I continued. "I had an older sister until she died. You're the closest thing I have to an older brother."

"Dammit," he muttered, and I swore I heard his voice crack for an instant. "I'd be a real prick if I turned you down after your little speech, wouldn't I? Of course, I'll do it."

"Thanks. We're hoping to tie the proverbial knot at City Hall tomorrow. Maybe you can suck up to the commissioner when the ceremony ends?"

"Is it too late to change my mind?"

"Yes," I said, and I broke the connection. I called a few more people starting with Joey, T.J., and Melinda. A short while later, Gloria came downstairs, grabbed me by the collar, and kissed me like she meant it. She tugged my shirt enough to get me moving—I didn't need a great deal of motivation—and led me upstairs where we stayed for a while.

"Davenport thinks we should be good for tomorrow," she said later as she rested her head on my chest. "His secretary is going to fill out the marriage license. We can sign it before the ceremony."

"Is he going to perform it?"

"Yes. We tentatively agreed on three-thirty." I gave a vexed grunt even after expecting the mayor would want to do it. I didn't like him, and he felt the same way about me. He was a big fan of Gloria, however, from the times she put on fundraisers for him in his former life as a business magnate and occasional philanthropist. "You need to be on your best behavior."

"Me?" I said. "Always."

"Uh-huh." She grinned and shifted, gliding on top of me. "This is a very short engagement. I think we need to spend as much time in bed as we can."

"You'll get no argument from me," I said as I rolled Gloria over and kissed her.

"Does this mean I can win all our disagreements by taking you to bed?" she said.

"Pretty much."

CHAPTER 31

THE NEXT TWENTY-FOURS passed in a blur. Gloria and I decided we didn't want a big formal ceremony—in terms of location and dress code. We were going to do this on the steps of City Hall with our parents, a couple other relatives, and a few close friends. No reason to break out the tuxes and ball gowns. I thought my mother would faint when I told her we were going business casual, but she recovered enough to express her displeasure. I knew she would come in formal attire regardless.

We headed downtown in separate vehicles. Gloria wanted time to get ready at her own house. I didn't hurry. She could primp and pamper with the best of them, and her drive from Brooklandville would be longer than mine from Federal Hill. I arrived early, which meant I needed to mark this day on the calendar for two reasons. My bride-to-be joined me soon after.

Gloria wore a nice pink dress, and I opted for a button-down shirt and a pair of pressed chinos. We let our upbringings show in our footwear, which was fancy and expensive in both cases. "You look beautiful," I said.

She smiled. "Thanks. You look like you're ready for your shift at Staples."

"I'm not hauling cases of paper in my Ferragamos."

A small matter remained: signing the marriage license Vincent Davenport rushed through for us. We found the appropriate office inside, affixed our John and Jane Hancocks to it, paid the registration fee—I knew the mayor wouldn't cover this—and returned outside to wait.

Baltimore's City Hall was a throwback to grand construction and opulence. The exterior was all pale stone, and arched windows covered the first three levels. Five columns loomed immediately past the stairs. A dome sat atop the building, lending it an architectural vibe similar to the US Capitol. It may have been the most proper building within city limits, and it definitely looked out of place with how most people perceived Baltimore.

Gloria's parents arrived first. Hugh Reading was clad mostly like me, whereas he opted to include a tie. Her mother Susan wore a similar dress to her daughter's, though hers was lavender. My folks arrived next. My father came in a sharp navy blue suit, and my mother wore a pink ball gown because of course she did. She made sure to catch my eye and look proud of herself. I offered a smile and a wave.

Rich's blue Camaro rumbled past despite the venue being two blocks from his office, and he walked up the steps of City Hall a couple minutes later. "Need some face time with the commissioner first?" I said as he shook my hand.

"I told him I'd wave. He prefers lieutenants to suck up from a distance." He slipped a slender gold wedding band out of his pocket. "Good thing you know her size. I'll send you a bill after the honeymoon."

"Might want to wait for me to take a case or two. She wants to go back to Hawaii."

"*Mahalo*," Rich said, and he walked away to say hi to my

parents. Gloria's maid of honor—one of her three friends named Courtney, none of whom I could keep track of without a program—arrived next, followed by Joey, Melinda, T.J., Gloria's other two guests, and the one friend from college I reached who could actually manage a day off on short notice. I hadn't seen Nick in at least a year. He came in a polo and a pair of dress pants, and he looked like he could still sprint up and down a lacrosse field a bunch of times.

At the appointed hour, Vincent Davenport exited the building. We first met when he served as the CEO of a major local corporation. I didn't much care for him, and he assured me the feeling was mutual. In the years since, he acquired a political bent, ran for mayor of the city, and won in a landslide. The office hadn't changed him much, at least on the outside. Davenport was in his mid-50s, most of his hair was still black, and a pair of glasses served as one of his few concessions to age. Despite the festivities of the day, he showed up in a black suit. He and Gloria embraced before he made his way to me. "Mister Ferguson." We shook hands. "Congratulations."

"Thanks," I said. "This day is a long time coming."

"Yes. I'd begun to wonder what Miss Reading was waiting for. I'm glad it all worked out."

This served as our most pleasant exchange in months, so I opted not to ruin it despite his barb. Might as well try to be nice on my wedding day . . . especially to the officiant. "Me, too."

Davenport walked away and talked to an aide, who handed him a few papers. I wondered how many ceremonies he performed. Probably not many. Gloria must have pulled an incredibly long string to make this happen. My soon-to-be-wife and I converged on the top step of City Hall. The five stone columns stood strong behind us. Ornate doors yawned behind the mayor. Our party assembled on the ample platform.

"I must say," Davenport opened, "I haven't done one of these before. 'Dearly beloved' sounds like we're in church rather than outside a city landmark." I fought the urge to roll my eyes. "Friends, family, and honored guests . . . We gather here today to join Coningsby and Gloria in matrimony." He looked between us. "Do either of you have anything you want to say?"

I shook my head. "No. This all came together kind of quickly."

"We just want to be married," Gloria added.

"Well, I won't keep you, then." Davenport paused for a few polite chuckles. Rich wasn't among them. I would need to remind him how to suck up to city officials afterward. "Do we have rings?" Rich and Courtney moved to flank us. I took the golden band from him, and Gloria beamed when she saw it. "C.T., place the ring on Gloria's finger and repeat after me." I breathed in the cool afternoon air, did as instructed, and repeated the standard wedding vows.

My cousin gave Gloria a light gray ring for me. I looked askance at it. "Titanium," he whispered. "I knew you wouldn't want plain gold."

"I like it," I said. Gloria slid it onto my finger and repeated her vows.

"By the power vested in me by the City of Baltimore," Davenport said, "I pronounce you husband and wife. You may kiss the bride." Gloria took a half-step closer. We embraced and shared a long, deep kiss.

"Get a room," Joey said amid a series of fake coughs.

"We plan to," I told him.

"Reception is at our house," my father announced. "Get the address from the happy couple if you don't have it already."

Davenport congratulated both of us before walking back inside, his aide rushing after him. Our party surrounded us to wish us well. Hugs and handshakes for all. "Welcome to the family," Gloria's father said.

"Thank you, sir."

"Please. It's Hugh."

As the crowd dispersed, T.J. ran to us and gave me a huge hug. "I guess you'll be on a honeymoon soon."

"We leave tomorrow," I said. "I suppose this means I'm putting you in charge while we're gone."

"I'll try not to burn the place down, boss."

"I appreciate it. Manny probably does, too."

"How long are you gone?"

"Two weeks. Plus a day or two for jetlag."

"What should I do if real clients come in?" T.J. wanted to know.

"Tell them what's going on," I said. "If it's something really easy and you can one hundred percent do it from your desk, go ahead. Bill appropriately. Pass on the harder ones. Oh, and extreme prejudice rules apply as usual."

"I'm on it." T.J. grinned. "No domestics or insurance companies. I'll tell them off."

"You coming to the reception?"

She shook her head. "Doesn't seem like my place."

"You should come," Gloria said. "If we wanted you here, you're welcome to eat with us."

After a moment of deliberation, T.J. shrugged. "Sure, why the hell not? Text me the address."

"I will," I said. She headed for the nearest parking garage. Gloria and I soon followed.

"I've done almost no packing," she said as we walked arm-in-arm.

"Does this mean we might get you down to a mere six bags?"

My wife—and it felt terrific to think of her as my wife—snorted. "Let's not get crazy."

"Let's at least wait until we're in Hawaii," I said.

END of Novel #12

Hi there,
Thanks for reading this book. C.T.'s adventures will continue, and he'll need to help his home city out of a dark situation—literally. You can read all about it in *Night Comes Down*, available for preorder now.

THE END

AFTERWORD

Thanks for checking out this novel! I hope you enjoyed reading the book as much as I enjoyed writing it.

I write mysteries and thrillers with action, snark, and flawed heroes. If this sounds like something you like, you can check out my catalog below.

The C.T. Ferguson Crime Novels:

1. The Reluctant Detective
2. The Unknown Devil
3. The Workers of Iniquity
4. Already Guilty
5. Daughters and Sons
6. A March from Innocence
7. Inside Cut
8. The Next Girl
9. In the Blood
10. Right as Rain
11. Dead Cat Bounce
12. Don't Say Her Name

13. Night Comes Down (Fall 2022)

The John Tyler Action Thrillers

1. The Mechanic
2. White Lines
3. Lost Highway
4. Four on the Floor
5. Forced Induction (Spring 2023)

(Note: C.T. Ferguson appears in *White Lines*. John Tyler appears in *Don't Say Her Name*.)

While these are the suggested reading sequences, each novel is a standalone mystery or thriller, and the books can be enjoyed in whatever order you happen upon them.

Connect with me:

For the many ways of finding and reaching me online, please visit https://tomfowlerwrites.com/contact. I'm always happy to talk to readers.

This is a work of fiction. Characters and places are either fictitious or used in a fictitious manner.

"Self-publishing" is something of a misnomer. This book would not have been possible without the contributions of many people.

- The great cover design team at 100 Covers.
- My editor extraordinaire, Chase Nottingham.
- My wonderful advance reader team, the Fell Street Irregulars.

Made in the USA
Monee, IL
26 May 2025

18151993R20152